I0574436

THE COLOR OF PAIN

The Colors of Novice Ray: Book One

E. G. ROSE

STIRLING & STONE

Copyright © 2023 by Sterling & Stone

All rights reserved.

No part of this book may be reproduced in any form or by any electronic or mechanical means, including information storage and retrieval systems, without written permission from the author, except for the use of brief quotations in a book review.

The authors greatly appreciate you taking the time to read our work. Please consider leaving a review wherever you bought the book, or telling your friends about it, to help us spread the word.

Thank you for supporting our work.

THE COLOR OF PAIN

Chapter One

RAYMOND HAD no *real* memories of life before this place. His imagination would have to do.

He gazed out the frosty classroom window, his thoughts drifting with the falling snow. It was the fluffy kind. Crappy for snowballs, but prettier to look at. He wouldn't dare say that out loud, though. Especially around Kevin, who would call Raymond a fag for saying something was "pretty," then prove his point with a headlock or an arm twist — maybe even a gut punch, depending on his mood. Had to put on a good show for anyone watching. The bigger the crowd, the more it hurt, usually. Raymond learned that the hard way.

The nor'easter expected that afternoon had blown up Maine's coastline early. Only half-way through first class, and the playground was already dusted white like the powdered donuts they sometimes got with Sunday breakfast. Raymond's stomach let out a low, gurgling rumble. He cringed and sneaked a glance over his shoulder, but nobody looked up. Cool relief washed through him. If the other students had heard, they'd let it go.

Raymond turned back to the window and gasped, as a Jacob's ladder cut through the trees, shooting a spear of golden sunlight through the center of the snow-covered monkey bars. It was one of those weird times when the weather got confused. Like it sent the wrong guy for the job but didn't figure it out until it was too late. Raymond *loved* those moments — they made him want to drop everything and draw something beautiful.

Father Galen was the total opposite. Those moments seemed to scare him a little. Like something had gone wrong. Something *unnatural.*

"The Devil's beating his wife," he'd say, scowling and making the sign of the cross with his whole arm.

How dumb was *that?* He's the DEVIL. What *else* would he do to his wife? Kiss her on the cheek and hand her a bunch of flowers?

But Raymond would never dare say that aloud either, of course. Not to Father. That would be *very* "precocious." And Father Galen hated "precocious" almost as much as he hated "wasteful."

Raymond had looked up the meaning of the word, but it left him confused. He wasn't exactly sure what was wrong with being precocious. It sounded a lot like being smart. But Father said no, it was arrogance, which lead to conceit, a lack of humility, many other paving stones on the road to a "poisoned soul." *A poisoned soul?* That gave Raymond the creeps. He prayed that being precocious was just something he *did* sometimes, without meaning to, and not his "nature."

Because the sisters said there was no changing *that*.

Raymond leaned over his desk, settled his chin on his crossed hands, and watched the swirling flakes dance and sparkle in the yellow shaft of sun. It was so strange and beautiful, he wondered if he were dreaming.

A wave of sleepiness crept over him. His throat hollowed out and tried to stretch into a yawn, but he clamped his jaw tight to cut it off. Sister Connie had a ruler for anyone who yawned in *her* class.

He was *so* tired. His head ached, and his eyeballs felt too big for their sockets. Once again last night, he hadn't slept. Though he wanted to — so *badly* — his stomach had other plans. The instant he drifted off, a sharp pain in his belly jolted him awake. Then came the gross, acid burn in his throat and something that felt like an earthquake in his guts. His stomach would cramp, then growl like a huge, vicious dog. Loud enough to wake the whole room! As if his roommates needed another reason to hate him. And it kept happening all night, over and over again, like that dumb groundhog movie they'd watched for Friday's TV Time.

He'd have to try harder tonight to finish his plate. Maybe food would stop the growling. He *wanted* to eat. But lately, he *didn't* want to more.

Raymond sneaked a glance at Sister Connie, scowling over a stack of completed math tests, her blood red marker hovering above them, ready to stab and slash. Most of his classmates still worked, but he'd finished first — ages ago — and hadn't seen the pen slash out a correction even once. Just one squeaked-out checkmark after another for all the right answers, always. That's the way it was for him. He didn't even need to study.

Another reason they hated him.

Sister wouldn't notice if he had a little rest. He wouldn't fall asleep — no way! Just an almost doze. He could get away that.

Raymond's eyelids fluttered to half-mast, then he let the dreamy sun-snow scene take him. Soon, his thoughts gave way to whatever it was that made the pictures. The ones he loved so much. The memories he wanted.

An image formed in the snowy playground. A small figure. A woman, her coat too large. She's carrying … what? A boy, straddling her hip. He is very small, his shiny red boots dangling like Christmas ornaments. Snowflakes swirl as she trudges up the stone walkway to the front entrance of the Haven. The boy's cheeks are winter apples. A neat row of baby teeth, cherry lips stretched wide in a joyous, little kid laugh. It's the snow. For some reason, the boy thinks it's funny. He stretches his tiny mitten high and taps the bobble of the woman's knit hat. Sparkling white crystals spill down onto her cheeks and dark lashes. She pauses. When she turns her face to the boy, he bumps the tip of his nose on hers, then throws his head back in a fit of giggles. Her smile is beautiful, sad, painful with love. They share the same coloring

4

— red lips, shiny brown hair peeking out from under their knit caps, pale skin, root beer eyes, and a track of cinnamon freckles across their noses. A matching set.

The woman turns back to the path and gets moving, eyes down, until they reach the end. Her gaze crawls up the stairs to the heavy wooden front door of the Haven for Tender Souls. She bites her lower lip. Her eyebrows narrow. Then her right boot lands with a thud on the first step —

Another yawn-cramp gipped Raymond's throat. His hand flew to his mouth to smother it, but a little got out. His attention flicked to Sister Connie. Luckily, she was too busy scanning the class for "sneaky cheats" on her latest pop-up math quiz attack to notice. The rest of the class was still huddled over their desks, pencils scratching like crazy against the tick-tock above Sister's head.

It had been nearly twenty minutes since Raymond had finished, easy-peasy. It pissed Kevin off, big time. Raymond felt him shooting eye daggers into his back when he put down his pencil then walked his test up to Sister's desk. He felt the others, too, only they were softer. More like normal jealousy. Which was not exactly great, but not ... *dangerous*.

Not like Kevin.

The image of the woman and boy was fading. With an explosion of butterflies in his belly, Raymond raised his hand. "Sister Connie," he squeaked, "may I please draw?"

Sister Connie glared at him for a terrible moment before giving him a single curt nod. Yes! When Sister's focus returned to the papers in front of her, Raymond nudged his backpack out from under his desk with his toe.

Moving quickly but carefully, he slid his sketch pad from the bag, then thumbed it open to a fresh sheet. He dug back in, searching for his special tin of charcoal pencils. They were a goodbye gift from Miss Brenda. She'd taught art — his favorite class — and had been his favorite teacher until she left to have a baby.

Kevin said she got "knocked up" because she wasn't a nun and could "do it" whenever she wanted to. Raymond didn't have the guts to tell Kevin to shut up but boy, did he ever want to. He knew "doing it" meant sex, and sex was how you got babies. *That* was basic biology. Big deal. But somehow, Kevin made it sound like something shameful. Something … ugly.

Miss Brenda was as far from ugly as you could get. She was the most beautiful woman he'd ever *seen* — golden yellow and cornflower blue, almost all the time.

On her last day at the Haven, Miss Brenda gave Raymond a box of Silhouette Coals — professional, *real* artist, charcoal pencils in twenty-four colors! They were labeled in swirly print. Sunset Pink, Glowing Embers, Heather Mist, Mountain Blue, Ocean Deep, Forest Pine, Driftwood … The names alone filled his head with pictures he couldn't wait to capture. The gift was so beautiful, so beyond anything he'd ever called his own, Raymond fought back tears. He told her that he couldn't take them. A gift like that was meant for a *real* artist. Miss Brenda said it wasn't a gift but a trade — the pencils for Raymond's promise that he'd work hard on his art, no matter what. She called him a true prodigy. To Raymond, that sounded a lot like precocious, but in a good way. Everything about Miss Brenda was good. He loved her with his whole heart. And now she was gone.

The woman! He was losing her. Raymond focused on the falling snow and willed her back into his brain. There she was, one boot on the first step, one on the snowy path. Her face — sad, angry, frightened, but still so pretty — tilted upward toward the oversized double doors at the top of the stairs.

Afraid to lose her again, Raymond gripped the pencil and pulled it out the bag. His hand moved in slow motion, but it was no good. The rattle might as well have been an explosion. He winced.

"Shhhhh!" The hiss of a giant serpent.

Raymond didn't look up. He didn't need to. Sister Connie's glare was burned into his brain forever, wrinkles, mustache, and all.

He waited a full, contrite minute, then gently popped the tin open. Green moss? Elderberry? No. Glowing Embers. The woman and the boy *needed* red. He didn't know why, but he was sure of it.

Raymond slipped the charcoal from its cradle and wiped the tip with a cotton rag. He took a breath, let his shoulders go soft, and closed his eyes.

Raymond's hand began to move across the blank sheet like it was a separate, living thing. The image of the woman flickered against the dark screen of his mind, in and out like the weaker channels on the rec room TV. Finally, it held, still and strong. Raymond's hand pushed the charcoal up, down, left to right, faster and faster, capturing the woman and her boy, together forever, in the folds of his paper pad.

"Hey fuckwit, quit scratching," Kevin's whisper crackled with irritation, "some of us ain't done."

Sister Connie's voice, a razor slash on sun-burned skin, cut through the room. "KEVIN! There is a bar of soap waiting for that filthy mouth of yours, young man. Get back to work!"

Raymond's stomach flipped over, then released a gurgling rumble so loud he almost didn't hear Kevin's growl.

"You are so *dead*."

No. Oh, no. Not again.

"Twenty with Benny, freak!" he hissed.

White-hot fear tore through Raymond like he'd stuck a fork in a socket.

Kevin's sing-song whine floated through the room like the smell of burnt rubber, "Twennnty with Beeenny. Twennnty with Beennny ..."

Raymond's body began to tremble, harder and harder, until he felt like he was nothing more than a vibration. He gripped the pencil as hard as he could, but his fist bounced up and down on the desk like it didn't belong to him.

"Gawd, you are such a *pussy*. Try not to piss yourself this time, freak. Your panties'll freeze at recess." Kevin's laugh was low, ugly, and dripping with hate. Not quite loud enough for Sister Connie to hear, but just loud enough for the others. Kevin had that trick down.

A barely stifled snigger erupted in the aisle to his right, then blew through the room like a cloud of black confetti.

Sister's eyes snapped upward. "QUIET! You have two minutes, then pencils down!"

Raymond's face burned with shame. He wanted to shake off like a wet dog. He wanted this awful, embarrassing shaking to stop. He wanted to flee, run far away. But worst of all, Kevin was right. More than anything, he wanted to *pee*.

Please, no. Please, please, *please*.

Two minutes. It might as well be two hours. His bladder felt like a balloon inflating in his groin. His heart hammered in his chest.

Raymond squeezed his legs together as tight as he could. He tried to slow his breathing, sucking air deep into his lungs.

Don't think about it. Find something else.

He turned back to the window. The shimmering Jacob's ladder had disappeared, leaving the yard steeped in dull, smoke-colored light. The snow fell heavier now, mixed with hail. Hard, gray pellets bounced off the glass, filling the room with an urgent, nervous ticking sound that merged with Sister's clock.

Panic would claim him any second now. His body would turn on him, his bladder would let go. *Very* soon.

No, not again. Please.

His sucked in his stomach, squeezing the muscles until they ached.

He remembered his drawing.

He looked down at his desk, and his breath caught in his throat. The image was so beautiful, so ... *powerful*. He was stunned that it had come from his own hand.

There they were, the woman and the boy on her hip, nearly complete. They looked back at him from the sketch pad, and the sadness in their expressions hit Raymond like a rubber ball in the gut. He knew then that her left boot would find the second step. And the next, and the next. And when they reached the top step, she would gently lower the boy onto the porch. She'd pull him to her for almost a full minute, holding him so tight he would nearly faint. Then she would lift the heavy brass knocker, hesitating for barely a moment before rapping it against the old wooden door three times — quick, hard and final. As the last bang still echoed, she would turn, rush down the slippery stairs, nearly falling twice, then run back down the path without looking back. And the boy, confused, frightened, and suddenly so very cold, would never see her again.

Sadness swept over Raymond like a warm wave of urine. His bladder throbbed and squirmed like it was full of snakes fighting for space. He couldn't hold it. Wasn't going to make it!

He bit down on a whimper. But of course, Kevin heard. He *always* heard.

"If he cries, I swear I will puke in his pee-pee." Kevin snorted, then faked a cough.

The whole room tensed, on the verge of explosion. Raymond felt them choking back their laughter, fighting to keep it in like he fought to control his bladder. A trickle of sweat ran down his back and into the seat of his jeans.

Could he get up? Could he make it across the room? Maybe. *Maybe* ... but.

He had to risk it. He had to go. *Now*. Raymond raised his hand. "Sister Connie?"

She looked up, with an irritated "no" already waiting on her dry, thin lips.

"May I use the restroom, please?"

Sister squinted her eyes, studying him like an insect on a pin that may yet be plotting a way to sting her, one last time. She licked her lips, took a breath —

The minute hand on Sister's clock ticked twelve, and the rusty screech of the class bell blasted the room. Raymond jumped so violently, his last shred of muscle control evaporated.

"Noooo ..." He threw both hands over his face as his bladder gushed a flow of urine, soaking his pants instantly. It streamed down his leg onto the floor. The bright, yellow puddle spread quickly across the pale tile, flowed beyond Raymond's desk, and puddled in the next aisle, for all to see.

"OH, MY GOD!" Kevin pointed and held his nose, "He did it AGAIN!"

The room exploded into shrieks and laughter, and

a perfectly coordinated chorus of "*Ewwwww!*" that sounded like they rehearsed it once a week.

"Sister!"

"Raymond wet his pants again!"

"It stinks!"

"It's getting on me!"

They all lifted their feet. Even those way in the back nowhere *near* Raymond's mess.

"Look out!"

"Raymond's trying to drown us in peeeeee!"

The shrieks of laughter pierced his back like a volley of poison darts.

Sister Connie jumped up from her chair and clapped her hands, like she was about to lead them in song. "Calm yourselves! *Calm* yourselves! NOW!"

Raymond dropped his forehead on his desk and thew his arms over his head, knocking his box of charcoal pens onto the urine-soaked floor. He wanted to disappear. He wanted to die. He wanted to dive into his beautiful drawing and chase the pretty woman down the path. Beg her not leave him. To take him with her. Please! Please! Please!

Everybody simmered down, but a trickle of pinched giggles still flowed around him.

Kevin made a squeal-y fart sound like a balloon and let out another huge snotty burst of laughter.

"KEVIN!" Sister Connie screamed, "You will wait for me in Father Galen's office. The rest of you, OUT! Leave your test papers on my desk!"

"But why am I in trouble?" Kevin whined, "*I'm* not the one who peed my pants!"

The screech of metal made Raymond jump. He didn't have to look up to know that sister had opened her drawer. She'd taken out her ruler.

Crack! Wood on wood. One slap on her desktop was enough to shut Kevin up.

Kevin's chair scraped against the floor. Raymond felt him close by. He opened his eyes just a crack but didn't dare lift his head.

Beneath his desk, the tip of Kevin's thick, black snow boot came into view. They all wore them. Part of the Haven's uniform. But Kevin was so much taller than everyone else, his looked bigger. *Meaner.*

Raymond knew what was coming next. He could see it in his mind. His chest burned with panic, his shoulders cramped, his hands shook, wanting to move, to *do*, but he remained frozen in place, shaking, cowering, and stinking of piss.

Nothing to do but watch.

The scuffed toe of Kevin's boot hovered over his beautiful Glowing Embers charcoal pen. Then it came down hard, twisted right, left, then right again, until a blood red smear was all that was left of it. Then Forest Pine, Burnt Earth, and Lavender. Kevin's boot found and crushed every pencil — twenty-four colors!

Raymond stared at the rainbow swirl of piss and charcoal, the last piece of Miss Brenda he had. And certainly, the last box of professional artist charcoal pencils he'd see in a hundred years. He wished for anger. That would be so much easier than the waves of sorrow crashing over him, again and again, until he was sure he would drown in it.

Raymond let out a sob, and then another, and another. He didn't care if Kevin or Sister or every stupid kid in the hallway heard him.

Until the swish of Sister Connie's skirt cut him off.

Raymond sucked in his breath and waited.

CRACK!

Wood on flesh. The soft flesh of Kevin's palm.

Raymond sputtered out a breath, then sucked in again. Waiting for the next crack. He knew it would come. Kevin did, too.

Maybe Kevin figured it was worth it.

Chapter Two

EVERY KID at the Haven for Tender Souls eventually heard the Benny story. Not all of them believed it was true. Some just didn't want to — it was pretty gross. Others *swore* it was the God's honest truth. But all of them, believers and non-believers alike, were terrified to spend "Twenty with Benny."

Thanks to Kevin, Raymond knew why.

No one knew how it started. Nobody knew the name of the first poor kid who was tied up and left in the pitch-black darkness of that musty old cellar for twenty endless, horrific minutes. But he probably pissed his pants. Raymond wanted to think he did, anyway.

He didn't want to be the only one.

The worst of it was, Raymond believed in science. *Loved* it, in fact. And science didn't believe in ghosts. Science would *laugh* at the dopes blabbering on about Benny in that stinky old basement. And Raymond wanted to laugh, too. The story of Benny couldn't be true. He was *sure* of it.

But the person who told him the story was sure it *was* true. She believed it, one hundred percent. And because he loved her, part of him believed it, too.

Her name was Sandra. She wasn't a resident of Haven — you could tell that by looking at her. Her hair was long, shiny, and the color of fresh corn. Her clothes always looked brand new, like she wore things once, then threw them away. Her skin was soft and smooth, like fresh rose petals. Her eyes were sea-blue, and she smelled liked vanilla pancakes. She had a way of looking at you — like you were sharing a secret, just the two of you.

Sandra was a senior at Casco High School. Her colors — honey-gold, cream, rose petal pink — took Raymond's breath away. He fell in love with her on sight. All the boys did. Kevin said he'd "seen better." But Raymond saw the way he looked at her.

Sandra was a temporary inmate at Haven. She'd been caught in the football locker room at Casco "doing something she shouldn't." Of course, all the boys were dying to know what the "something" was — Kevin had some gross guesses — but that wasn't something you asked a nun. The high school principal sentenced her to a month of weekends working on Haven's cleaning staff. Even at seven years old, Raymond knew that four lost weekends in an orphanage was brutal punishment for a high school girl. Especially one as beautiful as Sandra — she probably had a thousand friends.

She was nice, too. Friendly. Never acted weird or uncomfortable around them. And that was something new. Usually, normal kids couldn't stand to be in the place for *five* minutes, like orphan-ism was a contagious disease they were afraid to catch. You could see it on their faces on Pick-Up Day when the families came to take their newly adopted family member home. They'd mumble their hellos, stare at their shoes, and stay as close to the door as possible.

Like everyone else, Raymond was curious to know exactly what Sandra's crime was. He couldn't stop wondering if any of Kevin's guesses were right. One afternoon, while Sandra was wiping down his table in the lunchroom, Raymond accidentally asked her.

He was the last one left in the dining hall, as usual, trying to get through his plate while Sister Ann glared at him from the nun's table. Raymond had sat there so long, the greasy fat on his meatloaf had gone white. Suddenly, he was surrounded by the smell of something warm and sweet.

"Excuse me, sweetie, if you're done, can I just get that spot in front of you?"

Raymond looked up, and there she was, her pink lips smiling down at him, golden hair shimmering like she'd swallowed a piece of the sun. So close, he could have kissed her on the cheek.

He knew he was staring. Knew he should reply. But his mouth wouldn't work.

She laughed and asked him again. "So … you're done?"

"Uh-huh," he managed.

Sandra looked at his plate and wrinkled her perfect nose. "You didn't eat much. Aren't you hungry?"

He shrugged, like an idiot, and pointed to his aching, empty belly. Like that was supposed to make any sense to her!

She smiled again, just for *him*, and his heart sang. As she reached around him, swiping the table with her rag, a fresh cloud of vanilla pancake smell made him dizzy. He was suddenly desperate to know her, to share her secrets, to hand himself over, right then and there, and belong to her forever. He *had* to know.

"What were you doing in the boys' locker room that you weren't supposed to?"

The moment the question fell out of his mouth, he regretted it.

The smile dropped from her lips. Streaks of inky purple blotches shot across Sandra's beautiful field of honey-gold. The change was so sudden, so *ugly*, he felt like he'd been tipped upside down and spun by the ankles. Around and around, until his stomach began to creep up his throat.

Raymond jumped up, knocking his chair to the floor. He just managed to make it outside, to the bushes in the back yard, before a shower of foamy puke burst from his guts. He heaved, over and over, so hard he thought his back might break.

When he was nearly finished — there wasn't much in his stomach to throw up — he felt a hand on his back. He cringed, waiting to be scolded by one of the sisters.

"Hey, kid. Are you okay?"

Raymond looked up to see Sandra hovering above, a deep frown of concern — and maybe a little disgust — shadowing her pretty face. But her colors were honey-gold again. And her hand on his back was warm. *Kind.*

Tears pricked the corners of Raymond's eyes.

She crouched down beside him. "Aw, you poor thing. Don't cry. You probably just got a flu or something."

Shit! Now she thinks I'm a baby.

Sandra pulled a small pack of tissues from the pocket of her apron. "Here, let's get you cleaned up."

She started to wipe his face, but he pulled back. Sandra stared at him a moment, then smiled with one side of her mouth. "Okay, I get it." She handed him the pack of tissues. "You better go see the nurse."

Raymond dragged a wad of tissue across his eyes, and then his mouth. "We don't go to the nurse for puking."

"Okay, then a nun, or whatever you do when you're sick here."

"We don't do anything."

The way she looked at him made him want to cry all over again.

"C'mon," she held her hand out to him, "I got a soda in my bag."

He took her hand, and she pulled him up to standing.

"Feeling better?"

He nodded. "Are we friends now?"

She laughed. "You're kind of weird."

His heart sank. He couldn't look at her.

"Sure, yeah, we're friends now. But don't ask me about … *that* ever again. Okay?"

"Okay."

And he didn't, though he never stopped wondering. Once again, his imagination would have to do.

And Raymond's imagination did fine. So well, in fact, that describing his imagined pictures of Sandra, inspired by Kevin, doing "things she shouldn't" in confession got him fifteen Hail Marys, ten Our Fathers, and a good Act of Contrition. It also got him his *own* month-long sentence on the cleaning staff, which was pretty awesome because he got to be around Sandra on the weekends. Father Galen didn't really think that one through. And for once, Raymond was glad he was so crappy at lying.

On Sandra's final day, a stormy Sunday afternoon, she and Raymond were picked to scrub the salt stains off the chapel floor. The people of Brunswick, Maine wore boots, even on nice, dry days. And the weather that day was nuts. Snow, rain, sleet, thunder, *and* lightning. But they still showed up for church and "brought the weather indoors," as Father Galen liked to say.

When Raymond walked in, Sandra was already there with her bucket, staring up at the stained glass above the dais.

"Don't they usually have Jesus up there?"

"I think so."

"Who's that, then?"

Raymond looked up at the carved statue floating

high above the pulpit, and, as always, goosebumps slid along the back of his neck. His chest felt like it was full of light. "This is the Chapel of Jophiel. That's her. She's an archangel. Of beauty. And wisdom. They say she's the fountain of inspiration for all artists."

Jophiel. His favorite of all the angels and saints.

Sandra nudged his shoulder with her own. "Figures you'd know. She's pretty. But isn't that breaking some Catholic, church-building kind of rule?"

"A rich ship captain built this whole place. He chose Jophiel."

"Why her?"

Raymond stared up at Jophiel's enormous wings, each feather carved in such perfect detail, the marble looked soft to the touch. He drank in the intricate drape of her pacific-blue robes as her arms spread wide and reached outward as if to embrace the whole world. The creamy-peach skin tone of her face, warm and alive, caught in a gentle smile that radiated comfort. "Because he loved his wife."

"Lucky her." She nudged Raymond's shoulder with her own. "Come on, Brainiac. Let's get this over with."

For the next two hours, it was just the two of them on their hands and knees, each with a rag, sharing a bucket of soapy hot water. Raymond was in heaven. They scrubbed slow circles, making the chore last so there wouldn't be time for another. Sandra told him she hoped to run out the clock, then get the heck out of there. Every few minutes, she sighed like a grump, sat back on her heels, and frowned at her phone.

"Only 4:15?" she puffed out and squeezed her eyes shut, "Shit!"

A sharp crack of lightning made them both jump. Thunder rumbled the stained-glass windows, and the lights in the chapel flickered. Sandra's eyes snapped open wide, and she looked up, comically. "I mean shoot!" She leaned close to Raymond and whispered, "I think He heard me."

They both cracked up.

"Kind of weird," he said, "thunder and lightning in the winter, huh?"

"I like weird." She flicked her wet fingertips at him. "That's why I hang out with you."

Raymond grinned so wide, it felt like his lips would split. His chest was warm with amber, liquid happiness.

The storm went into high gear. Lightning flashes and rumbling thunder mixed with the ping of hail against the stained-glass windows. It sounded like a giant shaking out his boots after a walk on the beach.

Sandra dropped her dirty rag into the bucket, then wiped her hands on her spotless sweatshirt.

Raymond looked at the muddy trail she'd left across her belly and shrugged. "You'll be throwing it out anyway."

She frowned at him. "Yup. You're weird." Sandra smiled. Warm honey, vanilla pancakes. "Hey, Ray."

Ray.

"Yeah?"

She winked at him. "I say it's break time."

Raymond winked back and dropped his rag in the

bucket, too. When that made her laugh, his heart soared. He'd never heard such a beautiful sound.

They scooted back against the wall, stretching their legs out on the damp floor. It was chilly, but Raymond felt like warm toast. A huge boomer made them jump again. Lightning sizzled, the lights flickered, and this time, just for an instant, they went out completely.

"Wow. It's friggin' spooky here, Ray."

"You want to go back to the house?"

"No way. They'll put us on laundry. I'd rather wait it out here. I hate that cellar. It freaks me out."

"Why? It's just a cellar. Historic, because the stone was cut —"

"Ugh. Don't care. It's haunted."

Raymond laughed. She was joking. Right?

"Laugh if you want. But it is. Can't you feel him?"

"Feel who?"

Sandra swung round to face him, then tucked up her legs, crisscross-applesauce. "You don't know about Benny?"

"Who's Benny?"

"Oh, wow." Sandra smiled, mouth closed, sighing out of her nose like she had the *best* secret ever. She opened her mouth to speak. Then shut it. "How old are you?"

"Going on nine. But I'm precocious."

"What?"

"I'm smarter than everyone else, and it doesn't matter how old they are."

"Who says?"

Raymond shrugged. "Everyone."

"Okaaay." The lightening flashed in her eyes. "But do you scare easily?"

Kevin's face popped into his head, red, mean, smiling but angry underneath, a tight fist held up by his ear, ready to fly. Raymond coughed. "Sometimes."

He wanted to say 'no.' But he couldn't lie. Not to *her*, especially.

She stared at him. He drank in the blue of her eyes.

She shook her head. "Nah, forget it."

"Awww, c'mon. No fair. You have to tell me now."

"Promise you won't freak out? This is my last shift in this shithole. No offense."

He shrugged.

"I'm SO not into getting another month of —"

"I promise," he said.

She looked at him sideways. "You better mean it."

"I totally do."

"Okay." She cleared her throat and leaned closer, "About, fifty, or a hundred years go —"

"Well, which? Fifty or a hundred?"

"I don't know, whatever —"

"But that's like half-a-century difference —"

"Do you want to hear the story or not?"

"Yeah."

"Then shush." She started again. "So, *some years ago*, Benny was an orphan here —"

"Resident. We don't say orphan. Well, we *do*, but —"

"Dude."

"Sorry, I won't say another —"

Sandra held up her hand up and froze. The patter of hail shifted to pelting rain. It hammered the church roof and rippled down the windows in windblown sheets. She frowned, her eyes shifting left to right in concentration. "Did you hear something?"

He shrugged. "Rain?"

She nodded, peeked at her phone, then stuffed it back into her pocket. "Where was I?"

"I was saying that we're supposed to say resident but —"

""Fine, resident. So, Benny was a *resident* here his whole life. Nobody knew when he showed up or how old he was. Not the priests or the sisters or any of the teachers … he'd been here longer than any of them. He'd just always *been* here."

"That's sad."

"Not sad. Creepy."

"Why, creepy?"

"Because Benny was still a kid. He *stayed* a kid. Never got on any older, no matter how much time went by."

"That's impossible."

"It's true. Ask anyone. He was all kinds of weird. And the longer time went on, the weirder Benny got. He hated being alone. Hated it! But because he was so creepy, nobody wanted to be around him. No matter how hard he tried, the other kids pretended he wasn't there. Eventually, he quit trying. He stopped talking completely."

"To everyone?"

"Yup. Just stared at anyone who tried to talk to him. And he always had this spooky smile on his face, like he had some kind of dark secret that just amused the shit out of him."

"What secret?"

"Well, once he stopped talking, Benny started to be able to ... *do things*."

"What things?"

Sandra leaned in a little closer. Her voice was half-talk, half-whisper.

"Benny could walk through *walls*. He would be there one minute, just sitting at a desk or strolling down the hall. And then, just like that, he'd be ... *gone*. Then some kid in another room would look up, and there was Benny, right next to him. Staring and doing this crazy giggle thing. He had this weird, gross laugh. Everyone says it was like he was gurgling blood. And he smelled like blood, too."

Raymond's mouth went dry. Even if it was just a story, it was "scary as fuck," as Kevin would say.

She tugged on his sweater sleeve. "You okay?"

"Yeah. Why wouldn't I be?"

"You look a little ... pale. You want to hear the rest?"

He wasn't sure he did. But he nodded anyway. He couldn't stand for Sandra to think he was a coward.

"The kids said that if Benny touched you, that night, you'd have a terrible dream that you were in a boat, on a dark river, under a black sky. And along the river are these horrible, dead trees. And the tree branches are slithering because they're full of snakes.

26

The snakes all drop into the river at once. Then they come for you."

The image flooded Raymond's mind like rushing water. Hundreds and hundreds of wet, writhing snakes, their green, iridescent scales glowing in the moonlight. Their fat bodies snapping s-curves along the surface of a dark, oily river.

Raymond swallowed hard. "Go on."

"They swamp the boat. Tip you into the water. Except it isn't water," Sandra's voice dropped to a whisper, "It's *blood*. A river of blood." She paused for a breath, then picked up speed, the words coming out in a rush, "And you try to swim. You try to *breathe*. But all you can do is suck the blood into your lungs. You thrash and kick, but the blood is too thick. The harder you fight, the weaker you get. You try to scream but your mouth fills with blood. You can't breathe, you're suffocating. Drowning. You start to go under. And if nobody wakes you up?" She leaned toward him, so very close. "You choke to death in your sleep."

"What happened to him?"

"After two kids died, everyone got scared. Even the *sisters* were scared of him. Nobody wanted Benny in their dorm. So, they moved his bed into the cellar. But the kids would wake up to the sound of Benny's creepy laugh. And there he would be right by their bed, just staring. Laughing at them."

"What did they do?"

"The priests were getting fed up with nobody getting any sleep and everyone being freaked out. So, one night, they tied Benny to his bed. They prayed over him for, like, an hour, and doused him in holy water. Then they put a padlock on the cellar door and locked him down there for the night. But in the morning, they found Benny in the dining hall, dressed for breakfast, with the cellar door still padlocked. And Benny, just sitting there, giggling like crazy."

Raymond could see it all in his mind, just like a movie. A terrifying, horror flick that would *never* make the sisters' approval list.

"Then what happened?"

"Well, then … they discovered the bodies."

"What bodies?" The question came out as a whisper, though Raymond hadn't meant it to be.

"Five kids and three nuns were found in their beds. All dead. *Stone cold*. They just went to sleep like normal the night before but never woke up."

A violent thunder crash shook the walls, and the lights flickered on, off, on … OFF. Sandra gasped and grabbed Raymond's hand. She scooted closer to him, and his heart nearly exploded. She squeezed tight enough to make his fingers ache. But in that moment, as frightened as he was, all Raymond wanted was the velvet darkness and Sandra's warm, soft hand wrapped around his own, forever.

The lights flickered on again.

"Yikes!" She burst out laughing. "That scared the shit out of me!" She dropped his hand, then fished out her phone to check the time. "Yes! Let's go, Ray. I am OUT of here."

Grief flooded Raymond's chest like bog water. "Wait! You have to tell me the rest."

28

"That's it. That's the story."

"*That's it?* Didn't they, like, call the cops or something?"

"And tell them what? You think the cops would believe that story?"

"But what happened to Benny?"

"I told you. He's still down there. In the cellar."

"And *that's* why you hate to go down there?"

"Yup." Sandra stood, then grabbed the wash bucket. "And I'll never have to go down there again … hopefully!" She laughed. "Ready, Freddy?" She held out her hand, then yanked him up, just like she'd done the day they became friends.

"Wait." Raymond took a deep breath, reached into his pocket, found the small packet wrapped in tissue paper, and pulled it out. "I have a present for you. 'Cause it's your last day."

Her eyes went soft. Her colors glistened. Dappled sunlight on wet, green leaves.

He watched her open it. The butterflies flapping in his belly felt more like bats. When she saw what was inside, her eyes filled with tears.

"Oh, my God, Ray. It's *me*."

He'd found the shell on a school hike around the bay. It was pure white, smooth, and nearly as big as his hand. Perfect for painting. And he couldn't think of anything more beautiful to paint then Sandra's face.

"Jeez, you are *talented*. I mean it, Ray, really. You're … you're something special." She kissed him on the cheek.

Warm honey flowed through Raymond's veins. He stared at her. Memorizing every detail.

"C'mon." She put her arm around him as they walked up the aisle to the front hall. Sandra pushed open the door, then froze, sucking in her breath. A scuffling sound, then the slap of boots on wet stone echoed in the narrow lane through the churchyard.

Raymond's stomach cramped. He recognized the coat, slick and shiny under the lights of the walkway. "It's Kevin."

"Spying on us? Why?"

Raymond shrugged.

Sandra stared at the shadow form running toward the main house. "You stay away from that, kid, Ray. He's … not right."

Raymond laughed. The idea that he had a *choice* to stay away from Kevin seemed funny.

"I mean it."

They headed along the path to the main house.

"Hey, Sandra. You really think it's true? About Benny … and all that stuff?"

Her eyes were bright and round with honesty. "Absolutely, I do."

She was *not* lying; he knew that for sure. She believed every word of that Benny story.

And because he loved her, because that was probably the last time he would ever see her, and because he *knew* what loneliness could do to a person, Raymond half-believed it, too.

Chapter Three

NOT COUNTING ADOPTION, Haven kids were allowed off-grounds for exactly three reasons: doctor, dentist, or field trip. Field trip was the first choice, of course, but even a trip to Haven's dreaded dentist — so popular, they called him Dr. Bloodgums — was worth it just for the change of scenery.

The Haven had just four field trips a year, one per season, and no more. Field trips were expensive, and Father Galen hated expensive. They were also a lot of work — Father Galen hated that, too — so no "babies" allowed. You had to be eight, or close enough. Some of them, like Raymond, had no idea *exactly* when they were born, so an estimated age was the best they could do. But most importantly, if you were on a Haven field trip, you were expected to "look after your own person."

Raymond chose to celebrate his birthday on December 26th, the day he arrived at Haven. So, for the first time, he finally made the cut, age-wise, for the

January field trip. Best present ever, as far he was concerned, because the upcoming trip was to the the Portland Museum of Art! Or PMA, as it was called on-line.

Raymond had memorized the entire PMA Wikipedia page and spent hours on the library computer. He knew the name and artist of every exhibit currently on show in the museum's 112,000 square feet of gallery space. And he was hoping to squeeze in as many as Father Galen and the sisters would allow. He'd never been more excited about anything, ever.

But after what happened in the cellar, and the thing in math class — Sister Connie told, because of course, nuns *always* told — Father Galen called him into the office.

"Raymond," Father spoke without looking up, "the sisters are concerned about you. They say you're having some trouble. Nervous … episodes." Father Galen liked to wander around a key word before finally deciding to spit it out.

Raymond tried to make his face a blank page. "Episodes?"

Father took off his glasses and sat back in his chair. His eyes trailed down to Raymond's crotch then back up. "Containing your …" He coughed. "Maintain … control, son."

Father Galen would rather tie his tongue in a knot than say the word "pee." Or "piss." Or even "urine." Like certain words would permanently stain the inside of his mouth.

"No, not really, Father."

"No? Do you want to tell me what happened?

Raymond couldn't look at him. With his thumbnail, he scratched a square into the dry skin on the back of his hand.

"What's all this business with the cellar?"

He filled the square with X-shaped stars. Like a tiny window to another galaxy.

"Come, now. God helps those who help themselves, yes?"

Raymond nodded, but the idea pissed him off. Shouldn't God be helping those who *can't* help themselves?

"Sister said the bigger boys locked you in the cellar. In the dark. Is that right?"

Raymond scratched curtains into the galaxy window.

Kevin's voice in his head said, "Gay!"

He rubbed them out.

Father Galen let out a big, fat annoyed sigh. "Raymond, you know we have strict rules about bullying here, but there's not much we can do without information. So, you need tell me what, or who."

"Nothing, nobody … I just don't like it down there."

"Why not?"

"I'm claustrophobic."

"You are not. Do you even know the meaning of the word?"

"An irrational fear of small places."

Another annoyed sigh. "Sister said she found you,

quite upset. That you had" — Father wrinkled his nose like he smelled something bad — "*wet* yourself."

Raymond's face caught fire. He wished he could disappear, walk through walls … like Benny.

"Help *me* help *you*, Raymond, yes?"

No. Noooo way, in fact. He wanted to tell. He wanted help. But it wouldn't work. It never did.

"Do you *remember* what happened?"

Of course, he did. He'd remember it for the rest of his life. Every. Single. Detail.

Sandra smiling at him from the back seat of her dad's car. How she had waved his shell in the air, then kissed it. The blinding red taillights, cold and mean, as they disappeared into the misty darkness, rolling out of his life forever.

Raymond stood in the damp, frigid air in the front yard, listening to the distant rumble of the car engine until he could hear it no more. He made sure to wipe his eyes before climbing the steps to Haven's front door.

When he stepped into the hallway, Kevin was waiting for him. He had his usual audience there, too. Brandon, a big kid, like Kevin, but slow and dumb. Joey, who was small and weaselly, with a wide, toothy mouth. And Derek, who was quiet, and smarter than the others, but always seemed mad about something. They worshipped Kevin, but at the same time, you could tell they kind of hated him, too. He made them laugh, though, usually by making someone else look stupid. Or worse. At Haven, a guy could be bored into meanness.

Kevin sneered. "Hey, lover boy, did you kiss your girlfriend goodbye?" He made wet, slurpy kissing sounds, and the others cackled.

Raymond's stomach churned like he'd swallowed acid. He knew where this was going.

Kevin's colors pulsated, always. Wavy bands of purple and magenta, swirling and crashing into each other, over and over again. Smash, smash, smash.

"You know she's like, *the* major slut of the high school, right? That's why they sent her to this shithole."

"That's not true!" Raymond's stomach cramped so hard, he nearly folded in half. But no way was he going to let Kevin see that happen. That would be warm blood in the water for Kevin the shark. "She's … nice."

Kevin stepped closer. "You calling me a liar, freak?"

"No."

"Sounds like you are."

Raymond looked at the carpet and shook his head. But his body locked up. The first punch could come any time now. They were getting to *that* part of Kevin's show.

The swinging doors leading from the kitchen whooshed open. Sister Ann. Raymond nearly cried with relief.

"Boys! What are you doing here? It's TV time in the rec."

"We were just helping Raymond finish up his chores."

Sister frowned, "Oh, were you?"

"Yes, Sister. Father gave Raymond extra for punishment because —"

"Yes, Kevin, I know all about it."

Sister stared for a moment, gaze traveling among Raymond, Kevin, and the other boys. "Good Samaritans, huh?"

She walked over to Kevin. "All right, then. Here you go."

When Raymond saw what Sister Ann shoved into Kevin's arms, he almost fainted.

"Do NOT mix the whites with the colors." She turned and pushed open the sliding doors. "We've had gray sheets all week, and you know how Father dislikes …"

Her voice trailed off down the hall, though Raymond wasn't listening to her, anyway. He couldn't do anything but look between the laundry basket in Kevin's arms and the mean, ugly, sickening smile across his face.

He knew Kevin had heard Sandra's story. He knew Kevin was spying because he was jealous.

And knew what Kevin would do to him once he stepped through that cellar door.

There was no "staying away" from Kevin …

"Raymond? I'm waiting, son."

Father Galen was staring.

"Uhm … I, uh —"

"Raymond! Speak up. Please!"

"It was my turn to switch the laundry. The lights went out. I couldn't get the door open. And … I think

... I *thought* I felt someone touch the back of my neck."

Even the *memory* of his screams hurt Raymond's ears.

"Someone? Who?"

Raymond winced as another cramp ripped through him. When he spoke, his voice sounded small, weak, pathetic. "Benny."

"Oh, Raymond, really. Not that silly story again. I would have thought you, of all people, would know better. Look, imagination is a good thing when it comes to your art and creativity. But it's becoming too much of a good thing in your case. Do you understand? So, brass tacks, now. What exactly happened?"

"I told you."

"The lights just went out? The door just locked? By themselves?"

Raymond shrugged.

"And you were so frightened you ... lost control?"

Raymond nodded.

"What about in class? What happened there?"

Shit. Shit. *Shit.* Of course, Sister Connie told. Nuns *always* told. "I ... fell asleep and had a nightmare."

Father Galen said nothing for a while. Raymond could tell he was getting ready to say something crummy.

"Well, I'm sorry Raymond, but I think it's best that you sit out this field trip. We simply can't have these issues ... off grounds. The Haven has a reputation to uphold and —"

"Oh, please, Father."

"There will be other trips. Let's just see how you get on, and hopefully you'll have ... matured out of this by —"

"Oh please ... *please*. I can't miss this one. Not *this* one. It won't happen again. I just ... I'm over it. Honest."

"I'm sorry, son, but —"

"But ... but ..." Raymond fired his memory, scrolling through quotes like links from a Fetch-It search, "Lamentations, 3:21-23!" The words came out like a bubbling stream after downpour, "But this I call to mind, and therefore I have hope: The steadfast love of the Lord never ceases; his mercies never come to an end; they are new every morning; great is your faithfulness."

Father Galen froze, his mouth half-way open. He stared, frowning, like Raymond was a puzzle with a missing piece.

Raymond felt him sliding one way, then the other, then back. He flickered, like the church lights during Sandra's storm. On, off, on, off?

Another huge sigh. Then, *finally*, words.

"I need a solemn promise, son. No dithering — it's not fair to the others. Will you ... are you ... you *will* manage to hold your person? Off grounds?"

"Yes, Father."

"Because we simply can't expect the sisters to be —"

"I know."

"I mean, there won't be a change of clothing handy and —"

"I know."

"We must grow out of these things, yes?"

"Uh-huh."

"What?"

"Yes, Father Galen."

"You're sure?"

Was he sure? Not really. He *wanted* to be. But … "Yes, I'm sure."

Raymond held his breath, waiting.

"All right. We'll exercise a little faith. You may attend the museum field trip."

Father put his glasses back on.

Raymond jumped up, ready to head for the door.

"Raymond?"

He froze.

"The meet and greet. You're one of the boys tonight, yes?"

"Yes. My time is just after dinner."

Father dipped his chin and eyed Raymond over the top of his glasses. "You be at your best, now. Sensible, hmmm? This could be the one."

Father Galen didn't even bother to hide the eager look on his face. As much as he wanted a family of his own, it hurt to know that Father wanted him gone so badly.

"I will, Father."

"I'm taking you at your word, son. We have a reputation, here. No more … histrionics. Yes?"

"Nope. I mean, yes! Totally. Yes."

"Good." Father turned back to the papers on his desk.

Raymond headed for the door. "Thank you, Father." He never looked back. Light-headed and trembling with relief, he forced himself to close the office door slowly, carefully. A slam could get him called back into the office, and who knew what could happen? Father Galen had a way of shifting gears without warning. Raymond wanted out of there before Father changed his mind.

Plus, the longer he was in Father Galen's office, the more they'd think he was tattling on Kevin and his goons.

"Remember, freak," Kevin had whispered in his ear at breakfast, "snitches get stitches."

Chapter Four

As SOON AS the office door clicked shut, Raymond whirled around, then took off down the hall.

Laughter bubbled up from his chest and burst out of his mouth. He was *so* sure that this would be taken from him. Most good things were. But not this time. This time he'd *won*! He was going on the field trip!

Ignoring the cramp in his belly, Raymond ran full out, arms pumping, faster and faster, down the long empty hallway leading to the dining room. His legs felt like rocket engines that could shoot him off to the moon if he wanted.

He barely slowed at the end of the hall, just enough to round the corner —

"Raymond!" Sister Ann's nasal screech rang through the hallway.

Raymond's boots squeaked to a dead stop. He snapped back, falling on his butt, smashing his tailbone on the marble floor. A jolt of pain ran up his spine, and the air drained from his lungs. But it was better than crashing into Sister Ann.

Raymond squeezed his eyes shut, and gulped air into his lungs, waiting for the fiery sting in his tailbone to cool off.

"Are you okay?"

It was a high voice, one he didn't recognize. Full of surprise and ... concern? For *him*?

Raymond opened his eyes and looked up. Sister Ann stood above him, her eyebrows lifted in surprise and confusion. Beside her was a small figure, half the sister's height. A doll? No. The figure was moving, eyes blinking, weight shifting nervously, side to side.

It was a girl. But she was so perfectly formed, she could have been mistaken for an incredibly life-like doll. Her eyes were pure blue, almost cerulean, like the last charcoal pencil to disintegrate under Kevin's boot. They radiated like small, matching lighthouses from the smooth, glowing, milk chocolate of her face.

A black girl.

Person of color! Raymond corrected himself silently, automatically. But in truth, the phrase was silly to him. All people were people of color. Many, *many* colors. Weren't they?

But *her* colors, winter star blue against creamy warm cocoa, *stunned* Raymond. She certainly wasn't the first "non-white" resident at Haven, but he'd never seen beauty quite like hers. It hurt to look at her.

She spoke again, a talking doll.

"Are you okay? Did you hurt yourself?"

Her smile was brilliant white. Nervous, but *real*.

Raymond pushed himself up off the floor. "No, I'm okay. Just didn't see you."

"Well, what did you expect, tearing around the halls like a wild banshee." Sister's voice was sharp, but she wasn't too mad. Lucky for him.

"Sorry, Sister, I thought I was late for dinner."

"Hmph." She looked at her watch, "Well, we're all going to be late for dinner if we don't get a move on. Raymond, this is Keisha, a new resident."

Keisha wiggled her fingers. A tiny wave.

C'mon, dummy. A wave back. A nod. Something.

But no. All he could do was stare, lost in the pale blue of her eyes, her milk chocolate skin. Stunned silent. Stupid. Once again flummoxed by the colors of a pretty girl. Would it always be this way?

"Raymond, please take Keisha to the dining hall, show her where the trays are, plates and so on?"

"Yes, Sister," he mumbled.

Sister Ann bent down, getting eye to eye with Keisha. "Raymond's going to show you the ropes, okay. Just follow the crowd. Now don't be shy, we're all friends here. You'll do just fine."

Keisha's nod was sharp and tough. She pushed her chin out and up so high, it must have hurt. She *so* wanted to be brave. And it made Raymond want it for her. But the trembling in her lower lip gave her away. She sucked it into her teeth and waited, staring a hole right through him, freezing him solid.

Fat, awkward seconds passed until Sister lost her patience.

"Oh, for goodness's sake."

She grabbed Raymond's hand and turned it upward. Then Keisha's, pressing their palms together, before closing his fingers over Keisha's tiny knuckles.

Raymond's cheeks went red hot. He hoped Keisha didn't see.

"Off you go, before you miss the whole thing!" Sister shooed them, like they were a couple of seagulls begging a clam belly, then hurried down the hall, "Get moving!"

Raymond got moving, burning with embarrassment that he was holding hands with a girl. He hoped like crazy that they didn't run into Kevin. Or anyone else.

His eyes were glued to the shiny marble floor as he led Keisha toward the dining hall, hand-in hand. It was like holding a soft, little bird in his palm. Keisha's hand pulsed like a heart. Thump-thump, thump-thump. Speeding up, getting warmer by the second.

Then something strange happened. His hand felt like it was swelling, a fleshy balloon. And the warm bird in his palm began to flap its wings. It grew a sharp beak and began to peck the thin skin of his palm. Faster and faster, like a needle, stabbing into him over and over, until his entire hand went numb.

A sharp pain burst in Raymond's lower belly. He doubled over, hearing a grunt that must have been his.

"Hey!" Keisha's voice sounded muffled and far away, like she was underwater. Or *he* was underwater.

"Hey, not so tight. That hurts!"

He looked up at her face. It floated in front of

him, her eyebrows all screwed up, like she was in pain, too. It rippled, wavy, bobbing on a current.

They were both underwater now.

More voices, more faces flowed toward him on shimmering, iridescent waves. They were *Keisha's* waves, he suddenly understood, rippling from her to him.

Sharp, jagged rainbows, crisscrossed with gray and black slashes, streamed from her tiny body. They turned dark brown, like overflow from the sewer cap in the Haven's courtyard. Pictures began to break the surface, flash and sink, riding the dark stream like paper boats. A woman, a man, eyes like slits. Needles, like the doctor uses. A dirty, bent-up spoon that looked like it had been dug out of a campfire. A clump of mud? Dirt? Click! A flame flickered. The dirt got smoky. It stunk! Then dissolved into a spoonful of brown liquid.

Raymond's arm caught fire. The heat raced up his arm and shot through his body. He was burning up!

He felt Keisha trying to pull away, and he wanted to help, to release his burning grip on her tiny hand. But his fingers were melted together, fused with hers.

Her face changed. The eyes — so calm, and beautiful moments ago, now bulged with fear, and confusion.

Fear of what? Me? She's afraid of *me*!

"LET GO!"

Her scream smacked his forehead, stabbed his ears. And he wanted to scream, too. But when he opened his mouth, it filled with water.

Then Keisha's bulging eyes filled with blood. It spilled over into two tracks of crimson tears streaming down her cheeks. They flowed faster, gushing, until thick, red trails covered her face and dripped from her chin.

Raymond froze, horrified, as the blood poured from Keisha's ears, ran down her shoulders, splattered across the front of her sweater.

He gagged. The room spun. His stomach lurched.

He was repulsed. *Disgusted*.

Raymond tried, again and again, to rip himself away from her, but he couldn't.

Blood trailed down Keisha's arm now, soaking their hands. Unable to turn away, he watched it drip onto the dirty floor.

The kitchen floor? Linoleum. Like downstairs in the basement. Not the gleaming marble floors of Haven's hallways. Keisha's kitchen floor.

He realized he was shivering, chilled to the bone. But how? When he was burning to death from the inside out?

You're not cold. You're scared, you big fat baby. You pussy. You're fucking terrified.

But he wasn't feeling his own terror.

Keisha's?

He didn't know. It didn't matter. They were one.

What's happening? What is this? What is WRONG with me?

A distant scream, barely audible at first, rushed up at him like someone hit fast-forward on a remote

46

control. His forehead throbbed. Like the thump of a soft, round fist between his eyes, over and over.

Someone was crying. A man? And a little girl's voice, too — that had to be Keisha's. Both of them, screaming, crying, sobbing, over the wail of police sirens.

So loud, so ... *shrill*. Fingernails ripping his eardrums to shreds.

"I'm sick."

Raymond didn't know why he needed to say that. To *try* to say that. His mouth was mush, his words slurring like a cartoon drunk.

"LET GO OF ME!"

"I'm dying, Keisha. *Dying!*"

Keisha's screamed, doubling the one in his head. Her eyes were horror-movie wide. Her terror, his shame ... both crashed through him in sickening waves.

The throb in his forehead sharpened, like the tiny fist had found its knuckles, only to grind them into his skull until he was so dizzy, he couldn't tell the ceiling from the floor. He was spinning in circles, faster and faster, and the screaming, louder and louder still.

His terror broke into a run. Panic grabbed him in its sharp teeth and shook him, back and forth, like a shark in a feeding frenzy.

He had to stop looking, stop listening, stop feeling. He had to LET GO.

But he couldn't.

You're a *freak*. That's what wrong. You're weak and screwed up.

"I'm sorry Keish —"

Raymond's mouth filled with blood. *Mama's blood*.

He wanted to scream. But he was tired. Suddenly, so *very* tired.

A tremble started in his knees and spread upward. Then Raymond felt himself begin to dissolve. Like sugar in hot tea. He was wet paper, melting ice.

He slid downward.

With the last of his strength, he yanked his hand free of Keisha's. No need to drag her down too, right? Not where he was going.

A moment later, he was back on the floor. The images began to thin and ripple. The horrible shrieking drifted away, further, and further, until all that was left was an unpleasant ringing in Raymond's ears.

His was *so* tired. He'd never *been* so exhausted.

Well, he was already lying down. Why not just sleep?

Keisha was sobbing. For real, now. Here, in the hallway.

"Get up! You stop that!"

If he got up, he'd puke. Sorry again, Keisha.

Keisha grunted. A sharp pain exploded in his ribs.

"GET UP!"

He forced his eyes open. Keisha's face floated above him, nostrils flaring in and out, wet, snotty … furious.

She'd *kicked* him. And her face said she was about to do it again.

Raymond rolled to one side and pushed himself

up to sitting. His brain sloshed in his skull. The hallway did a somersault. He took a couple of breaths. The room went still. But his mouth tasted of salt, metal … blood.

"Keisha." His voice was back, but barely more than a croak. "Is your Mama … sick?"

"Not sick. Not *dying*. Dead. My Mama's dead. Happy?"

Why would he be happy about that?

"I … huh?"

"You have fun?"

"No —"

"That nun tell you what happened to her?"

"What? No!"

"They're not supposed to tell nothing. To nobody! That's what they said."

"No. I … I … she didn't —"

The clack of shoes drifted toward them. A man's voice. Father Galen!

Raymond pushed up onto his knees. Then to standing, breathing deep to keep his stomach from spilling out all over the place. He swallowed hard, but the salty blood taste was still there.

Keisha looked toward the sound, then back at him. She wasn't happy, but her furious look was now more nervous. Better.

"Don't say anything," he whispered, "Please."

Raymond almost grabbed her hand but caught himself just in time.

Keisha took a step back from him.

Father Galen's voice was louder now. It was high

and fake — the voice he used for the parents. He was yakking on his phone.

And walking right toward them.

"Keisha. Please. Don't tell what happened okay? *Okay?*"

Keisha lifted her chin in that tough way again. A good sign. But the fear was still there in her eyes. Along with hurt.

He had hurt her, though he hadn't mean to.

Keisha's pointed a tiny finger at him. Her nose twitched in anger. "You don't tell anyone what happened to my Mama."

"I won't. I swear."

Keisha's big round eyes became slits.

"And you never, ever touch me again. *Ever*. Right?"

He had no problem with *that*.

"Right. But …"

"But what?"

"Just … I'm sorry. About your mom."

Keisha's chin dropped. "Shut up."

"You must be sad."

She shook her head, but her bottom lip disappeared between her teeth. Without a word, she turned and ran in the direction of the dining hall.

Raymond waited a moment for the worst of the dizziness to clear, then started after her. He walked slowly, carefully, the taste of blood still on his tongue, the pictures of fear and death still pulsing in his mind. Awful, *horrible* images he wished he could un-see. And worse, they were *real*. True things that had *actually* happened. He *knew* they were. But how did he know that?

His body shook. He wanted to cry but was afraid if he started, he'd never stop.

Whatever had just happened to him, he knew it was wrong. Terrible. Not *normal*. Maybe even dangerous. The kind of thing a kid should talk to someone about.

But what would he say? Who would ever believe him?

As Raymond walked through the foyer, the hot soup smell of the dining room filled his nostrils. His stomach rumbled, but, for once, it didn't *burn*. Though he was still shaken by what he'd seen, the relentless, stabbing pain in his gut had softened to a dull ache. Not exactly fun, but tolerable.

Then a realization, so simple, so *ordinary*, nonetheless, caught Raymond by surprise.

He wanted food.

Chapter Five

Meet & Greet smelled like rotten fruit and wet paint, thanks to Mr. Gregg. "Air freshener" was the wrong name for whatever he was spraying around.

"Stuffy as hell in here, right?"

Mr. Gregg looked over at him and nodded, which meant Raymond was supposed to nod back. He did, of course. But the smell of "stuffy" was better than the gross stink coming out his can.

That thought was in Kevin's voice.

All the swear thoughts were in Kevin's voice.

I hate that stupid room, and all the fake-as-fuck cozy shit.

Raymond shifted on the scratchy sofa and looked around him. He'd never noticed that all the decorations had something to do with farming. A milk can filled with dried herbs and paper sunflowers took up too much space on the coffee table in front of him. Beyond that were two almost-matching rocking chairs with faded, plaid cushions and fat wooden arms covered in scars. The thin, flowery curtains hanging

E. G. ROSE

over the plastic-covered windows looked like they were put up one summer and forgotten about. And the walls were covered with pictures of cows, haystacks, fall-colored trees, and old-timey looking people smiling at each over dinner tables full of food.

Ugh. The last thing he wanted to think about was food.

The greasy chicken Raymond had chowed down at dinner was now a ball of writhing slugs in his belly. He eyed the trash bucket in the corner. Five, maybe six steps away. If his dinner finally made the decision to come back up, he figured he could make it. He *hoped* he could, anyway. He didn't get too many chances to be in this "fake-as-fuck" room anymore. Not like when he was *really* little. A big pile of chicken puke was not going to help his chances with Mr. and Mrs. Devlin.

For a second, Raymond forgot where he was. He burped, long and gross.

Mr. Gregg froze mid-spray and shot him a disgusted look.

"Sorry," Raymond mumbled. He took a deep breath and silently begged the Vomit Gods to let him off the hook this time.

The Meet & Greet room *was* fake, like Kevin said. It was stuffy, too. Mr. Gregg was right about that. And boy, was it hot — *way* warmer than the other rooms in Haven. All the thermostats had locks to make sure nobody "wasted heat," and Father Galen had the only key. They were all used to wearing double sweaters from fall through late spring. But this room was for outsiders. It might be their first, and sometimes only, peek inside the walls of the Haven Home for Tender Souls. Nobody wanted to think of poor orphans freezing their butts off.

Raymond was sleepy, and the weird thing with Keisha had left him with a headache. That and the heat made his whole body feel heavy, like he could sink into this itchy, ugly sofa and disappear. His eyelids fluttered closed.

A metallic creak made Raymond jump. His eyes snapped open. Mr. Gregg sat in the rocker across the coffee table, watching him in that weird way of his, through the corner of one eye, his face half-turned away. His dark suit and glossy black hair reminded Raymond of the crows that gathered on the roof above the playground during recess. They'd stare, sharp and menacing, like they'd peck a hole right into your chest if there was anything in there worth seeing.

Mr. Gregg had taken over as Raymond's case worker five months ago when his last one, Mr. Dillon, got a "better offer" from Boston. Raymond didn't care much either way. Mr. Dillon was sort of okay for a guy that didn't want to be there. But he acted like everything was pointless, and that made Raymond feel pointless, too.

Mr. Dillon had a bushy beard and wore big, floppy suits with sneakers. He grew up in Topsham, not too far from Brunswick. But he talked a lot about his favorite books and movies and where he'd traveled, like "out west," New York City, and even Europe. Raymond liked to hear about those faraway places and dreamed about going himself someday. Even though they were *supposed* to meet every Monday for Weekly Counsel, they hardly ever did. Mr. Dillon was always cancelling, postponing, or just plain forgetting their sessions. Eventually, Raymond just gave up. He spent the time painting and drawing, or in the library looking around online, which was fine with him. But Raymond just didn't get it. How did a guy who didn't do the job he had manage to get an even better one?

Mr. Gregg was the total opposite of Mr. Dillon. He wasn't a Mainer. He was from New Jersey. Sister Ann said *that* was obvious every time he opened his mouth. But Raymond had never been to New Jersey, either, so it wasn't obvious to him. In fact, the only obvious thing about Mr. Gregg was that he was never looked comfortable. He wore neat, slim suits, always black or dark gray. His movements were small and precise, as if he'd planned them all out at the start of his day. He walked in slow, careful steps, like his skin was stretched too tight over his skeleton and he worried it would tear. Raymond couldn't even *imagine* him in sneakers.

Mr. Gregg never talked about his favorite books or movies, where he was from, or where he'd traveled. He never talked about himself at all. The man was a mystery and seemed to like it that way.

Raymond did his best to respect that. It was the right thing to do. And he was grateful, in a way. In the five months that Mr. Gregg had been around, this was the third time he'd gotten Raymond in this room.

Which was three more chances than Mr. Dillon ever got him. And he had more than two *years* to try.

He caught Mr. Gregg's colors, of course. He couldn't help that. But Raymond never looked *too* hard. Never tried to see beyond the colors in the way he sometimes could. It was happening more often now. Like something was reaching out for him. A set of invisible hands, one pulling back a heavy curtain, the other waving him inside, to the place where the pictures came from. With Mr. Gregg, he never went beyond what he was *supposed* to see.

Mr. Gregg was yellow. Definitely yellow. *Usually* a safe, happy color. But Mr. Gregg's yellow was sickish and pale. Like a plant that hasn't been watered for a long time.

There's more, Raymond …

Stop.

He had to tell her to stop sometimes.

Her. What if Kevin knew?

The thought was like a punch in the stomach.

"Hello? Earth to Raymond?"

Mr. Gregg was still staring.

Raymond pushed down into the couch to sit up straighter. His stomach gurgled, like the water draining from a huge bathtub.

Mr. Gregg frowned and switched his stare to the other eye.

"Are you feeling … *well*, Raymond?"

Raymond wanted to smile and shrug. Like Kevin would. Like, no big deal, it's all cool. Kevin could get away with *murder* just by smiling in the right way. But

Kevin was confident, good-looking — everyone thought so. And that stuff never worked for Raymond. All he had was the truth. Whether it helped him or not.

"Sorry, Mr. Gregg. Just … my stomach, you know. And my eyes … my head. They just hurt."

He leaned in closer. "Right now?"

Raymond nodded.

"Since when?"

He shrugged. He honestly couldn't remember since *when*. What difference did it make?

"How often does it hurt?

A picture flashed in Raymond's mind. The crows, shining in the winter sun, iridescent rainbows on midnight black, leaning out over the edge of the gutter to stare.

"My stomach, almost always. My eyes, just when the colors are … a lot."

"Have you been wearing your reading glasses?"

Raymond nodded. He didn't think the glasses did anything to help his headaches. But he wore them most of the time.

"And no better?"

"Worse. They're getting … stronger. And there are more of them."

"More of what?"

Peck, peck, peck.

Raymond sighed. He didn't get it. He never got it. All those questions, and he *never, ever got it*.

"More of what, Raymond. Explain."

"*Colors*. More of them."

"How can there be more of them?"

"I don't know. But there are. And … other things."

"What other things?"

Raymond looked down at his boots. Dark, black, quiet, calm.

"Raymond, I'm up here."

He looked up. "Shapes, like. I don't know. Like the colors."

"And the other thinker?"

That's what he called her — the woman's voice in his head.

"Still there. Sometimes. I tell her to stop." Raymond couldn't stand to say "her" out loud.

Mr. Gregg sucked in air then puffed it out again, a little orange-red flare in his sick-yellow field.

Shit. He's annoyed. He's going to cancel the meet-and-greet.

"Sorry. I guess I'm just … nervous to meet them."

"That's understandable. *Normal.* But—" Mr. Gregg peeked at his watch. "Shoot. Okay, they'll be here any minute. I want you to —"

"They're not going to like me."

The orange flared again, but less red this time. "Then just *be* likable. Be the best version of yourself you can imagine."

"My honest self?"

"Of course, but … look, Raymond, not everything needs to be *out there*. Sometimes, to get through, we just have to —"

The knock on the door was shy, but Raymond still jumped.

"Just … be polite, pleasant, natural. Talk about your art, your interests. Relax. I'm sure they're going to love you. Just be yourself. All right?"

Raymond nodded.

Mr. Gregg stood, then smoothed the front of his pants. "Show time." He crossed the room and opened the door.

In the hall stood a small woman in a big, furry winter coat. It looked like she was wearing a bear suit. Her lipstick was fire-engine red and made the rest of her face look pale. Beside her was a big-jawed, tall man with brown hair like wire. When his eyes met Raymond's, the corners of his mouth went up.

"Mr. Devlin, Mrs. Devlin, welcome." Mr. Gregg spread his arm wide. "Come on in."

Raymond stood and, like Mr. Gregg, brushed the front of his clothing. He immediately felt stupid, and phony, like the fake-cozy farm shit around him.

Mr. Devlin moved toward him, hand extended.

"James Devlin."

The memory of meeting Keisha ran through him like an electric shock. Her tiny hand in his, beating fast like a bird in a trap, the fear, the blood …

LET GO!

Raymond pulled away from Mr. Devlin's extended hand and caught his heels on the edge of the sofa. He fell back into the cushions with a plop. He immediately straightened, sitting up as tall as he could, but his face burned with embarrassment.

Mrs. Devlin peeked out from behind the square

block of Mr. Devlin's frame. "Aww, he's shy, Jimmy. Not so fast."

Mr. Devlin looked back at his wife. When he turned around to face Raymond again, his careful smile had wilted. "Nice to meet you, Raymond." He stepped to one side, and his wife moved forward. "This is my wife, Debbie."

Mr. Gregg raised his eyebrows at Raymond and flicked his fingers upward. Raymond rose again. "Hello, ma'am."

"Oh, I'm not a ma'am! You make me feel old!"

"Sorry, Mrs. Devlin."

"Debbie." Her smile was too wide. Too bright.

"Sorry, um, Debbie."

She flapped her hand at him and laughed. "And he's Jimmy. Okay?"

Her laugh, her *everything*, was too bright. But Raymond felt her kindness and began to relax.

Mr. Gregg gestured to the rocking chairs. "Please."

Debbie and Jimmy settled into the rocking chairs, and Mr. Gregg sat beside Raymond on the sofa. He started talking in that adult-chat way — the one that always made kids tune out. How was the drive up from Rhode Island? Get much snow this season? The Sox got some great picks this year, eh?

Raymond put his "pay attention" face on, knowing this would go on for a while. But in truth, he was glad for the chance to take them in.

When Debbie spoke, her face moved through so many expressions, it was hard to keep up. Raymond wished she'd settle on one or two only, so he could really see her. It took a while, but eventually, she came through.

Her colors were red-brown, but dull, like an old copper pot that used to be shiny. Still warm and soft, though, and Raymond liked them.

Mr. Devlin — *Jimmy* — sat in the rocking chair with his knees spread wide, like he didn't want to waste an inch of seat. He did a lot of nodding but didn't always look like he was listening. He had red hands with fat fingers, and the hairiest knuckles Raymond had ever seen. They flexed and twitched as he gripped the wooden arms of his chair. He wore a suit and tie, but the suit seemed wrong. Like it belonged to someone else. There was something "someone else" about Jimmy in general. Hollowed, shadowed, like a crater on the moon. Raymond wanted to draw him.

His colors were smoky, mushroom truffle, dusty dark, midnight sky ... charcoal-purple.

Charcoal-purple? There isn't a charcoal purple.

There's more, Raymond. There's more, there's more.

As hot and stuffy as the room was, a chill when up Raymond's spine.

As Mr. Gregg spoke, Debbie leaned forward, hanging on his every word like a little kid. But occasionally, she'd sneak a grin at Raymond. Sometimes, she'd add a wink, like they were already good pals, sharing secrets. It made him like her even more. Pretty good trick.

A sudden prickling at the back of his neck made Raymond look at Mr. Devlin. Sure enough, Mr.

Devlin was watching him. Normally, when someone catches you staring, you turn away. But Mr. Devlin did not. He waited for Raymond to do it first.

After what felt like ages, the adult-chat became a car running out of gas. Mr. Gregg turned toward him, and Raymond's stomach tingled.

It was his turn.

Don't mess it up.

"So, as you know," Mr. Gregg said, smiling too much, just like Debbie, "Raymond has been very excited to meet you."

Jimmy nodded and smiled, for real this time. "Well, likewise. Debbie and I are pretty thrilled that we, uh, passed the test."

Raymond frowned, "What test?"

"For Haven. To be able to adopt. You know.

"They make you take a *test*? How do you study for getting a *kid*?"

Jimmy started to say something, but his mouth stopped halfway and just hung open, like he was waiting for a few words to drop in there. He looked at his wife, then Mr. Gregg, and suddenly all the adults were laughing.

Jimmy clapped his fat hands together, only once, but it was a loud crack. "That's awesome."

Debbie leaned forward and squeezed Raymond's knee, still chuckling. "We had to be approved. You think they're going to let just anyone take you?"

Raymond shrugged. "I'm not picky."

"Raymond!"

Mr. Gregg kind of shouted, but he was mostly

laughing. Jimmy and Debbie were still cracking up, like he was the funniest thing they'd ever seen.

Debbie leaned toward Jimmy, and gave his knee a squeeze too, "He's too cute, huh?"

It was weird. Him, cute? Funny? He was just being honest. Being *himself*.

But Mr. Gregg was smiling. Even gave him a little nod. So, he must be doing okay. Right?

As if to answer his question, Mr. Gregg stood and smoothed his pants. "Welp, I'm going to step out and give you all a chance to chat."

Raymond smiled. He'd never gotten *this* far before. They only left you alone with them if it was going well.

Mr. Gregg stepped into the hallway, then leaned back in, whispering, like he had a special bit of news, "Did I mention that Raymond is quite the talented painter?"

"Oh, yes." Debbie beamed. "We saw the photos in the file. Amazing!"

Mr. Devlin nodded, "Very nice, very nice."

The door shut. Then he was alone with them.

But it was okay. They were smiling. They were happy. They *liked* him.

Debbie scooted onto the couch beside him. "I was *so* impressed with your artwork, Raymond."

"Yeah," Jimmy said, "She couldn't stop talking about it. Hung it up on the fridge."

Raymond tried not to blush. But that wasn't really possible, was it? Faces just did that, like there was no such thing as a private feeling. "Thanks, Debbie."

"Oh, you don't have to thank me. It was really, just … I was SO impressed."

"You were?"

"Uh-huh. I teach art for primary school."

No way. An art teacher for a mom?

"You *do*?"

She laughed, and this time it wasn't too bright at all. It was just right.

"I paint some myself, you know. And draw. And sculpt a little."

If he were a girl, he would cry. This was it! It was too perfect! And they *liked* him. Mr. Gregg was right about just being himself. "That's amazing. I would love to try sculpting."

"I'm sure you would be great at it. But your paintings, your drawings … the use of color and shading. Your perspective. So unusual. So vibrant and *emotional*."

Jimmy groaned. "Geez, Debbie. He's eight. You're way over his head."

Raymond couldn't have shaken his head any harder. "No, she isn't. She's … " He smiled at her, "She's just right."

Debbie broke into a wide grin. Her shoulders lifted, then dropped down, quick, like she was excited and happy. Just like him.

"Life looks different to artists. It's how we see and feel the world. That's what I tell my students. Color is … our *language*, isn't it, Raymond?"

"I never thought about it as a language. That's cool."

"It *is* cool. Colors tell a story."

"Yes!" He wanted to jump off the couch and hug her so hard. "It's like, the doorway."

Debbie chuckled, but not in a mean way. "The doorway to what?"

"Well … I don't know exactly. People. First it's just colors — *their* colors."

Something made him stop. He looked from Debbie to Jimmy. They were both still smiling. And Mr. Gregg's advice was working. But …

"It's okay Raymond. I understand," Debbie opened her arms wide, "Colors just pop out at me, whether I like it or not. People make such *unflattering* choices. Drives me crazy sometimes."

"Me, too!" He'd never met anyone who *got* it. She really was like him. Which meant he wasn't the only one. He had butterflies in his stomach, but for once, they were happy. "I get *so* crazy. And I get sick, too. Do you?"

"Sick?"

"Yup, sometimes. It depends on the story that comes after the colors. Like I said, it's a doorway, sort of. You go through the colors. And on the other side are the stories."

Debbie's face moved from one expression to another, super-fast this time. Eventually it landed on one he could identify — confusion. "Stories?"

"Yeah, like you said. Secrets, too. Sometimes."

Raymond looked from Debbie to Jimmy. He was frowning hard. *He* didn't get it because he wasn't an artist. Obviously. Not like him and Debbie.

"What kind of stories do you see, Raymond?" Her voice was soft.

"It depends. Like, the new girl, Keisha. Her colors were pink, like a lot of girls, and that's okay. But then, her *story* was scary."

"She told you a scary story?"

"No, she didn't tell me. It just came from her. I wasn't spying. It just … happened. Like a movie — Keisha's movie — but I was in it. Sort of."

"What was so scary about it?"

Raymond hesitated. He didn't want to think about those awful pictures. Not now, when everything was going so well.

Debbie blinked at him and half-smiled. "What was so scary?" she asked again. Her voice had gone a bit quiet, but it was gentle.

Raymond took a deep breath. "Well, it had screaming. And lots of blood and … it made me really sick. She yelled at me to let go of her. And I wanted to — I *tried* — but I couldn't."

"She wanted you to let her go, but you wouldn't?"

"I *couldn't*."

Debbie's face was now the opposite of too bright. She sat back. *Away* from him. "Oh. Isn't that interesting?"

Jimmy looked like he smelled something putrid. He spoke from the side of his mouth. "No, it's fucking weird, Debbie. *He's* fucking weird."

"Wait, Jimmy —"

"There's two more to see."

"But …"

Jimmy stood up. "Nope. I heard enough. Done."

Debbie looked at Raymond. Her face was sad and suddenly very tired. Like she'd lost another round of a game that she never seemed to win.

Raymond knew how that was.

"Let's go, Debbie," Jimmy snapped, "I need some air." He gripped her elbow and pulled her up. "This room stinks."

They walked to the door. Jimmy yanked it open and waited for Debbie to step out first. He looked back at Raymond, his eyes hard and cold, his lip upper curled in disgust.

Another chill, stronger than the first, shot up Raymond's back bone, lifting the hair on the back of his neck.

There's more, Raymond.

There's more. There's more. There's more …

Chapter Six

RAYMOND PULLED his knees tight against his chest and clamped his jaw shut. His teeth would chatter, otherwise, and the sound made him think of creepy skeletons. Jophiel's Chapel was dark and cold, but he liked being there. It reminded him of Sandra. The damp from the stone wall seeped through his jacket, chilling his back. But he didn't want to move. This was where they sat, the last time he saw her. He wondered how she was doing. He'd never know, and that thought made him even sadder.

His stomach hurt. It felt hollow, empty. And in all that space was something sharp, digging in him, trying to dig *through* him, like it wanted out.

The *clack-clack* of footsteps on the path caught his attention. They were coming for him, and he didn't even care. He knew who those shoes belonged to. Only Mr. Gregg wore shoes with a *clack-clack* heel.

The chapel door opened. Sure enough, Mr. Gregg

stood in the doorway. He switched on the light. "Raymond. What are you doing in here?"

Raymond squinted up at him. "Nothing."

"Nothing, huh? Because it looks like you're feeling sorry for yourself."

Raymond wanted to scream at him. He imagined the sound of his voice, huge and booming, bouncing off the stone walls over and over.

But he said nothing. Just stared at the floor.

"What happened with the Devlins? You seemed to be hitting it off."

"They hated me. Just like I said they would."

"They did not *hate* you. But they did seem … rattled."

"What's rattled?"

"Disturbed. What did you say to them?"

"It doesn't matter."

"I'm not going to be able to help you if you don't tell me what went wrong."

"I don't *know* what went wrong. We were talking about art, like you said." He looked up at Mr. Gregg. "Debbie's an artist. Like me. Did you know that?"

"So, then what?"

"She said colors were our language. And that they told stories. I thought that was *so* cool. And I told her I saw the stories, too. Like her. Except I guess it wasn't like her."

"What did you say? About the color thing."

Raymond suddenly felt too hot in his winter coat. Irritated. Frustrated. Whatever the right word.

Jimmy Devlin. Charcoal-purple and —

There's something else.

"*He* said I was fucking weird."

"Aw, Raymond. Tell me you didn't go into that crazy talk about colors and —"

"I told the truth. I was myself, like YOU said to be!"

Raymond wasn't irritated. He wasn't frustrated. He was *angry*. He was really fucking angry.

"No, I told you to be normal. To use some common sense."

"You said to relax! Be myself! They'd love me —"

"Raymond, calm down."

"YOU said that, and I did it and now you're blaming me because you are just … shitty at your job!"

"Raymond!"

"It's not my fault!"

"Yes, it WAS. It was your fault, and you're never going to go anywhere if you don't start being honest with yourself. Face your problems —"

"Look who's talking! You left her for dead!"

Mr. Gregg froze. "What?"

Something cracked open. It wasn't his fault. He'd done as he was told, followed the rules. No, he was red hot with fury. Never before had he *been* so angry, and it cracked something open.

Then all at once, Mr. Gregg came spilling out.

Raymond saw it all.

Mr. Gregg in jeans, a black shirt, a leather jacket. Night-time. Rain. A woman waving on the side of the road. Head-lights passing as he knelt beside the flat tire, trying to work the lug wrench. But he couldn't. He was seeing two tires and rocking side to side, like he was on a boat. Because he was drunk and high. And his head hurt from the loud music and the lights, so he'd left the club. He shouldn't really drive, but home wasn't far. And she seemed nice, poor woman, stuck on the side of the road at night. Alone. A waitress, late shift. Good night? It was okay. Live far? Not too far, just a few exits off—

The blare of a horn, screech of tires. A sickening thud, then the woman was flying. Slammed against the guard rail, flopping, like a doll, onto the road when the van pulled back. On the guard rail, a bright red smear in the glow of the headlights. Blood flowing from her nose, ears, spreading like a rose in bloom, on the slick road. The lights go out. Tires screech on wet ground. Then the van is gone.

She's moaning, sobbing, reaching a bloody hand toward him. A broken, bloody pile of bones in a red-soaked coat. Help. She wants help. "Help. Please, help." But he's drunk. He's high. He's got to be at work in the morning. He has clients. There'll be cops. A statement. They'll think it's him. If she dies, she can't tell them. They'll blame him. His heart is pounding so hard, he can't think. Can barely stand. But he does. He stands over her. "I'm so sorry." He digs the keys from his pocket, climbs in the car, then pulls onto the road. Not too fast — has to stay in the lines — but go, go, go. Oh, my God. Don't think about it. Just go.

"You left that poor woman to die, all alone."

Mr. Gregg covered his mouth with both hands. His eyes bugged out like he was staring at a monster.

Raymond didn't care. *He* wouldn't have done that. Left that poor woman.

Mr. Gregg's hands fell from his face. "You can't know this. It's … it's not possible."

"You're a coward!"

A tear fell from Mr. Gregg's right eye. His expression cracked. He squeezed his eyes shut. His mouth fell open, but there was no sound. Not for a long moment. Then he let loose a moan that became a hard, sputtering sob. He dropped to the floor and bawled, full on, like a little kid.

Raymond stared, in shock. He'd never seen a grown-up cry before. It was awful. He pushed himself up from the floor, desperate to get out of there.

Mr. Gregg grabbed his hand on the way out the door.

"Raymond? *Please*. Don't tell."

Raymond yanked his hand away, then ran out. He tore down the path toward the main house. It was TV time in the rec room. They'd be looking for him. His whole body trembled, but not from the cold of the night air. It was like he'd been shot full of sugar. His skin tingled. He was electric, buzzing with liquid heat. It slid through his veins and pooled in his belly.

And slowly, for the first time in weeks, the pain dissolved completely.

Chapter Seven

RAYMOND USED TO LOVE PIZZA. It was his favorite, along with applesauce and chicken fingers. But after yesterday's Meet & Greet, the two slices on his plate looked like greasy triangles of melted wax. He just didn't feel like celebrating another Pick-Up Day for someone else. One of the little ones, a girl named Jordan, was leaving this time. She was young, and cute, and sweet ... *normal*. Exactly what all the hopeful parents were looking for.

He's fucking weird, Debbie.

Jimmy Devlin's disgusted face.

Charcoal purple.

A zing of pain shot through Raymond's jaw. He was grinding his teeth.

Was he loud?

He looked around the dining hall to see if anyone had noticed, but even those closest to him acted like he wasn't there.

Raymond sat on the end of the bench at the very

last table, closest to the wall. That had been his spot for almost two years now. The other kids moved seats every week in rotation. Father Galen said it was so everybody got the chance to "make friends." But everyone knew that wasn't true.

The problem was nobody wanted to sit next to Raymond. Or anywhere near him. Ever. They'd fake being sick. Maybe knock his tray on the floor. Sometimes just plain whine to the point where the sisters didn't want to deal with it anymore. Father Galen *and* the sisters wanted order and ease. And they'd use any shortcut they could think of to maintain it.

So, they put Raymond on the last bench against the wall and announced that seating would now be determined by weekly rotation. Period. Anyone who complained forfeited dessert and got double chores.

It was Monday, the start of a new week, and the spot beside Raymond was still empty. He looked around the room, wondering who was stuck next to him this time. His heart leapt when he spotted Keisha heading his way.

Of course. The new girl got the crappiest seat in the house. Right next to *him*. And he could tell by the way she dropped her tray on the table and sunk into the seat beside him that she wasn't happy about it.

He didn't dare speak to her, and Keisha didn't even glance at him. She sat with her legs clamped together and her arms squeezed in close to her sides, like she was trying to make herself even smaller than she already was.

Anything not to touch him.

Raymond focused on his plate but watched her out of the corner of his eye. He noticed, with a dark satisfaction he wasn't proud of, that nobody talked to Keisha, either. It took a while to make friends at Haven. That's just the way it was.

Keisha ate like a person twice her size, tearing big bites out of her pizza then gulping them down so fast, he thought she might choke. When her two slices were gone — portions were small at Haven — she tapped her fingertips all over the plate, then stuck them in her mouth, making sure she got every last greasy crumb. How could somebody so small have such a big appetite?

Raymond felt sorry for her. She probably got as much pizza as she wanted in her old life. Having less of everything must be a big adjustment. Especially for a young girl.

Being careful not to graze her elbow or bump her hand, Raymond slid his plate in front of her. For a few seconds, he said nothing. But he sensed her staring at those slices and wanting them. *Bad*.

Finally, she turned toward him. "You're not going to eat 'em?"

He shook his head.

"Aren't you hungry?"

He shrugged and felt her gaze on the side of his face. It made his skin tingle. Out of the corner of his eye, he saw her fingers stretch out to pick up a slice, then hesitate.

"What?" he said, not caring if he sounded mad.

"They're all scared of you."

"So."

"They said stuff."

"Like what?"

"They say, 'ooh girl, don't look in his eyes, he knows things, he can do things,' stuff like that.

"That's stupid."

"Is it?"

He turned to make a mean face at her, but he couldn't. She was just too beautiful. He looked away before she could and shrugged. "Think what you want."

Nobody said anything for a few seconds. But she must have been more hungry than scared because she picked up his pizza and went at it.

"So" — she talked between chews — "you like to be called Raymond ... or Ray ... or Ray-Ray — "

"*Ray-Ray*? Gross."

She stopped chewing. "Hey! That's what we called my uncle. So shut up."

"Called?"

"Yeah. *Called*. He's dead. Happy?"

Wow. She sure had a lot of dead family in her life. Maybe that was worse than never having a family at all.

"Sorry. That sucks."

She took in a long, loud breath and let it out. It sounded kind of wobbly. "What about your family? They dead?"

"I don't know. I guess so. Never met them."

"That sucks, too."

He didn't know what to say to that. Of course, it

sucked being an orphan, having no mom, no dad. But nobody had ever said it to him out loud — *that sucks* — just like that.

She reached for the second slice. "They give us pizza here a lot? It's my favorite."

Raymond almost said, "Mine, too," but it didn't feel true anymore, no matter *how* hungry he was. "Not a lot. But always on Pick-Up Days. It's supposed to be like a party. To celebrate."

"Celebrate what?"

"Getting adopted. The day they come to pick you up. We have a pizza party. We get ice cream. Then we all have to line up in the main hall to say goodbye."

"That sounds kind of weird."

Out of nowhere, a pizza crust came sailing through the air and smacked Raymond on his head. Keisha looked all around, then back at him, her eyes popping.

A loud burst of laughter two tables over told Raymond who it was.

Raymond sighed and brushed the crumbs out of his hair.

"Who threw that?"

"Kevin," he mumbled, hating the feel of Kevin's name in his mouth.

"Who's Kevin?"

"The *asshole* of the school."

Keisha slapped her hand over mouth and looked at him with big eyes. Her giggle sounded wet and sputtering, smushed up against her face. It made him giggle, too. He felt stares on him and looked around, sure the people close by must be looking. They must have heard him swear. And he just *knew* they were wondering why the new girl was talking to *him*. Even *laughing* with him. But no. Everyone was focused on the cart of ice cream that was just wheeled in from the kitchen.

But still, he felt ... *something.* Some*one?*

"Why is Kevin the bleep of the school?" Keisha giggled again.

Her question hovered in the air. He'd heard it but was too distracted to take it in. It was like an invisible hand was tapping his shoulder.

"Why is Kevin the a-hole of the school?" she repeated.

"Shhh! Quiet Keisha." His reply came out meaner than he'd meant it.

"Fine. Screw you."

Keisha let out a loud huff, then made a big show of turning her back on him. She tapped the kid beside her on the arm. "Hi. I'm Keisha. What's your name?"

Her voice sounded far away.

A cool breeze blew up around him, though the windows were closed, lifting the hair on the back of Raymond's neck. He turned around in his seat to face the big double doors at back of the dining room. They led to the long hallway, where he'd had his horrible first meeting with Keisha. The tall, wide doors boasted large, glass windows. He could see through them the dark hallway beyond — all the offices were closed by this time. But a blurred outline, a shimmering cloud of silver smoke, seemed to fill up the glass window of the door. It never settled on one shape, just hovered there, its mass thickening, swirling, growing wide, then narrow, as if it was struggling to stay present for as long as it could.

After a few moments, it thinned in the center, and its edges broke into wispy trailing fingers until it disappeared.

Raymond had no idea what it was ... *who* it was.

But in some dark place deep inside, he knew it was there for him.

Chapter Eight

THE CRUNCH of tires on snow never failed to send a tingle up Raymond's spine. It was a regular kid sound. At least, what he imagined regular kids heard all the time. Riding to school, catching a ballgame with Dad, running to the store with Mom, heading out on family vacation — it was the sound of having somewhere to be. The sound of "normal."

It was also probably the sound of "boring" if you heard it all the time. But for a Haven kid who didn't, it made you want to bounce off the ceiling. Just knowing it was moments away made Raymond feel a little better.

He didn't want to think about Mr. Gregg crying.

Or the poor woman, in the dark, reaching a bloody hand to nobody. Raymond dreamt of her.

He just wanted to think about the museum and the amazing things he would see there. If he didn't freeze to death waiting for it to happen.

It had to be the coldest morning of the year.

Maybe even the coldest morning of every year he could remember.

Raymond stood in line, shivering with the other kids lined up alongside the rumbling rented school bus, waiting to board. Nobody got on until Father Galen showed up, and he always took *forever*. But Raymond didn't mind so much. Keisha was in front of him. She didn't talk to him, but she turned around and kind of smiled once.

They stomped their feet, jumped up and down in place, anything to keep warm. The older boys started huffing frosted morning air through V-shaped fingers, then blowing it out like they were "smoking." The girls laughed into their mittens as though it was the funniest thing they'd ever seen. Why did girls like such dumb stuff? Just looking at them made his stomach hurt. But lately, everything did that.

He turned away and noticed poor Sister Ann was shivering so hard, her teeth chattered like old skeleton bones.

"Jeezum, hasn't been this cold since eighteen-hundred-and-froze-to-death! Where on earth *is* that man?"

"Shush, now," Sister Melinda said, "that's disrespectful. He'll be here when he's here."

"Easy for you to say. You don't feel the cold like I do."

"Well, that's hardly my fault. You got no fat to keep you warm. Should have eaten your breakfast."

Sister Ann should have eaten everyone's breakfast. She looked like a rake in a black dress. She never ate.

And because of that, she always noticed what others *didn't* eat, too. Raymond felt her gaze on him in the food hall more often than he liked. She caught him, a couple times, dropping food into the napkin on his lap. Her eyes were two fire-red question marks so bright, they almost burned. But she never asked him why he wasn't hungry. Maybe she'd heard that enough herself and decided to let him be. Which was fine with him.

Sister Melinda, on the other hand, could have skipped breakfast for a month and it wouldn't matter. She had the look of someone who was just born heavy, shiny-faced and always out of breath. And Sister Ann was right — she didn't look the least bit cold.

When Father Galen finally stepped out onto the porch with his clipboard, everyone cheered, including the sisters. Father smiled and held up his hands like he was the most popular guy in town. Kevin called him Father Dork and sometimes, and in times like these, Raymond could really see why.

Father always went for outdoor field trips when he could. State parks, discount boat trips to the islands of Casco Bay. He loved the Freedom trail in Boston because it was pretty much "gratis," the man's favorite word. Raymond looked it up and learned it was a fancy word for free. Made sense. But January's trip was always indoors because, as Sister Ann, a genuine Mainer always said, "Winter in Maine was not meant for sissies."

Raymond didn't like the word "sissy." He knew it meant "fag," which was *Kevin's* favorite word. But in this case, he was all right with it. Because it meant they had to be indoors. And the destination for his first ever field trip couldn't have been more perfect if Raymond had picked it out himself.

They would be split into groups and cover as many exhibits as they could with either Father Galen or one of the sisters leading the way. Raymond prayed he'd get Sister Ann. She was strict and wicked grouchy half the time, but at least she was fast. Sister Melinda walked around like she had a two-ton anchor attached to her butt.

Father Galen tapped a pen on his clipboard, which meant they all better shut up or they'd be out in the cold for another hour.

"I hope I don't have to remind you children to pay attention and take notes on each exhibit you view," Father Galen warned. "This is not just fun and games. There *will be* a test."

Nothing was ever just fun and games when it came to Father Galen. Raymond often wondered what he had against them.

"The Portland Museum of Art is the largest and oldest public art institution in Maine," Father Galen yelled down at them, "and houses more than fifty thousand objets d'arte." He smiled proudly then, like he'd collected every item himself.

Raymond smiled back, and he meant it. He didn't care about the test or that the museum was old or big or whatever. He just knew it was full of fifty thousand pieces of real, actual art by real, actual artists.

He knew it was full of colors.

It was going to be *epic*.

"We will board the bus in an orderly fashion as soon as —"

The bus doors hissed open before Father could get out another word. Then the far-right corner of the bus bounced up and down like someone was rocking it from inside. They all stared as the biggest guy Raymond had ever seen hauled himself down the steps. He had to turn sideways to squeeze his shoulders through the bus doors.

The guy wasn't fat big, like Sister Melinda. More like a grizzly bear or a silver-backed gorilla. He was two heads taller than Father Galen, who was pretty tall himself, and had a thick, wide neck, which was good because his head was huge. His chest looked like an overinflated tire. He filled up his bus driver uniform like an overstuffed sausage, the coat sleeves barely covering his forearms. Raymond caught a glimpse of faded tattoo ink that looked like a strip of barbed wire, but he couldn't be sure.

The man hitched up his pants and lifted his chin, frowning down at them like he'd expected more. "My name is Bob. You can call me Bus Driver Bob, Mr. Bob, or Mr. Bus Driver Bob. Not 'hey, you' or 'mista.' Got it?"

Of course, they *got it*. An orphan's whole life was being told what to do. But Raymond knew right away that Bob wasn't his real name. The moment he'd said it, Mr. Bob's field of orange-brown flickered like the bare bulbs in the laundry cellar. Then rows of ugly, black spikes marched across it like a battalion of tiny soldiers heading into battle.

For a moment, Raymond thought he might puke, so he closed his eyes. When he opened them again, the spikes were gone. Why would Mr. Bob lie about his real name? What was wrong with it?

He must have been staring because suddenly, Mr. Bob's attention narrowed on him and stayed there. His face took on a weird expression, like a dog wondering whether to bite you or run.

A current of fear shot through Raymond. His body locked up, and a terrible image of Mr. Bob sinking his yellow teeth into Raymond's throat made him shudder.

He looked down at his boot. Black, shiny, calm.

Don't shake. No shaking. This is supposed to be a *good* day.

It was huge relief when Father Galen clomped down the steps, hand extended for Mr. Bob to shake. Father Galen wasn't used to anyone bossing them around but him. He put a stop to whatever bossing Mr. Bob was about to do.

Raymond took a quick peek. Bob went back to *mostly* orange-brown after that, and Raymond's chest and limbs relaxed.

Father Galen waved the sisters up into the bus then followed them. Bus Driver Bob stood at the door like Captain Bligh as they climbed board, giving each of them the hairy eyeball coupled with a squint that said, "troublemakers will not be tolerated." When it was his turn, Raymond kept his head down. But he felt the heat of Bus Driver Bob's gaze on his back as he climbed the steps.

When the last kid had pounded up the aisle, Mr. Bob hauled himself up, crashed down into the driver's seat, then yanked the doors shut. He looked over his shoulder at Father Galen, sitting in the first row, who gave him a nod. Mr. Bob jammed his enormous boot down on the gas pedal, making the bus growl like a hungry animal. When he jammed it into drive and pulled out, the kids exploded into whoops, cheers, and bus honking noises that were beyond irritating. Raymond watched the back of Father Galen's head, waiting for him to turn around. But he let them get away with it this time.

Maybe he knew they couldn't help it. That sound. They had somewhere to be. Somewhere that wasn't a gloomy old house filled with unloved kids, stern women, and an old guy who who'd forgotten what it was like to be young.

Raymond watched the snow-heavy trees that lined the Haven's driveway slide past his window then disappear. He smiled. The big fat tires of the bus crunched, devouring the snow faster than it could fall. Whoop, whoop!

His gaze drifted to the front of the bus, and his smile faded. A circular mirror was mounted to the left of the steering wheel. It was full of Bus Driver Bob's face. And his red, squinty eyes were staring right at him.

Maybe Mr. Bob had decided to bite after all.

Raymond's chest tightened. Next would come the anxiety, the fear. Little ripples at first, then waves would crash over him, drag him under.

NO. No, no, no. Stop.

Mr. Gregg's voice filled his head.

They're just panic attacks, Raymond. Your imagination working overtime. Breathe. Tell yourself it's not real, you are safe, all is well —

"Oh, just shut up, Mr. Gregg!"

The angry words came out of his mouth before he could stop them.

The girls in the seat in front of him turned around to stare. Raymond looked away and focused on the scenery whizzing past his window for the rest of the ride. He did breathe, and it did help calm him. But when they filed off the bus at the museum, he scooted past Mr. Bob as fast as he could.

As luck would have it, Raymond ended up in Father Galen's group. He didn't mind too much because Father was almost as excited about being there as Raymond. He wanted to see as much as possible and would because he "liked to get his money's worth."

Being in the museum was a waking dream. Raymond had never seen such intense beauty, one room after the next. He felt a humming beneath his skin, his blood was flowing faster than it ever had before. His head swam with shapes, textures, shadows, and forms. And the colors seemed to be multiplying by the minute. Shades split into new shades, hues layered over each other to create wheels of color he'd never seen before. At times it was too much, and he had to his close eyes. He hated to miss a single thing, but it was either rest or fall and have

Father Galen accuse him of embarrassing the whole group.

Just before they stopped for lunch, they reached the exhibit Raymond had been looking forward to the most — a collection of Jackson Pollack large scale pieces. They had to wait for the group ahead them to finish. He practically vibrated with excitement as he stood in line.

At last, the group ahead of them shuffled out, and it was their turn. Raymond stepped into the room and felt liked he'd been whacked between the eyes with a baseball bat. A huge work, the showcase of the room, seemed to rush up at him like it had wings. He stumbled backward a few steps, just managing to stay on his feet. But he had to get out. If he lost it, Father Galen would ban him from field trips forever.

Raymond slipped back out the door and found an empty bench in the hall. Even seated, he felt like he was spinning in circles. He squeezed his eyes shut. Armies of colors jumped and swirled against his eyelids, crashing together before exploding into bright, whirling spirals. His skull felt like it was shrinking, squeezing his brain on all sides.

He pulled out his sketchbook and began to draw, fast and wild, his hand moving in wide arcs and circles, covering the whole page. He swapped out pens, red to blue, blue to yellow, yellow to green, until, finally, the painful tightness in his forehead and the back of his skull began to soften.

Raymond leaned back against the wall, afraid to close his eyes in case it all started up again, but unable to keep his lids open. The colors were there, but softer now, moving slowly, bumping into each other in a lazy way.

He needed to get back to the group before Father noticed he'd snuck out. But just for a moment, he let himself drift.

As his breath deepened, the vibrant swirl of color faded until all he saw against the black of his eyelids was a rippling current of pale gray. It was wispy, like smoke, curling into shapes he almost recognized before pulling itself apart to form something else entirely.

An intense feeling, a *chill*, weird but familiar, ran up his arms. The skin prickled across his back and down his legs. He bolted upright, looking around him, up and down the hallway.

Had he fallen asleep?

The image was still there in his mind, floating weightless, shapeshifting, like a jellyfish in a pool of black ink. But the movement seemed … on purpose. Like it was trying to tell him something. Raymond picked up his pen and began to sketch, but it was impossible to capture. Like smoke itself. Then, like the colors, it began to fade.

This is stupid.

Raymond snapped his sketchbook shut. He shook his head to clear it. Just a leftover from his dream.

The hallways lights flickered, and a rumble of thunder shook the skylights above him. The glass doors leading to the parking lot whooshed open, and a group of old women rushed into the hallway. They were laughing and all talking at once as they shook out their umbrellas and brushed wet snow off of each other's shoulders.

As they took off their coats, one pointed at the door to the Jackson Pollack exhibit. "Perfect! It's right there."

Lucky break! Raymond stuffed his pens and pad in his bag. The ladies were heading into the exhibit. He'd just sneak back with them. Hopefully, Father Galen wouldn't notice he'd left.

A movement behind the women caught his eye.

A fresh rush of chills prickled his skin from head to toe. He stared at the parking lot doors, his heart pounding against his chest.

Raymond squinted, not sure if he was really seeing what he thought he was seeing. Then it moved again. And he knew.

The shadow had followed him.

Its outline was clear against steel-colored clouds behind it. Her features were impossible to make out in the late afternoon darkness. But her eyes seemed large and round, like an insect or a giant fly.

Her? Yes. Raymond felt — he *knew* — the shadow in the window was female, and she was there *for him*.

He knew it for certain, though he didn't know *how* he knew.

Raymond trembled, anxious for what could come. For the colors.

But … nothing. Nothing at all.

For once, he tried to will them. He *reached* for them. And the strangest thing. For the first time in his life, all that came to him was pale gray. Wispy, like smoke. A nothing color.

It was all the shadow would allow him.

The group of women passed and entered the exhibit. Raymond was alone in the hallway, watching the shadow watch him, waiting. For what, he didn't know.

Eventually it came. A half-nod. Barely a movement. *Hello.*

A gust of wind sent a sheet of hail ticking against the glass doors. The shadow thinned, then disappeared, as if it had been blown away.

"Hey," Raymond whispered. "Are you there?"

There was no reply. He was all alone.

Chapter Nine

SISTER ANN DIDN'T SAY one word to Raymond on the walk to Father Galen's Office. She didn't even look at him. Raymond figured she was saving it all up so she'd have a big pile to spill on Father Galen's desk. Nuns always tell.

His heart was still pounding, and his right hand felt hot and puffy from his run-in with Kevin. Raymond replayed the scene in his mind, over and over, not quite believing it had really happened.

It had started with the snoring. Someone in the back row was sawing wood. *Loudly*. And in huge, sputtering snorts. In fact, if Raymond had turned around and seen a full-grown pig flopped over a desk sound asleep, it wouldn't have surprised him. Sister Olivia had either gone deaf or was so determined to get through the Periodic Table of the Elements by the end of class, she was *pretending* she had.

The chart was a hand-me-down from Bowdoin

College. It was huge, covering nearly the whole side wall of the science lab, with colors that practically jumped off the paper. Pacific blue, fern, butterscotch, peony — it was beautiful. Raymond thought so, anyway.

Everyone always groaned when Sister got her pointer out for memorizing drills. Raymond already knew the table by heart and had since he was three. But he still liked to look at it. He loved the idea that everything in the universe could be broken down into its purest state, and placed in neat, colorful rows and columns. It made him feel better. Like there was someone in charge of the universe and that, someday, everything would make sense. It made him feel less … alone.

Since his fight with Mr. Gregg, Raymond had been feeling more alone than ever. He'd spent the weekend dreading their Monday morning counsel time. Part of him wanted to apologize for making Mr. Gregg so upset. He really hadn't meant to do it. Mr. Gregg was a good guy and doing his best to find Raymond a permanent home. But Mr. Gregg was also a crow. He couldn't help himself. And the crow would want to know exactly *how* Raymond saw what he saw, knew what he knew. He would peck, peck, peck, digging for a deep, down-inside answer that Raymond couldn't give him. Because Raymond didn't know how. He didn't know why, what or when about *any* of it. And that scared him.

Maybe Kevin was right. He was just a freak, and that was that.

Mr. Gregg couldn't help him. Nobody could. What was the point of counseling sessions?

So, Raymond had skipped their session and hid in the library until chemistry. When Sister Ann poked her head through the door toward the end, Raymond knew she was there for him.

"Raymond," she'd snapped, "Father Galen would like to see you. *Now.*"

The class let out a group, "Ooooooooh."

Jerks. Stupid jerks.

Raymond packed up his schoolwork and tried to ignore them.

Kevin cupped his hands around is mouth and bellowed, like a dying cow, "Buuuusted!"

"Quiet, Kevin!" Sister Ann snapped. She tapped the spot on her forearm where a watch would be and glared at Raymond, "Today, boy!"

Raymond picked up his bag and hurried up the aisle. Suddenly, his upper body lurched ahead, but his foot was caught up in what felt like a tree root behind him. He fell forward, smashing his face on the floor with a loud crack! His nose exploded in firey pain, like someone had jammed a burning torch into his face.

Raymond pushed himself up onto his knees. Fingers trembling, he carefully touched his nose, sure he would feel something wet and mushy, like raw hamburger. His nose hurt plenty, though there was no blood. But something sharp was scratching against his cheeks on both sides. He reached up to take off his glasses and found himself with a half of a piece in each hand.

The room erupted in laughter and whooping noises that sounded like feeding time at the zoo.

Raymond's whole body burned with embarrassment.

He looked behind him, knowing what he'd see. Sure enough, Kevin's big, ugly boot was sticking out into the aisle and he was doubled over, his face bright red, shoulder shaking, as he snorted with laughter.

In that instant, Raymond's embarrassment, the burning in his nose, even the constant, nauseous ache in his belly drained from his body. They were just *gone*. And what replaced it was something new. Anger. *Fury*. A blood red rage that exploded in Raymond's chest like a pipe bomb.

He charged at Kevin, one hand cocked behind him. He swung his arm wide, and smacked Kevin's face. The crack of his hand against Kevin's cheek was so loud, the entire room gasped. Kevin stared in complete disbelief. He looked so surprised, so shocked, so *stupid*, that Raymond nearly burst out laughing himself.

"Raymond!"

He turned toward the front of the room. Sister Ann and Sister Olivia looked almost as shocked as Kevin. Again, he nearly laughed. But when he spoke, his voice was so calm it surprised him. "Yes, Sister?"

Neither answered him, they just stared. After a moment, Sister Ann shrugged. "Well, Kevin, you can't say you didn't have it coming." She snapped her fingers at Raymond, "Come! Father's waiting."

Raymond picked up his bag and followed Sister Ann out the door. It took a lot for him not to steal one more look at Kevin's freshly slapped face. But he had Father Galen to worry about now.

He waited one pace behind while Sister knocked on Father Galen's door. "Father Galen? I have Raymond."

Father's voice rumbled through the door. "Come!"

Sister Ann opened the door, then stepped aside so Raymond could pass. He waited for her to sweep in and spill the whole story, slap and all, with breathless annoyance. But she stepped back into the hall and quietly closed the door behind her. Not a word to Father Galen, not even a *look* at Raymond.

For as long as he lived, he'd never understand the sisters. They'd jump to pull out the ruler for a dumb word like "dick," but when it came to actual violence, they couldn't be bothered. It made no sense.

"Raymond, sit!" Father Galen always sounded like he was training a dog.

Raymond sat.

Father Galen's office was gloomy in the dull afternoon light. It was raining again — Raymond couldn't remember the last day it *hadn't* rained — but as dark as it was, Father Galen was too cheap to turn on an extra light.

He squinted at Raymond across the desk. "Well, now. How are we doing?"

"Fine, Father Galen."

"Good, good." He leaned back in his chair,

crossing his fingers over his chest, and sighed, "So … I have some unfortunate news."

Hmm. That didn't sound good, but it didn't sound like he was in trouble. "Okay."

"Mr. Gregg has left his position."

There was a hollow pop between Raymond's ears. He was confused. "Wait. He left? Or he's doing another job here?"

"He quit. He no longer works here."

"But … why?"

Father Galen shook his head and rolled his eyes. "Who knows? Another flake. He just dropped his keys at reception and walked out. No notice. Very irritating."

A wave of dark, sticky guilt rose in Raymond's chest. He felt sick. "But … did he give a reason? Did he … say anything about me?"

Father Galen frowned. He tilted his head to one side, then the other. "You? What might Mr. Gregg have to say about you, Raymond?"

"Umm — "

Someone knocked on the door. Raymond could tell right away it wasn't one of the sisters. The knock was too soft.

"Come!"

The door swung open slowly.

Raymond's mouth went dry.

A tall woman stood in the doorway. She wore simple, dark clothes and black leather shoes that shone with fresh polish. Her dark hair had a thin swoop of silver along one temple and was pulled back into a long ponytail that draped over one shoulder. She held a white stick and wore dark sunglasses — large oval shapes, like the eyes of a giant fly. It was impossible to tell if she was old, but her skin was smooth.

"Ah, Miss Dagon. Good timing. Scoot over, Raymond."

Raymond shifted to the next chair over, leaving the closest for Miss Dagon. He looked her up and down, his stomach fluttering with nerves. He'd never met a blind person before, but that's not what bothered him about her. It was … something else.

"Please." Father Galen held out his hand toward the chair beside Raymond, then quickly pulled it back. His eyes flicked to Raymond, clearly embarrassed. "There is a chair just a few paces —"

Miss Dagon held up her hand, palm first, "No need. I'll follow Raymond's voice."

She turned toward him and nodded.

A half-nod. Barely a movement.

He shivered.

She raised her eyebrows above her glasses and smiled.

"Um …" Raymond's voice trembled. "Just here. Beside me." He tapped the seat of the wooden chair with his knuckle. Miss Dagon walked forward, without hesitation, then took her seat like she'd sat in that chair a thousand times.

Raymond studied her profile. Her *outline*. He waited for her colors to display. Though part of him already knew what he'd see. As her colors rushed into his mind like a storm-swollen mountain spring, Raymond's whole body went cold.

Miss Dagon's colors were silver-gray smoke. They were *nothing*.

Father swept his hand outward, like he was giving Raymond an awesome present. "Raymond, this is Miss Ada Dagon."

"Nice to meet you, Raymond." She stared straight ahead as she spoke, without looking at him.

Why would she look?

Raymond made no reply. He couldn't.

Father gave him a quit-being-rude look. So, he nodded in her direction. Then immediately felt stupid.

A deep, annoyed scowl settled in the lines on Father's forehead. "As luck would have it, Raymond, Miss Dagon happened to inquire about a position barely an hour after Mr. Gregg put in his notice."

Father lifted his eyebrows at him and waited.

What the heck was he supposed to say?

Raymond looked down at his lap. His hands were shaking. He clasped them together and squeezed.

Father Galen lost patience. "Come on, Raymond! You know better than that. Say hello properly."

"Nice to meet you, Miss Dagon," he mumbled.

She smiled. "Ada."

"Oh, no," Father wagged his finger, "We prefer formal names only at Haven. It reflects a — "

"I prefer Ada." She turned her face toward, Raymond. "Ada." She nodded once, like that was the end of the matter.

Father Galen stared for a moment, his mouth slightly open. "Well, then."

"Wait. So Miss Dagon is my case worker now?"

"Yes, she is. And you're lucky to have —"

"No."

Father Galen's face flushed. He was getting mad, and his temper was legendary. "Excuse me?"

But Raymond couldn't help it. "I don't — I think it would be better if it were someone else."

"What has gotten *into* you, Raymond? You owe Miss Dagon an apology."

"Oh, that's not necessary," Ada's voice was like warm honey, "I'm sure Raymond is upset about Mr. Gregg. All this change, so sudden. Perhaps he just needs some time to process."

"He can process without being rude."

Ada Dagon seemed to glow for a moment, like headlights through a gray mist. Raymond closed his eyes, and concentrated, hard, to see beyond the gray. There were always colors. *Always.*

"Raymond?"

He opened his eyes. Father Galen was staring at him, confused. And aggravated.

Ada Dagon sat facing forward with a strange smile, like she was somewhere beautiful, maybe on a beach, staring out at the sea.

"I'm sorry, Miss Dagon."

She turned toward him again. "Ada."

Raymond peered at her, trying to see if her eyes were open behind her dark glasses. But all he saw was his own distorted reflection.

Father Galen cleared his throat. "Miss Dagon is a behavior specialist, uniquely trained to work with children just like you."

"Like me? What am I like?"

Ada laughed — a pretty, happy sound that surprised him. Raymond wasn't sure what she found funny. And he wasn't sure he wanted an answer to his question.

He just wanted *out* of that room.

She touched his arm lightly. "Social skills. That will be the main focus of our work."

"What kind of social skills?"

It's not like he went to parties or fancy dinners.

Father Galen looked at his watch. When he spoke, the words came out fast. "To improve your relationships with people, friends, and —"

"I don't have any friends."

Father Galen puffed air through his nose like an angry bull. "Of course, you don't! And why would you, with *that* attitude?" He stood up, "Miss Dagon, you have your work cut out for you. I'll leave you two to chat for a minute, eh?"

"Fine idea."

"Best behavior now, Raymond. We don't want to lose another one, do we?"

Raymond felt Father Galen's dislike like a cold, damp breeze as he walked past him to the door. When he stepped out, Raymond's heart sank. Sister Olivia stood in the hallway looking grim and serious. Kevin stood beside her, staring at the floor. The slapped side of his face glowed bright pink. Raymond couldn't take his eyes off it.

Kevin looked up at him. His eyes narrowed, burning with hatred and violence.

Raymond's guts squirmed.

Father Galen's punishment was going to suck, he was sure of that.

But that would be *nothing* compared Kevin's.

Chapter Ten

Mr. Gregg's office looked just like it always had. His books, and folders were stacked on the shelves neatly, according to height. The photo of his yellow lab, Brady, in mid-leap over a sparkling blue ocean, was still propped up on his desk. Beside it, the blue tin of butter cookies — his favorite — was still in its usual place. His raincoat and umbrella were hung on the coat rack in the corner. It was as if he'd just stepped out to the bathroom and would be right back.

Except he wouldn't be back. Ever. Raymond had scared him off for good.

This was Ada's office now. Ada's desk. Ada's cookies. Ada's chair. Except she wasn't in her chair. When Raymond walked into the office for their first session, he found her standing at the window, her face tilted upward toward the late-morning sun.

"I can't see it, but I like the way it feels." She sighed.

"Oh." He hadn't asked, but he *was* wondering what she was looking at.

She turned toward him. "Sit, please."

Raymond sat in his usual chair and waited for Ada to take her seat at the desk across from him. But instead, Ada gripped the back of the chair and rolled around the desk to the spot right next to him. She sat, spine straight, and crossed her ankles, like she was posing for a photo.

"So, you have no friends." Her voice was low, like a man's, but soft and definitely female.

She waited for him to answer, but it wasn't a question. So, he said nothing, and she let him.

Instead, Ada reached out, hovering her hand over the desk. She gently touched down with her fingertips, moving them right to left, in slow arcs, until it landed on the cookie tin. She slid it onto her lap, popped off the tin, then held it out. "Cookie?"

"Those are Mr. Gregg's."

"Were."

"What if he comes back for his stuff?"

Ada chuckled softly and leaned closer, waving the cookie tin just under his nose.

How did she know where his nose was?

The sweet, vanilla smell made him want to gag. "No, thank you."

"You're not hungry."

Again, not a question — not the way she said it. This time, Ada waited for him to answer.

Too bad, shadow lady.

After a long moment, she nodded. Then she

dragged the waste basket out from under the desk. Holding the cookie tin high, she smiled then dropped it. Her grin widened at the loud clatter of metal against metal.

Raymond stared at her in shock. He'd never seen anyone waste perfectly good food. Father Galen would have a heart attack.

She sat back in her chair and folded her hands together. "Why don't you have any friends?"

"Everyone thinks I'm weird."

Ada smiled again but it was warm ... kind. "Do you know another word for weird?"

He shrugged. When he realized, *again* that she couldn't see him, he blurted, "Creepy!"

Ada's head tilted back as she laughed — a nice sound.

Raymond felt a warm flare inside, like someone had lit a tiny candle in his chest.

"No. Not creepy. I have a better word. *Special*. As in, unlike anyone else."

"I'm not special."

"Yes, you are." She said it like it was fact. No point in even *trying* to disagree.

Raymond had never thought of himself as special. And he certainly had never been *called* special. Not by anyone.

The candle flame glowed a little brighter.

"Nobody *here* thinks I'm special."

Ada leaned toward Raymond and laid her hand on top of his. "We're going to change that, you and I."

Raymond fought the urge to pull back, worried

she'd feel that he was trembling. After Keisha, he'd come to hate being touched.

But Ada's palm was warm and soft against his knuckles.

"How do you change a thing like that?"

"First, we need to convince Raymond that Raymond is special."

She really did have a pretty voice, especially when she spoke so soft and sure.

Ada continued, "We're going to meet twice a week."

"Twice?"

She nodded in that tiny, sharp way. "We've got a lot of work ahead of us."

"What kind of work?"

"Just talking. At first. About what *makes* you special."

"Then what?"

"We'll work on developing new skills — a few little tricks — to help you share those special traits with others … comfortably."

"Tricks to help me make friends?"

"Yes. And more than that. You'll learn to really connect. With people, foster parents."

"*They* don't like me. At all."

She shrugged. "You just haven't found the right fit. But you will. *We* will. We'll find the right people. A family of your very own."

The candle flame flared. Her words echoed in his head.

A family of your own.

"Would you like that, Raymond?"

Raymond's cheeks burned. He looked away from her, then down at his shoes, embarrassed, even though Ada couldn't see the blush on his face. He peeked up at her. She was smiling like she knew.

He closed his eyes and tried a third time to really *see* her. But still, in his mind floated a thick silver-gray cloud. And nothing more.

Ada's hand on his shoulder made him jump. Her grip felt like the claws of a very strong bird.

"We're going to be good friends. I can already tell. Stop worrying."

"I'm not."

She chuckled and gave his shoulder an extra squeeze before releasing him. "Now tell me, why do you suppose Mr. Gregg ran out on you?"

A nest of butterflies hatched in his stomach. "He wasn't happy here, I guess."

"You guess?"

"Do we have to talk about him?"

"Father Galen says you think he left because of *you.*"

Raymond's heart crept up into his throat. He couldn't speak if he wanted to.

"Well, did he?" She looked right at him, as if she could search his face for the answers his mouth wasn't giving her.

"We had a fight."

"About what?"

"Something weird happened. I guessed a secret. By accident. A bad one."

"You *guessed* a secret?"

Raymond was so dry, his tongue made a clicking noise when he pulled it from the roof of his mouth. "May I have some water?"

"Later. What happened, after you guessed Mr. Gregg's bad secret?"

Raymond's throat cramped.

Don't you fucking dare cry. Not in front of her.

"Tell me."

The shock on Mr. Gregg's face. His eyes swollen with tears, sobbing. A grown man *sobbing*.

"He started to cr —"

Just saying the word out loud pushed Raymond over the edge. His eyes brimmed with hot tears that spilled down his cheeks. He choked on them as the first sobs broke through. Raymond burned with embarrassment, hating himself for cracking so fast. So *easily*.

Images rushed into his head, spinning, and overlapping. A woman's bloody skull, Mr. Gregg bent forward, sobbing into his hands like the world was ending, his face angry, horrified, frightened — glaring at Raymond like he was some kind of monster. A *freak*.

Ada said nothing. She didn't comfort, she didn't tell him to stop, she wasn't even looking at him. She just sat there, her face pointed upward, like she was stargazing or trying to remember where she'd left her wallet.

Or waiting for him to grow up.

Raymond tried to pull himself together. He wiped his eyes and dragged his sleeve over his nose. He knew it was gross, but Mr. Gregg didn't leave his box of tissues.

Because he'd used them all himself.

The sadness of that realization got Raymond blubbering again.

Ada turned in her chair to face him. She held out her hands, palms up. "Give me your hands."

"Why?"

She wiggled her fingers impatiently.

Raymond did as he was told, wiping his wet hands on his pant legs before lightly touching his palms to hers. When Ada wrapped her fingers around his, goosebumps pricked the back of his neck and ran across his shoulders. His face burned — he'd never held hands with anyone before. Not like this, anyway.

"Take a big breath in through the nose, then blow it out, softly." Ada demonstrated, a deep, slow breath in, then a long, smooth exhale through her mouth.

He tried to copy her, but his nose was snotty from crying. He tried again, but his breath came in wet sputters, like motorboat running out of gas.

"I can't —"

"Again. In through the nose, breathing up from the belly, then out, nice and relaxed."

He tried again. It was a bit better this time. His nose had cleared some.

She squeezed his hands and nodded for him to continue.

He kept at it, and by the seventh or eighth breath, the sputtering had gone. His breath was still ragged but was coming easier now.

"Good. Now we're going to count our breaths. Breathe in for four, hold for six, out for four, hold it out for six."

"I don't know how."

"Follow me. We'll do it together."

Ada breathed in, squeezing his hand four times. She held it, squeezing for six. Then released it, squeezing four. "C'mon now."

He breathed in with her, holding and releasing to her count. She nodded, and they began again. Over and over, together, each breath deeper and slower than the one before. Raymond closed his eyes and felt himself soften and relax. A feeling of space, a pleasant emptiness, started in his head, then moved downward, through his chest, belly, limbs, even his toes. He floated weightless, bodiless, like there was nothing to him but breath. Like he was made of air. He might even drift off to sleep if weren't for the ache in his belly, that constant pain that rarely left him in peace. Still, Raymond couldn't remember the last time he'd felt such ease.

He barely felt Ada's hands slide away from his own. But their absence, as his palm cooled, left him with a strange longing. Whatever they were doing, he didn't want it to end.

"How do you feel, Ray?"

Ray?

"Umm, dreamy, I guess."

"Very good. You need to practice. When you're upset, or angry or … guessing bad things. By accident." The corner of her mouth tugged up into a half-smile, like she'd thought of something funny but didn't want to say it out loud. "I'll see you next time."

"That's it?"

"You made a good start."

He stood and swayed a little. His head still felt like it was full of air but not in a bad way. He walked carefully to the door, passing Mr. Gregg's raincoat on the way.

"Are you going to keep his stuff around here?"

Ada reached again for the desk, scanned it with her fingertips until she found the framed photo of Brady. She stood up and handed it to Raymond. "What is this?"

"A picture of Brady, his dog."

"It's all yours."

Raymond stared down at the photo. Sunlight diamonds sparkling on blue, Brady's launch, his golden back arched, front paws stretching outward, his mouth pulled back in a happy dog smile as he's just about to crash through the cool crest of a wave.

And Mr. Gregg's woman, again, flashed in his mind. Her cracked skull, her bloody hand reaching upward.

Help me.

Raymond walked back to the desk and dropped the photo into the waste bin.

"Bye, Ada." He headed for the door.

"Raymond?"

He stopped but didn't turn around to face her. For once, he remembered that she was blind.

"Look at me, please."

"Why? You can't see me."

"But you can see *me*."

He turned to face her. "Okay."

"Don't you worry about what Father Galen said. *I'm* not going anywhere."

The candle flame in his chest ignited. *Ada's* candle. It glowed golden yellow.

Right then and there, Raymond decided to paint a bright winter sun for Miss Ada Dagon.

Even though she wouldn't be able to see it.

Chapter Eleven

FOR A GUY who devoted his whole life to the King of Peace, Father Galen sure had a mean streak when it came to punishment. *And* a good memory.

Raymond stared out the dining hall windows, pretending to eat breakfast. A storm was dropping a fresh coat of snow over the grounds of Haven. Perfect sledding weather. And on a *Saturday*. But Raymond was stuck indoors, thanks to Father Galen.

He could almost *taste* his anger at the unfairness of it all.

After Sister Beatrice had told Father Galen what she "saw," she'd hurried off to lunch. Kevin put on a big show after she left. He kept touching his face and wincing, like Raymond had hit him with a rock rather than the palm of his hand. Kevin was so convincing about his innocence, Raymond wondered whether he honestly had no idea what a jerk he really was.

Sorry, Father, but I'm getting sooo tall. My legs are long. I didn't stick my foot out on purpose. Why would I do that?

Raymond didn't think Father Galen totally believed Kevin. But in the end, Father didn't see it like Sister Ann did, either.

"Even if Kevin *did* have it coming," he said, "violence is never the answer."

Father grumped a bit at Kevin. He told him to be more careful and to stay out of trouble. But when he turned toward Raymond, the look on his face said it was going to be bad.

"Raymond, I want you to see this not as a punishment, but as an opportunity to get over your nonsense, once and for all."

Father Galen gave him Twenty with Benny.

He didn't say those *exact* words. What he said was that Raymond would be "responsible for completing *Kevin's* chores on Saturday." Father pretended to look up Kevin's Saturday chore on the calendar, but Raymond could tell he already knew what it was.

Laundry.

Raymond crossed his fingers and prayed that it was "fold and put away." But the mean little smile on Father's face sucked all the hope out of him.

Raymond was sentenced to "wash and dry."

In the basement.

Benny's basement.

Father was lucky Raymond hadn't puked all over him.

Here it was, Saturday morning, and Raymond hadn't slept at all last night. Even Ada's breathing exercise hadn't helped. Instead, he huddled in the covers, his stomach on fire, counting the hours until dawn like a prisoner on death row. Now, as he pushed his French toast around on his breakfast plate, it was down to just minutes.

If it was your week for Saturday chores, you were supposed to get started right after breakfast, and be done by noon. Then you were free until Sunday morning services.

The kids at his table — including Keisha, who was still ignoring him — had already cleared their trays and taken off, either for chores or excited to get out into the snow.

Skinny Sister Ann, his own, personal *food spy*, was staring at him from the sisters' table. She looked up at the clock, then back at him, frowning.

Why can't she worry about her *own* eating problem instead of his?

Raymond stabbed a piece of soggy French toast and stuffed it in his mouth. He stole a glance at Sister Ann. Still staring. He forced his mouth to chew, but it was no use. He gagged and spat it back out on the plate.

"Raymond!"

"Sorry, sister."

"You're done. Clear your tray."

He couldn't put it off any longer. And there was no getting out of it.

Raymond stacked his tray on the dirty rack. Then, with legs that felt like rubber bands, he headed to the cellar.

As he crossed the main hall, the pounding of winter boots on the floor above stopped him in his tracks. Kevin and his stupid friends came running down the stairs, dressed in their winter coats, hats, and gloves.

Raymond's heart, already thumping hard, sped up. He looked back toward the dining hall, hoping the sisters had finished up. But on Saturdays, they drank a second cup of coffee and hung around the table yakking. Raymond was on his own.

Kevin turned the corner of the stairs, then jumped from the lower landing, skipping the last three steps. He slammed down like an Olympic gymnast, forcing Raymond to take a giant step backward. He wanted to keep walking, but there was no way he was turning his back on Kevin.

"Hey, Raymond, comin' sledding? Oh wait, you can't because you have to eat my shit."

Kevin and his goons cracked up, smacking their gloves together in high-fives. They headed to the door, whooping and shouting at him on the way out.

"Have fun in the cellar, sucker!"

"Give Benny a kiss for me!"

"On the ass!"

Raymond replayed his Kevin smack in his mind a few times as he watched them go.

He turned toward the cellar door. The dark wood gleamed with fresh polish. It seemed to almost breathe with impatience. Like it had been waiting, just for him, holding its terrible secrets, and couldn't wait to share them.

Raymond shook off the thought. *Silliness.* Just like Father said.

He pulled the door open. It creaked like he was in some dumb horror movie. The smell of dampness and dirt trailed around his face like cold fingers. His mouth went dry.

With a shaky hand, he reached into the darkness, feeling along the wall for the light switch. When he flipped it on, a dusty yellow light filled the stairwell. He waited, listening ... for what? There was nothing but the click and hum of the furnace beneath him and his heartbeat, thumping loud and hollow in his ears.

He peered through the gloom to the bottom of the stairwell. The narrow wooden steps came to a landing, then hooked right, with three more steps leading to the laundry area. But first, you had to pass the doorway to the furnace room, directly at the bottom of the stairs. The room had no windows and either no overhead light or Father Galen was cheaping out on bulbs. Raymond had never seen it illuminated. Its entrance was a cold, black rectangle, leading to utter darkness. Anything could be in there, waiting, unseen, at the foot of the stairs, close enough to reach out and touch ... or *grab*.

Raymond swallowed the dry lump in his throat and started down the stairs.

The musty odor rising from the basement's dirt floor — like wet mittens and dirty socks — filled his nostrils. His heart raced as he crept downward, past the shelves of dusty glass jars, and tin cans that lined the walls of the narrow stairwell, their yellowed labels curling off the cans, like they'd given up waiting to be used as food a long time ago. The air grew damp and cold, seeping into his sweater and through his flannel shirt, chilling his skin. Raymond shivered, wishing he'd worn his coat.

He paused on the last step before the landing, just an arm's reach from the furnace room. Raymond peered into the nothingness beyond the doorway, watching for the slightest movement, a fleeting shadow, any sign of life. But all was black, as if the world ended where the room began. Still, he sensed … something. A sound, maybe? Was that scraping? No, *scratching*? Like fingernails on something smooth. Like glass. Like a glass *jar*.

NO. No. It was just a rusty bolt in that clunky old furnace. Or a rat, maybe, huddled down for the winter. Right?

Raymond stared into the dark opening, his body tingling with dread. There was no getting to the laundry area — and getting this whole stupid thing over with — without passing that doorway.

But he couldn't bring himself to move any closer.

Raymond looked down at the dirt floor beneath him. The last three steps to the laundry area were high, but not too bad. And the dirt was softer than marble or wood. He'd be okay. Before he lost his nerve, Raymond ducked his head under the railing and jumped. He landed hard but kept his footing. He looked back at the black furnace hole just once before sprinting into the laundry area.

There were three large washing machines and two

dryers set atop thick wooden pallets. It raised their height by at least six inches. In the shadow of the bare bulbs overhead, they looked like square, metal monsters, their round, glass mouths open wide in toothless laughter. Like they knew Raymond was scared and found it funny.

His job was to fill the washers in intervals, so they'd be timed right for the dryers, and not left wet in the machine to "sour." And no overloading! The dryer load had to be shaken out as soon as it was finished, and not left to wrinkle. Otherwise, the sister might make you do it all again. A week's worth of Haven laundry added up to *way* more time in the basement than anybody wanted to spend, but at least nobody had to iron.

The laundry was stacked in plastic hampers, already separated into whites and colors. That was someone else's chore — someone who was probably outside playing, like everyone else. They were full, but not overflowing. If he moved fast (and overloaded a *little*,) he could get all three washers going at once, then run back upstairs to wait it out in the library. Nobody would be there on a Saturday, especially with a fresh blanket of snow to play in. He'd have to cram three loads into two dryers after. There might be some wrinkling, but hopefully not too bad. And getting in trouble for *that* was better than —

No. Don't even think it.

The cold breath on the back of your neck —

STOP.

Fingernails, scratching, just light at first, but then digging

—

Raymond bit down on the edge of his tongue hard enough to make his eyes water. The pain was brutal, but it shut down the rising panic that wanted to send him back up the stairs as fast as his feet would go. His boots made no sound as he crossed to the laundry area, where he scooped up the first basket.

He worked as fast as he could, gathering up the dirty clothes and towels in armfuls, throwing them into the machines, stuffing and cramming, until the big mouths were full. He tossed a cup of soap powder into each load, spilling white granules along the edges and onto the floor. The pallets made the machines so tall, Raymond had to stand on tip toe to reach the back panel of switches. He leaned over the first machine, stretching to reach the controls, then spun the wheel to "big load." He punched the "on" button and the pipes came alive with the sound of rushing water.

He moved quickly to the second machine.

One more before he could bolt up the stairs.

The third washer was the oldest and biggest of the three. It was also the hardest to reach. Raymond heaved himself up, laying his belly on the edge of the machine. His arm ached as he locked it out, but he could barely graze the buttons. He shifted forward, stretching his two longest fingers as far as they could go. He'd just managed to grip the control wheel when he heard it.

A giggle.

Chills raced across his back and down his arms.

No. Not real. Imagination … *silliness*.

Raymond froze. He held his breath, listening. Was that … breathing?

He slid down from the machine and stared at the black hole leading to the furnace room. It came again, a soft, muffled laughter, like a hand covering a mouth.

Whose mouth?

You know.

No. Somebody was messing him. That's all. "Hello?"

Nothing.

"Who's there?" He spoke louder, stronger this time. At least, he *hoped* it sounded stronger.

The laughter bubbled up again, but high-pitched now, taunting him. Mocking his fear.

As scared as he was, it pissed him off.

"I know it's you, Kevin! Come out so I can slap you again!"

The laughter stopped, cut off mid-breath. Relief washed over him. It was Kevin. *Of course*, it was.

Then a new sound, worse than the laughter, raised the hair on the back of Raymond's neck. Whoever was there, hiding in the damp darkness of the furnace room, began to *sing*. The lyrics, if that's what they were, came out … *mangled*. Bits of broken melody mixed with grunts and hisses, as if there were no tongue to shape the words. In between, it took long, wet, spluttering inhales, as if the singer had once taken a big breath underwater, and his lungs had never dried out.

It sure didn't sound like Kevin. It didn't even sound *human*.

A tremor started in Raymond's hands and spread through his whole body. His heart slammed in his chest so hard, so fast, he could barely breathe. Everything in him screamed run, run, RUN! Fly up the stairs, slam the door, and never, *ever* come down here again!

But that would mean heading straight *toward* it. There was no other way out.

It was trick. Someone *had* to be tricking him! Raymond *knew* it.

But still, a scream was pushing its way up through the tightness of his chest. And — oh God! — he needed a bathroom *badly*. No, no, no. He could NOT let the sisters find him, terrified, humiliated, soaked in his own piss.

He *had* to get out. He had to go past *it*.

With his eyes locked on the open blackness of the furnace room doorway, Raymond took a wobbly step forward. Was it deep within the room? Or there, at the doorway? Ready to snatch him, as he passed, and drag him into the dank darkness of the cellar forever?

And God! That disgusting voice, he wished it would stop! But it went on and on, choking and sputtering out its song, until Raymond's skin felt like it was crawling off his bones.

He took another step toward the stairs. Toward *it*.

As if in response, like a fat sewer rat in a pile of dead leaves, the thing *scuffled*.

It was moving. Toward *him*.

Raymond's scream broke through, ripping his vocal cords to shreds. Panic exploded in his chest like a pipe bomb. He raced toward the stairwell, then dove for the platform.

He landed in darkness. *Pitch-black* darkness.

For a moment, confusion took over his fear. Had he hit his head? Knocked himself out? He touched his fingertips to his eyes. They were open. He was awake.

Which meant that the lights were out.

He was alone, in the cellar, in utter darkness, with that *thing*. And it was close. *So* close. It had stopped singing — thank God — but Raymond could *smell* it. A dead-thing stink, like the half-rotted, maggoty squirrel he'd found under the porch last spring, that made him want to gag.

He had to move. Maybe, if he was quiet, and careful, he could find his way up the stairs and run before the thing knew he was gone.

Raymond held his breath as he reached upward, feeling for the step above him. His hand landed on the splintery wood. He began to crawl upward through the darkness, his heart stopping with every creak of the old wooden stairs.

He'd counted four steps — nearly halfway up — when, he heard it take in breath — a snotty, wheezy rattle that seemed to go on forever. Then it spoke. Just one mangled, spit-soaked, *horrifying* word. "Raaaaaay …"

It *knew* him. That thing knew his *name*.

Raymond had read about people being "paralyzed" with fear. But he didn't believe it was possible.

Not any more than he believed people could be "scared to *death*." How very wrong he'd been.

His entire body locked. No trembling, no breathing, even the beating of his heart seemed to have stopped cold. But not his brain.

Move! *MOVE! GOOOOO!*

He wanted to. He knew he *had* to. But his body wouldn't listen. He was frozen. Stuck to those shitty wooden stairs like winter roadkill.

Another rat-leaf scuffle on the steps below him.

It was coming toward him. *For* him.

He wanted to scream, to rip his throat to shreds.

Raymond whimpered. It was all he could manage.

And once again, the thing from the furnace room laughed at him. But this time, Raymond felt its hot, wet breath in his ear. And the stink that breath carried with it smelled like a sewer full of blood.

The terror inside of him busted wide open.

Raymond's scream ripped from his throat and tore through his body.

He threw himself upward, boots scrabbling, and lost his footing. His chin slammed on the step above him. He tried again, clawing at the rough wood, screaming in pain as a dozen splinters slid into his palms and under his fingernails. Kicking and howling like a trapped animal, he scrambled upward, away from the gut-churning stink, the insane cackle, the sound of his name and that horrid thing's mouth as it called after him.

"RAAAAY! RAAAAY! RAAAAAY!"

His head cracked against something hard. The door!

Raymond thrashed wildly against the wood until he'd found the doorknob. He yanked and twisted, back and forth, his sweaty, bloody palms slipped against the cold metal.

It wouldn't open! It wouldn't open! Why wouldn't it open?

Because it's locked. It's locked. It's locked. You're locked in!

A feeling of weakness started in Raymond's legs and crept upward through his chest. His head felt like it was full of air. He was going to faint. It was happening.

He would faint. And that thing, with its putrid stink of death, would be on him. All over him.

Something stroked the back of his head. Fingers. Cold wet fingers. They trailed down his neck, along his spine ...

Raymond's lungs blew out a shriek so loud it pierced his own ears. He pounded on the door as hard and fast as he could. He yanked down on the door-knob, harder and harder, until the muscles in his shoulders felt they were tearing.

"HELP ME!"

He was sobbing, screaming, seconds away from being dragged by the neck, leg, arm, down into the darkness of that horrible death-smelling basement, when someone spoke.

"Let go!"

Relief washed over him when he realized the voice was coming from the *other* side of the door.

"Get me out!"

"Let go of the knob, you dummy!"

He knew that voice.

"It's locked!" Raymond shrieked.

"Let GO!"

Raymond slid his hands from the knob. His arms, heavy and aching, dropped in his lap.

The knob clicked and the door creaked open wide. Light spilled over Raymond like warm water. He clawed at the hallway rug, pulling himself out of the stairwell as fast he could.

"What are you *doing*?"

Raymond looked up, blinking until his eyes could handle the light.

Keisha.

"You okay?" She crouched beside him and pointed to the blood on his palms. "You're cut."

Raymond curled his fingers into his palms. "Kevin locked me in!"

"Your face is waaay too red!" She stretched her fingers out to touch his face, then pulled them back.

Still afraid. Of *him*.

"There was something down there," he choked.

"Nah."

The stink of that thing was still in Raymond's nostrils. He looked toward the cellar. The door hung open wide. Raymond kicked it shut with all his might.

"Hey, it's okay, dude. There's nothing down there. All right?"

Keisha's face … so beautiful. Staring down at him like he was some scared, little baby.

Pathetic. *Pathetic.*

The way she was looking at him — sad, worried, *kind.* He couldn't stand it. Not for one more second.

Raymond pushed himself up and ran. He didn't need to look back to see the expression on Keisha's face. Hurt, confusion, anger, disgust — one of those would be there.

Did it really matter which?

Chapter Twelve

SHOULD HAVE SNEAKED off to the library.

The thought played in Raymond's head, over and over, as he watched the rain drizzle down Ada's office window. It was definitely *Ada's* office now. Not a trace of Mr. Gregg remained.

Whatever. He didn't want to think about Mr. Gregg. He didn't want to be in this room. And he didn't want to talk. Especially about what happened in the basement.

Ada hadn't asked about it ... *yet*. She was in her chair, her body slightly angled toward him, sort of waiting, sort of not. It was hard to tell with her. The glasses hid her expression, and Ada hid the rest.

Raymond's stomach felt like he'd swallowed a sharp rock. Except he'd barely swallowed anything for days. And it was starting to show — had to ask Sister Connie to punch another hole in his belt. The butt of his pants was so loose, the kids were calling him

"Diaper Drawers." Raymond wasn't sure who started it, but Kevin was happy to take the credit.

As if on cue, his stomach let out a vicious growl. He crossed his arms over his belly, like that was going to help anything.

Ada smiled. "Did you miss lunch?"

"No."

"What did you have?"

Raymond thought hard, but he had no idea. "I can't remember."

"What's wrong?"

"Nothing, I just can't remember."

"Tell me what you're so upset about."

"I'm not."

Ada turned her chin upward, like there was something interesting on the ceiling. That meant Ada was annoyed. He'd learned that about her.

"Ray?"

He loved to be called that, and she knew it. She'd learned that about him.

He sighed. "I'm just sick of everything."

"Hmm. Me too, sometimes."

He looked at her in shock. That just wasn't the sort of thing grown-ups said. "Why? You can go anywhere, do whatever you want. You're not stuck *here*, in this, this …"

"This what? Say it."

"Shithole. I'm sick of it."

He waited for the reprimand.

But Ada *laughed*. "What else?"

"I'm sick of Haven, I'm sick of Father Galen and the sisters, I'm sick of ... feeling *sick*! I'm sick of being ..." His throat closed like a fist.

"Go on."

"Afraid." His baby voice. He hated it *so* much.

"What are you afraid of?"

The snotty, choking, singing creep in the basement that stunk like death and thought terrified boys were funny.

"I got locked in the cellar."

"By who?"

No way. Snitches get stitches. Besides, he hated tattletales. It happened to him too often. Raymond didn't answer, even though Ada waited a long time for it.

"Hmm ..." she said, finally. "Good for you. Loyalty is rare."

"I'm not loyal to *him*! I hate him." He spit out the words with an anger that caught him off guard. "Sorry," he mumbled. "I know it's a sin to hate."

"Rubbish."

Raymond glanced nervously at the door, as if Father Galen were out in the hall with his ear pressed against the wall. "You don't believe hating another person is a sin?"

"I don't believe in sin. It's a control word."

"I don't get it."

"Who decides what is sinful and what is not?"

"Father Galen, the sisters ..."

"And how do they know?"

"It's in the Bible."

"And who wrote the Bible?"

"God."

"No. Man. *Men* wrote the bible. They filled it with their own opinions, declared it the Word of God and themselves as his police department here on earth."

"But … *everyone* believes in the Bible. It's … faith."

"They gave people a choice. 'Faith' or death. Which do you think they chose?"

Raymond was shocked. This conversation was *dangerous* for both of them. Imagine if Father Galen and the sisters knew how Ada felt. But still, something clicked inside of him. Something that knew there was truth in what she was saying.

Father Galen would say Ada was wicked. But she was unlike anyone Raymond ever met. She saw things differently.

Should he tell her what happened? Would she laugh at him?

Raymond wiped the sweat from his upper lip and pressed his knee against the arm of the chair to keep it from bouncing. "If I tell you something, do you promise not to laugh?"

"No. But I promise to listen."

Not the answer he expected. Or wanted. But he'd barely slept a wink since it happened. Maybe she could help with *that*, at least.

"I can't sleep."

"Why not?"

"I don't want to close my eyes. I'm scared."

"Of what?"

"I got locked in the cellar doing laundry duty."

"And that scared you?"

"No, not just that. Th-there's something horrible down there."

"What are you trying to tell me, Ray?"

"There's ghost living in the cellar, Ada." The words spilled out of his mouth like wet fish from a torn net, "He's gross. He stinks, like blood and … dirty toilets and… and he knows my *name*!"

"So."

So? *So?* Raymond had no words for that. None.

Ada shifted in her chair and rested her chin on her hand, as if she were studying him. As if she could see him. "Knowledge is power, Ray. Have you ever heard that?"

"No. I — look, he's real! He's *down* there."

"So, what if he is? Why should he frighten you any more than the living?"

"Because … because …"

"Because you don't have the knowledge to understand it."

"What kind of knowledge?"

Ada laid her hand on his knee. It bobbed a few more times, then finally stilled. "Let's play a game." She walked around to her side of the desk, opened the drawer, then took out a brand-new pack of colored markers.

Raymond's heart did a little flip in his chest. "Oh, wow! I'll get my pad —"

"No, we're not drawing."

Ada took her chair beside him, then reached

under the desk for the wastepaper basket. She turned it upside down to empty it, but nothing came out. No papers, of course, she couldn't read them. But not even a candy wrapper, or a crumpled-up chip bag. She opened the packet of markers and, one by one, dropped them into the basket. Then she set it on the floor, and held out her hands, palms up.

Raymond laid his hands on top of hers. Again, the smooth, softness of her palms made him feel embarrassed, somehow, but not as bad as last time.

"Take a deep breath and blow it out."

He did as she asked.

"Now together, to my count, like last time."

Ada began to breath, squeezing his hands to the count of four, six, four, as she had before. He joined her, letting her rhythm take over his thoughts, his breath, everything. He liked this. He *needed* it. The space opened up in his head, and then his chest, wider this time, like his skin, muscle, and bones were falling away. Until he *was* the space, floating, warm and free in an endless field of golden yellow.

"Very good, Ray."

Ada slid her hands away but this time, the feeling stayed with him a bit longer. Not as strong, but soft and pleasant, like a nice dream that he could *almost* control.

She picked up the basket. "Okay, eyes closed please."

Raymond closed his eyes.

"Now reach into the basket and choose a pen." She rattled the can under his nose.

He felt the air shift and become cooler beneath his chin. He smelled metal. This is what life is like for her all the time, he thought. Sounds, temperatures, smells …

His fingers found the edge of the can. He reached in and chose a pen. It seemed to pulse, lightly in his hand, growing warmer.

"Now, without opening your eyes, tell me the color of the pen you're holding."

A sharp cramp stabbed Raymond in the groin. His eyes snapped open as he dropped the pen, sending it rattling back into the trash can. The peace he'd felt moments before drained away. And in its place was a tingling anxiety he didn't understand. "I don't want to play this game."

Ada sighed, placed the can on the desk and sat back in her chair. She looked upward.

He'd disappointed her.

A dark blue sea rose in him, washing away the last remnants of the peaceful yellow field. The game frightened him. He didn't know why. But he hated the look on her face. "Sorry, Ada."

"No need for sorry, Raymond."

Raymond.

"It just feels weird."

"Yes, new things do."

"Sorry."

"Maybe next time you'll be ready. Will you do one thing for me?"

Anything. Just please *like* me again.

"Yes, sure."

"Practice your breathing. Seriously. Three, four times a day. First thing when you wake, last thing before sleep. Until it's something you can do anytime, anywhere … whenever you need it."

"That's easy. I like doing it."

Ada smiled. "And you're very good at it."

A band of yellow-gold returned, not as wide or deep, but Raymond felt its warmth. If it weren't for the gnawing emptiness in the pit of his stomach, he would have been happy in that moment.

She squeezed his shoulder. That meant it was time to go. Another thing he'd learned about her in their short time together. Raymond stood, then slung his backpack over one shoulder.

Ada stayed where she was, still staring up, reading the ceiling. "You said you were locked in the cellar."

"Yeah. And it was totally dark."

"How did you get out?"

"Oh, um, Keisha." His face flushed with embarrassment remembering how she'd found him, scared out his mind and crying like a little baby.

"Keisha."

"She heard me yelling and let me out."

Ada stood, took Raymond's elbow, then moved him slowly toward the door. When it opened it for him, he stepped into the hall. "About Keisha, Ray …" Ada paused, mid-sentence, mouth half open. Then shook her head. "Never mind." She closed the door on him without saying goodbye.

Raymond walked down the hall, slowly, his head swimming with confusion. Ada hadn't asked for the rest of the story. Oh, there's a dead kid in the cellar? So, what. It was no big thing to her.

The weird part was, he *did* feel better. She'd helped him.

He just didn't understand how.

Chapter Thirteen

ADA GRIPPED the gate post leading to her walkway and swiped a paving stone with the toe of her boot. It was slick from the icy rain that had been pelting down since morning. She tested the next stone, relieved to feel the gritty scrape of sand against her sole. Roy, her handyman, wasn't the brightest, but he was reliable. And thorough when it came to her safety.

In Ada's experience, some men seemed to have a "thing" for blind women. As if the inability to see turned them into china dolls that needed to be wrapped up in cotton or stored under glass. Roy was like that. It was tedious, but she made good use of it when she needed to.

She moved carefully up the walk to her front door, then stepped inside. The house was too warm. Ada made a mental note to ask Roy to adjust the timer.

After slipping off her glasses, she placed them in bowl on the table, by the door. Her coat had its own hook, as did her scarf, and gloves. She sunk into the hall chair, slid her feet out of her boots, then placed them on the doormat.

A bath before bed, perhaps. Yes. That would help.

Ada ran the water extra hot, letting the enormous old tub fill to nearly overflowing. She eased in carefully, then soaked until the water grew tepid.

Dressed for bed, she enjoyed the heaviness in her limbs and hoped the drowsiness would last. She couldn't remember the last time she had slept through the night. Or even half the night.

Maybe tonight will be better. An hour or two, at least.

Ada's bed was king-sized — much larger than a single person required. Anything smaller, her decorator had proclaimed, was out of the question. It would be simply *dwarfed* by the room. If Ada had eyes, she would have rolled them. But still, the bed was comfortable, and she never worried she'd fall out of it.

Ada settled into the pillows, grunting softly against the pain.

"Breathe," she whispered. "Breathe through it."

With her arms laid out at her sides, palms up, Ada summoned the memory of Raymond's hands on hers. Their tingling warmth. The pulse of pure, raw *energy*. She inhaled deeply through her nostrils, softened her lips, and slowly puffed out. She counted — slow, slower, slowest. Deeper and deeper.

Extraordinary boy. He had no idea.

Ada began to drift.

Colors, shapes, textures, pushed through the velvet darkness. *Vision.* Oh yes. Yes!

They swirled and circled, arranging themselves together, gradually becoming a full picture ... a scene.

She was seated at table. Before her, a place setting made up of snow-white plates and fine silverware shimmered in the glow of a tall candelabra. The table and its elegant settings stretched outward on her right and her left, so far that she could not see where it ended. Plate after plate of rich-looking foods presented as if they were works of precious art. Ada looked around her, expecting to see a magnificent ball-room or the foyer of a splendid palace. But no. This splendid banquet was set in the dining hall of the Haven for Tender Souls.

The seats were occupied by men and women, dressed in opulent, vibrantly colored clothing from the Victorian era. A celebration. A masquerade? A costume ball? It didn't matter. Ada drank in the colors like nectar. Ruby red, peacock blue, greens and golds. And the textures! Velvets, silks, and satins shimmered in the candlelight like living things. Ada could have wept at the beauty of it. But the colors and shapes radiated, bright and prismatic, so intensely she couldn't stare too long without shading her eyes.

She looked down to admire her own elaborate dress of velvet, brocade, and lace, but was struck with confusion. Her body had shrunk. She was a little girl again. Eight or nine, perhaps? She looked up, bewildered, to see her merry dinner companions had shrunk too. They were now children, all of them, eating, laughing, stealing furtive looks in her direction, lifting their glasses to toast her. Though she recognized none of the faces, they treated Ada as the guest of honor. But a voice, like a tiny itch, in the back of her mind, whispered to her.

You're missing the joke.

Ada's stomach churned and emitted a loud, hollow rumble that turned heads all around her. Laughter rippled through her companions, like she'd said something clever and hilarious. But nothing was funny to her.

And she realized she was hungry. *Ravenous.* How had she not noticed? Saliva flooded her mouth as she scanned the vast array of beautiful steaming hot platters. But nothing — *not one dish* — appealed to her. In fact, they turned her stomach.

One dish, an oval-shaped tureen, was particularly offensive. She stifled a gag as its aroma wafted across the table. The smell was *rank*. What on earth was it?

Blood and ... and toilets.

Of course. She knew that. But why didn't anyone else notice? Who were they? Why would they celebrate *her*, a stranger?

A hunger pang, razor sharp, clawed at her gut. It made her woozy, seasick. She gripped the edges of her chair. She would certainly fall off it, pass out cold, if she didn't get something in her belly soon.

But *what*?

The table grew loud, more festive, as silverware

clinked and dishes were passed around. Ada watched in disgust as the guests piled their plates with the rotten food and dug in. How could they stand it?

You're missing the joke.

Ada's anxiety grew icy tendrils of fear that curled around her neck and shoulders, promising panic very soon. If she knew just *one* person, someone who could tell her what they were all celebrating?

"Ada?"

Ada looked to her left. Raymond! He gazed at her with a smile of deep serenity. His eyes glowed warm and incandescent. Sweet relief washed through her as she leaned over to hug him, wrapping her arms around his fine-boned shoulders.

He laughed and hugged her back. She'd never seen him so happy.

When Ada pulled away, she noticed that Raymond had a plate of food in front of him. It looked delicious, like a thick, rich, meat stew. He nodded at her, then picked up his fork and tucked in, stuffing huge forkfuls into his mouth so fast, she worried he would stab his tongue.

Ada's heart leapt. If he enjoyed it, surely she would, too.

She scanned the table again, looking for the serving platter of stew, but none of the dishes remotely resembled what Raymond had.

Ada leaned close to Raymond so she could whisper, though she didn't know why she needed to. "What are you eating?"

Raymond chuckled. No answer, just a chuckle between mouthfuls.

It annoyed her. She was *hungry*.

Ada laid a hand on Raymond's shoulder, gripping it tighter than she'd meant to. "Ray, *what* is on your plate?"

Raymond's shoulder, now bonier than "fine," shrugged beneath her hand.

"Raymond! You are being *rude*."

Laughter, like the tinkling of a silver bell, came from Ada's right. She turned to see that a woman, not a child, was seated next to her. The woman wore a full veil of exquisite lace. The glowing candlelight illuminated the fine detail of the hand-stitched pattern, which repeated over the woman's face. Even through the veil Ada saw the woman was very beautiful. But her eyes were ... *strange*. They were like clear, blue marbles, lit from within by a flickering, yellow flame.

Ada nodded a hello, but the gesture went unanswered.

Beneath the veil, the woman's cheekbones lifted slightly in a half-smile, bereft of warmth. In fact, the woman's smile *chilled* her. It triggered something in Ada's mind. Something horribly familiar.

Another hunger pang ripped through Ada, taking her breath away. It was so brutal, there was no hiding it. She doubled over, clutching her belly to keep it from ripping open.

"I need to EAT!" Ada gasped, "God damn it!"

The woman lifted her chin upward and laughed.

The sound was low, from deep in her chest, and echoed through the room.

Ada ignored her. She would NOT look at her again.

"WHAT is on your plate, Raymond?"

Raymond smirked and speared a a piece of meat from his plate with his shiny fork. The woman laughed again. Ada fought the urge to slap her face.

Raymond grinned at Ada like he knew what she was thinking. He spiraled his fork in the air, prompting another burst of mocking laughter from the veiled woman, which made him smile in obvious delight.

Ada's stomach was on fire. It burned with hunger, and now *anger.* White hot rage.

She snatched at Raymond's spiraling fork, but he pulled it back, evading her easily, and stuffed it into his mouth. He laughed while he chewed, like this was some kind of game.

"You STOP that, Raymond. What is on your plate? Tell me. NOW!"

The woman jutted her chin against the veil. A curt gesture. *Go ahead. Show her.*

Raymond shrugged. He stabbed a piece of meat from his plate, then a second, stacking his force with a double bite. Smirked, he twirled the fork toward her in a childish, "here comes the airplane" gesture. The fork looped closer and closer.

The veiled women's giddy cackle grated Ada's nerves. Still, she wouldn't look at her. Couldn't, in fact. All she could see, all that *mattered*, was Raymond's fork and the smell of roasted meat wafting from it.

Ada's hunger spiked, *exploded*, obliterated all sense and dignity. Her mouth hung open, warm drool slid down her chin. But she barely noticed. She swiped the air with both hands, snagging them on Raymond's forearm. Ada held tight. Digging her nails into his flesh, she dragged the fork to her mouth.

She snapped at the morsel, intent on ripping the meat from the fork with her teeth and swallowing it whole.

Raymond resisted, snorting with laughter at their tug-o-war. As the fork hovered under her nose, Ada focused on the two round balls speared on its tines.

She recognized them.

Her gorge rose, filling her throat with bile.

Ada's wide-mouthed bite became a wide-mouthed scream. The room erupted with laughter. The fancily-dressed children cackled and hooted. They clinked their forks against their glasses.

She stared at the two pieces of dripping horror on Raymond's fork. Eyeballs, like clear blue marbles lit from within by flickering golden candle flames, stared back.

Her eyeballs.

My eyes, my eyes, my eyes!

Ada woke to the sound of her own moaning, sticky with sweat and drool. She bolted upright, dragging the blanket across her slimy chin. She shook her head, desperate to fracture the dream images that lingered there.

Slowly she sucked in air, deeper and deeper, counting inhales against exhales until, once again, she felt fully in her body. A grown woman, sitting in her oversized bed, in the dark.

Blind, once again.

Tears spilled from the hollows above Ada's cheeks as her stomach rumbled with hunger.

There would be no more sleep that night. And she was glad for it.

Chapter Fourteen

RAYMOND DIDN'T KNOCK on Ada's office door. He just stood there on Mr. Gregg's old welcome mat, waiting to see what would happen. He didn't have to wait long.

"Good morning, Ray."

Even muffled by a thick, wooden door, Ada's voice was liquid warmth.

He stepped inside, then took his seat beside her.

When Raymond had slipped out of bed that morning, it was still dark. He'd gathered his clothes, careful not to wake the others, then tiptoed to the bathroom. As he dressed quietly, he'd whispered his morning prayers, then he'd made his way downstairs to his early session with Ada.

The hallways of Haven were still and shadowed, as if the walls and floors themselves were fast asleep, enjoying their last moments of peace before Monday morning erupted.

Ada had changed their meeting time to early morning. "We'll work better with less interference."

Raymond didn't understand who or what would interfere. He couldn't imagine anyone knocking on Ada's door uninvited. The office was tucked into the last corner of the admin hall. You wouldn't pass it unless you were snooping. But it wasn't just that. Ever since she arrived, everyone, even the sisters, seemed to just naturally give Ada … *space*. Maybe it was the fact that she couldn't see them. Like Ada might bump into them if they got caught in her path. But Raymond felt something more, beyond the usual jumpiness inspired by the "differently abled." That's what Ada called herself.

No, Ada made them nervous because of her Adaness.

She seemed tired today, sinking just a bit lower in her chair, her shoulders rounding forward. Raymond peered into the glossy black ovals of her glasses. He saw nothing but his own wavy reflection, of course, but imagined dark circles beneath her … what? Eyes?

Sockets.

He wondered, for the thousandth time, what happened to Ada's vision. Was she born blind? Had some kind of terrible accident? Or was it something else?

Raymond pushed the thought away, but as Ada's silence wore on, the question kept coming back. He dug inside his backpack for his sketchbook.

He drew an oval. The oval became a bowl. A bowl on a table.

"Are you nervous, Raymond?"

"About what?"

"Me."

"No."

"You were staring."

"I wasn't."

Ada huffed softly.

"Okay, I was. Sorry. I was curious."

"Curiosity killed the cat."

The heat rose in his cheeks. "I know."

"But we're *not* cats, are we?"

He said nothing. Some Ada questions didn't need answering.

"Why did your mother dump you here?"

Raymond's heart jumped into his throat. A fresh wave of acid washed through his belly. "I don't know. How could I?"

"Your theory, then," she snapped back, "You must have given it *some* thought."

"Ada, are you mad at me, or something?"

She sealed her mouth into a tight thin line.

Raymond searched her color. Pearly smoke, wispy, floating, silver on gray. Was that all the color Ada had? Or all she wanted to show?

"Well, this is scintillating," she sneered.

Her anger was a lead weight on his chest. He longed for her smooth, warm voice.

"I was thinking I could try today."

"Try what?"

"I'll play the game."

Ada smiled and dipped her chin in that sharp, decisive Ada-nod. "Very good."

The tension in Raymond's shoulders eased, though his stomach still burned.

She reached under the desk and pulled out the trash can. As she set it down on the floor between them, it rattled. Ada had the game ready to go before he'd even walked in.

Of course she did.

She held out her palms. He slid his hands onto hers and they settled into their breathing.

The space inside of Raymond opened almost immediately. It was immense. Wider than the sky. Infinite.

"Raymond."

Not yet. Please.

"Ray?"

Raymond's eyes opened. His hands were face down on his thighs. He hadn't felt her hands leave his. Ada held up the basket of pens.

"Eyes closed, please." The plastic and metal rattled under his nose as Ada shook the basket. "Okay. Just one. No peeking."

Raymond heart thumped faster he felt for the basket. He reached inside, closing his fingers on the first pen he touched. He took it out and rolled it between his palms. Tiny starbursts of colors, like miniature fireworks, dotted the darkness of his inner field of vision. He smelled sweet citrus.

"What color, Ray?"

"Orange?" He waited for Ada to tell him yes or no. "Well?"

After a few moments, it hit him — that rush of embarrassment he got when he remembered, yet *again*, that she couldn't *see*, stupid.

He opened his eyes. "Huh."

Ada's eyebrows lifted above her glasses. "And?"

"It's orange."

Her warm smile went straight through his chest. "Of course, it's orange."

Raymond let out a small giggle that probably sounded shy. But what stirred in him, just then, was undeniable pride.

"What kind of orange?"

Raymond stared at the pen "Regular orange. Like the fruit. Have you seen one?"

The question popped out before he thought it through. It was rude. He opened his mouth to apologize, but Ada held up a finger and shook her head.

"I have. It's getting harder and harder to remember. But … I have."

His heart ached for her. How *awful* it must be to lose all the colors, all the light, all the faces, the sky, the trees, the ocean … everything. All at once.

"So," she leaned toward him, "what is 'regular orange?'"

"A color?"

"And?"

"And what?"

"What does orange *mean*?"

"I don't know."

"You do. Breathe."

He closed his eyes and counted breath.

"What does orange say to you?"

Raymond filled his mind with orange. An orange ocean. He dove in, breathing it into his lungs. With each inhale, something inside him grew heavy, and began to sink downward, pulling him along. An anchor, nearly too much weight for the boat that bobbed along the surface of a gray misty bay. He let it pull him down, down, down to the ocean floor. He stayed there a moment, until he was certain.

Raymond opened his eyes. "It says lies."

Miss Ada clapped her hands together just once — a loud crack that startled him. 'YES! Excellent Ray."

Raymond lit up with pride.

No. Joy. This is *joy*.

Ada must have felt it, too, because she was glowing. "Do you see?"

Raymond shook his head.

Ada sat back in her chair. "Colors are feelings. Emotions. Memories. Secrets. Information. *Energy*."

"I don't get it."

"Energy flows everywhere. From everyone. All the time."

"Even if they don't know it?"

"*Especially* if they don't know it. Secrets, Ray. Those we keep, deep down inside. Those we *store* — they ferment. Getting stronger and stronger."

"*That's* what I'm seeing? In the colors? Peoples' *secrets*?"

"Emotions, memories, their essence. All of it. But our secrets, our *pain* — that's where the real power is."

Raymond shuddered. He wasn't sure he liked the thought of seeing pain.

"Secrets are funny, though. Deep down, most want to share them. To *release*. And even if they don't … they will. With *you*."

"Me? Why would anyone share that with *me*? What would I do with it, anyway?"

"Information. Is. Power. *Energy*. Remember?"

"I still don't get it."

Ada smiled. "You will."

"How do you know about all this stuff? Can other people see colors, like me? Can you?"

She flinched.

Raymond could have kicked himself. "Sorry, Ada. I meant to say, well, *could* you … before?"

"That's a long story for another time." She held out her hand for the orange pen. Raymond gave it to her, and she dropped it back in with the others. Ada rattled the basket and grinned. "Now, my clever boy, let's try again."

He was floating, glowing, vibrating with pleasure. *Her* clever boy.

Raymond closed his eyes and reached into the basket.

He could happily do this all day.

Chapter Fifteen

THE SNOW FELL IN FAT, heavy flakes through the night and all the morning. It was the wet kind that stuck. By the end of the school day, the sun broke through, lighting up the playground like an old-fashioned Christmas card.

Last bell set off a stampede for the mud room. They pulled on their boots and coats and charged out into the cold, excited to squeeze in as much play time as they could before dinner.

Most of the girls dropped to their knees and started in on snowmen while the boys picked teams for a snowball fight.

A clean, sparkling blanket of white — Raymond never tired of winter.

He brushed off a swing and sat, drinking in the clean, sparkling white world around him. Tilting his head back, he let his mouth hang open to catch the last of the freezing white flurries on his tongue. The sky was the color of the flakes it dropped on them, hiding its secrets in its frigid breath. Or maybe they were letters — thousands and thousands of frosted envelopes, little white messages for anyone who would read them.

Raymond thought of colors. And their voices.

And his voice? What would it sound like if he really used it? He wanted to hear it.

He began to sing the song, quiet and soft. And … incomplete. Either his mother never sang the whole thing to him, or a small piece was all that stuck in his baby mind. He *barely* remembered. Just three lines. But still, he loved the melody. So, he sang what he knew, over and over.

And the best thing I learned.
Is that this little bird.
Ain't a carrion crow, but a swallow.

"What's that song?"

Raymond jumped. He'd been so deep in his head, he'd forgotten where he was. He blinked his eyes into focus.

Keisha leaned on the post of the swing set, watching him.

He looked down at his boots. "I don't know."

"I liked it. Your voice is nice."

My voice is nice? Raymond couldn't hold back a smile. But … oh, God. How *loud* had he been singing?

"I think my mom sang it to me."

"Thought you never met her."

"I just remember a few things. I was only a baby."

Keisha brushed the snow off the swing next to him, then sat. "You been here since you were a baby?"

She looked at him in that way again. It made him want to cry, hug her, and scream at her to cut it out, all at once. "I don't remember being anywhere else. What about you?"

"What *about* me?"

"Your home before this?"

"None of your business."

Her reply stung. "Well, you started it." She'd asked him first, *right?*

Keisha scowled at him before looking away. She scuffed double tracks in the snow beneath her, dug in her boots, then pushed off and swung, but just a little.

Raymond watched her from the corner of his eye, wondering whether he should ask again.

Secrets are funny, though. Deep down, most want to share them.

He opened his mouth to ask her when a burst of color filled his mind. Pink.

Ballerina pink.

And creamy white.

The colors swirled together like a peppermint candy, separated, then swirled again. A shape formed in the center. A white horse with a golden horn. No, a *unicorn.* Then two unicorns, then many, in different poses, running, jumping, dancing on two legs, a patten, repeating over and over against a sea of pink. A window, then unicorns, a door, then unicorns, a ceiling, a ballerina lamp with a pink lace shade, then a sing-song voice calling, "Kei-kei! You can look now. Mama's got your —"

NO.

Soon Mama would be screaming. And bleeding.

And dying.

Shut it down! Shut it down, shut it down, shut it down —

"Aww, look guys, Raymond's singing a little song for his little *girlfriend*!"

The shout came from across the playground. That sneery, nasal voice could only belong to Kevin.

Raymond squinted through the glare of sun on snow. The boys stood in a pack, Kevin at the center. Their bodies cast long, late afternoon shadows across the field of white.

"You mean his snitch bitch girlfriend!"

They snorted ugly laughter and frosty breath through their noses.

Keisha whimpered.

Raymond leaned toward her to whisper. "You told? About the cellar?"

"Sister said she wouldn't tell it was me."

"They *always* tell."

"Hey snitch bitch! Want some cheese?"

Keisha started to make little hiccup noises, but her chin was pushed up high.

So brave for someone so small.

"I know what." Kevin stroked his chin like he was about to spill the smartest idea ever. "I bet she'd like to visit the cellar and hang out with the other rats."

"Yeah! *And* Benny!"

The side door to the mud room was about twenty yards away — an easy fifteen second run in the snow.

But they'd have to run through Kevin's pack to get there.

Please don't come over. Please don't.

Raymond's heart sank as they started to crunch toward them through the snow. Keisha started to sob. It hurt to see her chin, dipped low now against her chest, and tears trailing over her carmel skin.

It more than hurt. It pissed Raymond off, like Keisha's fear had somehow drained his.

"Hey, Kevin! Why don't you go kill yourself like your dad did!"

Kevin stopped cold in his tracks.

Keisha gasped. Raymond turned to see her look of pure shock. Her mouth gaped open as her shock turned to fear. He followed the direction of her eyes.

Kevin stood wide-legged in the snow. Huge bursts of frost-breath puffed from his mouth and nose, like a dragon about to throw its flame.

Despite the bitter cold, the heat of Kevin's rage prickled the skin on Raymond's cheeks.

This was going to be bad.

The words had just spilled out of his mouth before he knew what he was saying. He had no idea where they came from. Or why he'd said them. But he knew that they were true. And that they had done their job. He'd never seen Kevin so angry.

"Raymond?" Keisha's voice trembled, "What do we do?"

The *second-to-last* thing Raymond remembered about that moment was a quick breath before his mouth forming the word "run." He had no idea if he'd actually given voice to it.

The *last* thing he remembered was an explosion — a rock bomb, half fire, half ice — shattering against his forehead. He caught a short glimpse of frost-white sky as his body jerked backward. His back hit first, knocking the wind out of him. Then his head whipsawed and cracked against the ground, releasing a burst of multi-colored stars across his eyelids.

There was Keisha's scream, Kevin's mocking laughter, then nothing.

THE NEXT TIME Raymond opened his eyes, the upside-down face of Miss Zale, the school nurse, floated over him. She was swaying side to side in a slow swoop. He wished she would stop because it was making him sick.

"Raymond? What on *earth* are you doing?"

He had no idea how long he was out, but the sky was thick with steel gray clouds, and it was snowing again.

"Nussingmizsale." His mouth felt mushy.

"Get up out of there."

His arms prickled with pins and needles as he dragged them in toward his ribs. The world flip-flopped as he pushed up on his elbows and lifted his head. His coat crunched as he peeled his back off the frozen ground. His head ached and buzzed, like a big, fat wasp had gotten inside and built a nest between his eyes.

As his vision began to clear, Raymond realized he was staring at his knees. He squinted, trying to figure out why they were so close to his nose. And even more confusing, his bare feet floated above them. They were nearly as white as the snow piled up on his shins, and shriveled, like they belonged to a corpse. Perhaps they did because he couldn't feel them at all. He tried wiggling his toes, but they ignored him.

"Where are you boots and socks?" Miss Zale sounded as confused as he was.

"Gone?"

"Yes, I can see that."

Raymond squeezed his eyes shut, then opened them, willing his eyeballs to quit jittering.

Ah, the swing. He was still on it. Sort of.

He tried to slide his legs down off the plastic seat, but they were full of lead. Miss Shane grunted as she scooped one arm under his kneecaps, pulled the metal swing chain out of his way, then pulled him up.

"Come on! Let's get you inside before gangrene sets in, you silly boy."

Raymond laid on the hard cot under the bright fluorescent lights of the infirmary. His skull felt like it had cracked down the middle. Miss Shane sat beside him, dabbing his forehead with a cloth that must have been covered in red ants. Each time she touched him, his skin caught fire, and the smell of poison flooded his nostrils.

"What IS it about LITTLE boys that makes them

SO damn STUPID?" She punctuated the words with a hard cotton dab for emphasis that made Raymond's eyes water. "You think it's a JOKE, running around BAREfoot in the SNOW?"

"I wasn't."

"You weren't, huh? How do you explain that egg on your forehead?"

Raymond wanted to say — no *scream* — IT WAS FUCKING KEVIN! But where would that get him? Besides, he wasn't a snitch. And that reminded him.

"How's Keisha?"

"Keisha? The new girl? How should *I* know?"

"She's not hurt?"

"You SEE now?" Dab, dab. "HYPOthermia. THERE you go. You'll haven to stay the night, and that means I'm working late. Thank you very much."

"Can you ask Keisha to come see me? Please?"

Miss Shane dropped her instrument of torture into the wastebasket and looked at him. Her mouth was tight and tugged to one side. An annoyed little scrunch. But her eyes went soft. "I'll see. Meantime, you rest. Don't sleep. Just rest."

"Why not?"

She tapped the side of her head. "Concussion. No sleeping."

Raymond wanted to ask what she meant, but Miss Shane swooped out of the room. He hoped she was going for Keisha.

Raymond laid back against the pillows and drew mind pictures on the stained ceiling tiles above him. The old-fashioned radiator clinked and sputtered along the wall behind his bed, though the room was stuffy and already too hot. He tried not to sleep, but the heat and the rhythmic metallic ticking behind his head made him drowsy. His eyes slow-blinked, threatening to close no matter what his brain told them to do.

The click and twist of the doorknob sent a jolt through him that nearly made him jump out of bed. Had he fallen asleep? His heart leapt, then blew up like a balloon as the door swung open. Keisha!

Miss Ada stood in the doorway. Raymond deflated.

"Oh, it's you," he said.

"My apologies." She sniffed.

"I thought Keisha was here."

"*I'm* here." Ada's nostrils twitched. The fluorescent lights glared in her glasses like oncoming headlamps.

Raymond's mouth went dry. "S-sorry, Ada."

She turned her back on him.

"I didn't mean it, Ada!" Raymond cried out, wincing at the loudness of his voice.

But it was too late. Ada walked out, closing the door sharply behind her.

Raymond's stomach bubbled up with acid anxiety. He just wanted — what? He didn't know.

Sure, you do.

He did.

You have a nice voice.

He wanted to see Keisha.

Raymond waited, watching the clock … hoping.

The hours passed and Haven house quieted. Finally, it settled into stillness for the night.

Keisha hadn't come.

Around nine, Miss Shane handed him a little paper cup with two pills and a glass of water.

"For the pain. So, you can get some rest."

"I can sleep now?"

"A-yuh. I'll see you in the morning."

She put on her coat, shut the lights, then closed the door softly.

But whatever Miss Shane gave him didn't work.

Raymond spent the night wide awake, watching the shadows of the snow-covered trees that swayed outside his window. All night long, a jackhammer pounded his head, and his stomach churned from the smell of alcohol and the memory of Ada's face before she'd stormed off.

And the song — his *mother's* song — wouldn't leave him alone. The lines looped in his head, over and over, as the shadows shape-shifted across the water-stained ceiling.

And the best thing I learned.

Is that this little bird.

Ain't a carrion crow, but a swallow.

He didn't understand the song, but his heart clung to it. Always had. Because, somehow, he knew it was about him.

And because it was all he had of *her*. Not even enough to call it a memory. Just a tiny sliver of something sort of good.

Like Ada's smile when he guessed the right color pen.

Like Keisha leaning on the swing set. *Your voice is nice.*

Tiny pieces of good, like snowflakes on his tongue, that would melt into nothing.

Maybe that's just the way it was.

Chapter Sixteen

"OPEN, PLEASE."

Raymond opened his mouth and Miss Shane, still in her coat, shoved a thermometer under his tongue. She left the room then returned a couple minutes later with a tray of food. The smell of greasy scrambled eggs filled the room, blending with the stink of alcohol and antiseptic spray.

Raymond squeezed his lips tight and forced a burp back down into his throat.

Miss Shane pulled out the thermometer, peered at it, then nodded. "Good." After rolling the sick bed table over, she slid the tray under his nose and handed him a fork. "Eat it all up, now. Do you good."

"I'm not really hungry," Raymond mumbled.

Miss Shane ignored him, bustling around the room like she had twenty critical patients to tend to. She smoothed Raymond's covers, pushed the curtains wide, and put a fresh plastic bag in the trash can. Finally, she dragged a chair beside Raymond's bed before giving the room a once over. "Okay," she murmured. Miss Shane opened the door, then leaned her head out. "You may enter."

Raymond's heart lifted. Keisha!

No *way* was she going to see him in *bed*.

He sat up, threw the blankets off his legs, then swung his feet onto the floor.

"WHAT are you doing?" Miss Shane yelped, "Back in bed!" She glared at him and did not turn away until he was back under the covers.

She stepped out, and Ada walked in.

Disappointment crushed Raymond's chest, but he forced his mouth into a smile. "Hi, Ada!"

It was too loud, too … bright. But he was relieved to see her smile.

Ada's white cane was tucked into her elbow. He'd never seen her use it. "How are you feeling?"

"I'm fine."

"You're fine?" She tapped the cane, side to side, as she walked toward him. "May I?" She didn't wait for an answer. Just reached out and touched Raymond lightly on the top of his head. She trailed her fingers down his bangs, then pushed them aside. Ada's face darkened as she found the stinging, swollen lump that Kevin's ice ball had left behind. Her fingertips, warm and soft, paused on his cheek before she dropped her hand.

The door squeaked open slowly.

"Hello?"

Keisha! The small burst of butterflies in Raymond's belly made him giddy.

"Keisha's here, Ada."

His voice was wobbly and apologetic. He looked at Keisha, hoping she hadn't noticed, but she was too busy staring at his forehead.

"Wow!" Keisha was wide-eyed. "That must have *hurt*! Are you okay?"

"Yeah, I'm okay," Raymond brushed his bangs back into place, "Just a headache, is all. But Miss Shane says I have to —"

"Keisha," Ada's snapped. "Would you wait in the hall for a moment, please?"

"But ..."

Keisha looked at him, her face a big, disappointed question mark. He shook his head, just barely. Though her eyes said she understood, her expression was both sad and annoyed as she stepped back into the hall. She shut the door behind her.

"Raymond, it's our session time."

"I know, but — "

"*But, but, but.*" Ada sighed and turned her face upward. "Perhaps I was wrong about you." She let her cane slide from the crook of her elbow and into her palm. "All right then."

Ada turned and began to tap her way toward the door.

Raymond's heartbeat picked up speed.

"Wait! Don't go."

Ada flapped her free hand at him and kept walking.

"Ada! Please. I don't want you to go."

Ada stopped, her hand on the doorknob, but said nothing.

"I'll see Keisha another time," Raymond said to Ada's back.

"You're sure?"

"Definitely."

She returned to the chair Miss Shane had left for her.

"Can you tell Keisha?"

Ada shrugged. "She'll figure it out."

Raymond stared at the door, picturing Keisha waiting on the other side.

Ada pulled her bag onto her lap. "Now, close your eyes, please."

Soon, Keisha would get tired of waiting and walk away with that angry-sad look on her face.

"Are they closed?"

And she would never come back. Raymond's heart ached, but he forced a brightness into his voice as best he could.

"Are we playing the game? Shouldn't we breathe first?"

Ada smiled. "Eyes *closed*."

Raymond closed his eyes. "Okay. Closed." The rattle of paper and Ada's footsteps confused him, but he kept his eyes shut tight. He listened as she settled back into her chair.

"Okay, you can open them."

Raymond opened his eyes. A gift-wrapped box with a gray bow balanced on the edge of his bed. "What's this?"

"Open it and find out."

His fingers tingled as he pulled the bow from the package. He found the tape, unsealing it carefully to keep from tearing the beautiful paper. When Raymond slipped the paper from the box, he couldn't believe his eyes. A box of Silhouette Coals — professional, real artist, charcoal pencils — in twenty-four colors! "For *me*?"

Ada laughed in that pretty way. "Of course, for you, Ray."

Raymond's breath hitched in his throat. "Wow. Oh … wow! Thank you, Ada. I used to have these. The very same ones!"

"Really? Well, imagine that. What happened to them?"

"Um, they broke."

"Hmm. Well, you'll make sure *this* set doesn't … *break*. Right, Ray?"

He wanted to agree, but in truth, he wasn't sure he could.

Ada's chin dipped low, as if she could see him over the edge of her glasses. "Say, 'Right, Ada.'"

Raymond's neck and arms prickled with goosebumps. He hesitated, not knowing what, exactly, he was agreeing to.

Ada leaned forward. "Say it, Ray."

Her voice was somewhere between a low whisper and a growl. It sent chills down his spine.

"Right, Ada," he whispered.

What else could he do?

Chapter Seventeen

RAYMOND CHEWED the inside of his cheek as he watched the twin doors of the dining room swing open. The old door hinges screeched like a wet cat, over and over, as one kid after another filed in and lined up to take a food tray. None of them was Keisha.

Where *is* she?

He squirmed on his bench, craning his neck to see if she was already seated at another table. Maybe he'd missed her coming in.

Keisha's mandatory seat assignment next to him had timed out. This week, she could sit anywhere she wanted. But Raymond clung to a flicker of hope that Keisha would *choose* to sit next to him anyway. Fat chance. But he couldn't help wishing for it.

The dining room was nearly full, but the seat was still empty. This week's unlucky kid hadn't turned up yet, so Keisha could still take it, if she wanted to. Who would complain if they *didn't* have to sit next to *him*?

Raymond had been right about her not coming back to the infirmary. But *maybe* she'd tried. Miss Shane had released him an hour before lights out so he could sleep his own bed. Which meant *she* didn't have to stay late and come in early again. Fine with him. It was better than another sleepless night on plastic sheets that stunk of medicine.

He rested his head in the palm of his hand, careful not to press too hard on the bruised lump Kevin had given him. It ached, down to the back of his eyes. His bangs covered the worst of it, but he could feel everyone staring, hear them snickering behind his back. Kevin got put on bathroom duty indefinitely, but Raymond doubted that would change anything.

Raymond stared down at his plate. He was starving — exhausted with it — but everything on his plate just... *disgusted* him. Was the food always this bad here? Or was he just "growing out" of Salisbury steak and macaroni and cheese? He couldn't go on like this much longer — he was wasting away. He knew that. Maybe he had an ulcer. Or cancer? He might need a doctor. Or a shrink. Something.

Ada would know. She'll help.

Raymond looked up when the double door cat-screeched again, and his heart stopped.

Keisha.

She walked across the room to the stack of trays without looking up.

Raymond came half-way up off his seat and waved. The faces at his table turned his way, eyebrows up, then followed the direction of his wave. Raymond dropped back into his seat and tucked his waving hand under the table. He picked up his fork and pushed his food around, stealing peeks at Keisha as she lined up for food.

An iron band tightened around his chest when she turned with her full tray and scanned the room for a seat. Their gazes met, just for a second, then she looked away. Raymond fought the urge to reach for her colors. Ever since his talk with Ada, he felt weird about what he could do. It seemed ... wrong, somehow. Like a sin, maybe.

Anyway, he figured Keisha wouldn't like it, so he didn't want to do it.

As he watched her take a seat at table full of younger girls, a lead weight settled on his chest. His hands trembled, itchy to pick up his plate and fling it against the wall. His head and eyes throbbed as he fought the tears that were already blurring his vision.

A tray clattered onto the table next to him.

"Move over, freak." Derek, one of Kevin's goons, scowled down at him.

Raymond shifted closer to the wall.

Derek dropped down on the bench, picked up his fork and aimed it at Raymond's throat, "I'm stuck next to your ugly ass all week. You even think about touching me, this fork goes in your fucking neck."

Derek glared at him like he was a piece of dog shit in the tread of his boot. His eyes narrowed, zooming in on Raymond's forehead. He let out an ugly, spit-soaked laugh. "Shit! Kevin really fucked you up."

He leaned in closer, peering at Raymond's injury,

with an ugly, yellow-toothed grin. Then something —
the shadow of a memory — crossed Derek's face. His
smirk dissolved and his eyes glinted with pain.
Raymond could feel it — icy, cold, *sharp* — as if it
were his own. Then the colors! A thick, soupy swirl
began to flow from Derek's chest.

His heart space.

Raymond stared, mesmerized, at the vortex of
color churning in Derek's center. It flashed with tiny
sparks, like static electricity in a darkened room.
Purple, rust-brown, dull green, and dark metallic blue
— like a thunderstorm in a twilight sky. Like the
bruised knot on his forehead. Raymond's scalp and
arms tingled. His mouth went *sour*, like he'd swallowed
vinegar. It was the colors. He could *taste* them!

And he wanted *more*.

"Hey, freak," Derek snarled, "quit fucking staring
at me."

Raymond's stomach growled. A loud, acidic
rumble that seemed to go on forever.

Derek pointed his fork at Raymond's eye, "I said
quit fucking staring!"

"Derek!" Sister Ann screamed from across the
room, "WHAT do you think you're doing?"

"He won't stop looking at me, Sister!" Derek
whined.

And he was right. Raymond wouldn't. He *couldn't*.

His mouth filled with saliva, and his stomach let
out another powerful gurgle. He wanted more than a
taste. He wanted to *eat*.

The realization disgusted him. *Sickened* him. He was going to puke all over the table and on Derek, too, if he didn't get out of there fast.

Raymond swung his legs over the bench and walked out, leaving his tray behind. He'd hear about it later but, in that moment, he didn't care. His dorm would most likely be empty and, more than anything, he needed to be alone.

THE ROOM WAS cold and filled with the hard light of a rainy winter afternoon, but Raymond had it to himself. He stretched out on his bed with his sketch pad in his lap. With his eyes closed, he moved the pen across the page, willing the images to flow. But nothing pleased him. It was all jagged lines, warped circles, and sharp edges.

Raymond let it slide to the floor. He focused on his breath, counting slowly, breathing, releasing. But the rat eating a hole through his stomach didn't care. His anxiety seemed to notch up with every inhale.

He sat up and drew his knees in, hoping to ease his stomach. But the pressure on his gut only made the pain worse. Nothing helped. Nothing! What on earth was happening to him? Was he dying?

Raymond turned over, stuffed his face into his pillow, and sobbed as quietly as he could.

A sound slid into the room from the crack under the door. He held his breath to listen. *Click-click, click-*

click — the even, confident tap of plastic on marble. Ada was coming.

Did she know he was hurting? *Could* she know?

The *tap-tap* of her cane stopped at his door. Raymond slid off the bed, then opened it. Ada stood in the doorway in a long blue raincoat, wet and glistening under the hallway light.

"Ada," Raymond choked, "Something's wrong with my stomach."

Ada smiled, sad and soft, then opened her arms to him.

Raymond's breath caught in his throat. *Jophiel*, come to life, here in his hallway.

He fell against her, shivering, as Ada's damp coat wrapped around his shoulders. And though it shamed him, Raymond couldn't hold back the tears. He pressed his face against her shoulder and sobbed in big, stuttering gulps.

She rested her cheek on the top of his head, whispering soft words that he wouldn't remember later. His mind filled with pale gray smoke. It puffed and swirled, like the wind had somehow gotten inside of him, blowing the smoke apart until it was so thin, Raymond could nearly glimpse what lay beyond it. It was so close, so —

Ada pushed him away and stepped back. "Get your coat."

Raymond's head spun. His eyelids fluttered like tiny bird wings as he braced one hand against the door frame and caught his breath. "What ... why?"

"We're going for a walk."

He pulled on his coat, then followed Ada downstairs, outside, and down the stone pathway toward the chapel.

"The chapel? It's locked now." Raymond said.

"We'll be fine."

The chapel was dark but for the single lamp that always burned inside the foyer window. Ada took Raymond's elbow as he led her up the stone steps, slick with rain, to the tall wooden doors of the front entrance. Ada slipped a key from her pocket and handed it to Raymond. Raymond stared at her, shocked — only Father Galen had keys — but said nothing.

He unlocked the door and let Ada in first. She stepped inside, shook off her raincoat, and sat down in a window seat in the front hallway.

"It's warmer in the chapel," Raymond said.

"I'm happy here." She patted the seat next to her.

He sat. His head was mushy with confusion, and his belly ached like he'd been kneed in the groin. "Why are we *here*?"

"Veiling."

"What?"

"You need to learn how, and you need to make me a promise."

"I don't know what you —"

"Colors are vibrations, like sounds are vibrations, and vibrations make up all there is. Molecules, cells, galaxies, memories, emotions, time. *Everything*. Vibrations, color, life."

"I don't understand."

Ada slammed her hand down on the bench. "STOP saying that! You *do* understand. And you *know* you do."

Raymond trembled —with cold, with hunger. But mostly, with fear. Because Ada was right. Her voice, her words, were like memories he didn't remember making. But he *did* understand them. He *knew*. But he didn't know *how* he knew. And that terrified him.

"It scares me."

She sighed and patted his knee. "Nothing to fear. It's just information. And what is information?"

"Power," he mumbled.

"*Your* power."

"But what is *that*?"

"You see what others can't."

"But how?"

Ada shrugged, "Born with it. Your natural abilities."

"Then they're right about me?"

"They are."

"I *am* a freak!"

"Yes."

The way she said it. So … matter of fact. Like *so what*? Like it was *nothing*.

"Well, that just SUCKS, Ada!"

Raymond dropped his head in hands like a bag of wet sand. His whole *body* felt like sand, draining away, grain by grain. Yet his heart was pounding, like he'd just run the whole beach.

"Breathe."

"No."

He didn't want to *breathe*. He wanted to cry and wail and scream his head off. But he was *tired*. All cried out. And what difference would it make anyway?

"Ray. Inhale, 2, 3, 4 ..."

"My stomach hurts."

"We'll take care of it. First things first. Breathe with me."

Ada shifted to face him and held out her hands. He sighed but did as she asked, laying his palms on hers and focusing on her breath instead of his own.

When Ada pulled her hands away, he felt calmer, clearer.

"Better now?"

He nodded. "What's wrong with me? Am I sick?"

"No. You're out of balance. Too much of some things, too little of others. For starters, we need to control the 'too much.' Veiling will help."

"What is *veiling*? Where do these words and ideas come from? I haven't read anything about these things — "

"Of course you haven't. Not everything worth knowing is in a book or on the Internet. Are you ready to listen?"

"Is it going to help me?"

"Would I be wasting my time with anything else?"

"I guess not."

"Veiling is a skill, like anything else. You have the power to *choose* what you see. What you take in."

"But *how* do I choose?"

"Like anything else. Awareness. Conscious decision-making. By knowing you can, you simply *do*."

"I just *do* it. Those are the directions? Great!"

"You're not a *victim* of your abilities. So, stop acting like one!"

Raymond knew he sounded like a brat. But his head ached, and he was sick of this conversation. Keisha was probably in the TV room now, with everyone else. She might not talk to him, but he could at least look at her. Be near her.

"I just want to be normal."

Ada sighed. "Well, you're not. And you need to learn how to be what you are. I can help. But I can't do it for you." She stood up and felt along the window seat for her raincoat.

"Wait! Don't go."

"I'm not going to waste my time," she snapped.

"I'll try, I promise!"

Ada sighed again and sat down. "So, do it."

"What?"

"*See* me."

"What do you mean?"

"See my color field."

"I can't."

"You *couldn't*. Not in the beginning. But you're getting stronger. Isn't that true?"

"I guess so." It *was* true, but he hadn't realized it. "But I can't control it."

"When you look into the colors, what do you do? What does it feel like?"

Raymond had never thought about it before. It

just seemed to happen. He closed his eyes and tried to remember the moments with Keisha, with Kevin, and earlier, in the dining room with Derek. "It feels like … " It was so hard to explain, "Like I have to get myself out of the way. I pull myself *inside*, then focus *outside*."

"Yes. Very good. So, try it. See me."

Raymond took a deep breath in, then blew it out slowly. He drew himself inward. Then shifted his focus, placing it all on Ada. He had that sense of reaching outward, reaching *for* her, seeing only her and, finally, seeing *into* her.

There she was. Her wall of thick gray, silvery smoke. He tried to push through it, to scatter the density, but it flowed faster, billowing in thick masses, replenishing itself.

She was doing that. She was stopping him. Ada was trying to *block* him. The realization nearly rattled him out of focus. But even more, it *angered* him.

"Enough, now, Ray. Stop."

He was doing what she'd asked. Why was she shutting him down? Toying with him! He was sick of it! Sick of all the stupid words. Sick of *her*.

"I said turn it *off*, Raymond."

No! He didn't want to! He wanted to *see*.

Raymond drew himself inside even tighter, shutting down any thought, any feeling, that wasn't about Ada's gray wall.

"Raymond, I said enough!"

He reached down into the burning pit of his stomach and pulled up the pain, the anger, the hurt there. He let it spin, gathering strength with every rotation, until it burned white hot. Raymond let it fly.

It blew a hole right through! A shaft of pale blue light shot from the center of Ada's gray smoke blanket. Raymond moved toward it, ready to peer through to what was beyond, to *see* —

Crack!

His concentration shattered as his right cheek caught fire. His eyes snapped open to see Ada's palm, bright red from the slap she'd given him, still hovering, ready to strike again.

"What!" He shrunk back, shocked, his face stinging.

"I said enough." Ada spoke quietly, but there was a quiver in her voice he'd never heard before.

"But you told me to! Information and power and all that!"

"Exactly. *My* information. *My* power."

"But I can see it if I want to. You can't stop me!"

"That is correct. But you can stop yourself. *You* have a choice. And I do not. Unless you give it to me. Allow me to keep what is mine. *That* is veiling. And *that* is a friend skill. Do you understand?"

"No! I don't!"

"Are we friends?"

"Yeah, but you just *told* me to — "

"And would you like to *keep* my friendship?"

"*Yes*, but— "

"Then you have to promise that you will give me the choice. Promise you will veil me. Always. Otherwise, that's it."

"That's not fair!" Raymond burned with anger and frustration.

"Not *fair*?" Ada sputtered a mean little laugh and tilted her face upward. She meant it. She'd walk away from him. Even though she'd said she never would. Just like his mother. Just like Keisha.

He pictured Keisha walking past him in the dining hall earlier, purposely *not* looking at him. How he'd wanted, *so badly*, to reach for her colors, to see inside of her, to feel what *she* was feeling. But he'd stopped himself. He just knew, in his gut, that she wouldn't like it.

Ada was right. It was fair. *Of course* it was fair. He didn't have the right to take that from anyone just because he *could*. That would make him no better than Kevin and Derek and all those jerks.

"Okay. I get it."

"Do you promise?"

"I promise."

"Good."

She didn't make him say it twice. That somehow made him mean it even more.

"Now let's go take care of that belly."

"How?"

"Shush."

They locked up the chapel, then Ada led him back inside and down the admin hallway. He thought they were going to Ada's office, but she stopped outside Father Galen's door.

"What are we doing?"

Ada tapped her ear. *Listen.*

"But this is wonderful news. I thought you'd be more excited." Even through the door, Raymond recognized the edge in Father Galen's voice.

"I am excited. It's just …"

Kevin?

"It's just what, son?"

"Well, I'm used to being *here*."

Definitely Kevin. But Raymond had never heard him sound so small, so … *scared*.

"I know the Devlins will make you feel right at home. 'Course it will take some getting used —"

"But I don't *know* them!" Kevin sucked in a big snotty breath. Then, incredibly, let out a huge, rusty whine, followed by a sob. "I won't know *anyone*."

Raymond's jaw hung open.

Kevin. Whimpering like a scared, little *baby*?

A sharp cramp stabbed his lower belly, sucking the strength from his legs. A wave of dizziness and nausea crashed over him. His hand squeaked against the wall as he slid down to the floor. Raymond pressed his back against the wall to keep himself sitting upright. He clutched his stomach, breathing hard, and waited for the pain to fade.

Ada crouched down beside him. A sharp, double finger snap in his ear made him look up. They were nose-to-nose. His breath fogged her glasses.

"Read him," she whispered.

"Wha— "

"Kevin's field. Now."

Raymond shook his head, but he was too weak to argue. He breathed in and out. The count came automatically now, he didn't even have to think about it. He reached out for Kevin, through the door, zeroing in on the breathless rush of his words as Father Galen tried to calm him down. And then, it came, like a strange, cartoon sunrise in the darkness of his mind.

Kevin's color field. A mix of dirty blue-violet, green, and fire red. A bruised color, like Derek, but hotter ... *angrier*. It flashed and glistened, like a track of lava through a muddy swamp. And it was singing, it had a *voice*. An ugly purple mournful voice soaked in despair. Misery, pain, sadness ... *fear*.

"Do you see? Can you feel it all?" Ada's low whisper dampened his upper lip.

He nodded, suddenly aware that his chin was wet with drool. Shame rippled through him but from somewhere far away.

"Good," Ada breathed, "Now take some ... just a taste."

Take some? A taste? The thought disgusted him, yet ...

He shook his head. "I can't."

"You can."

He opened himself to it, just a little, like cracking a door. A current, like the trickle of a narrow mountain stream, flowed toward him, *inside* of him, cooling the burning pain deep in his belly.

Raymond's eyes snapped open. He stared in horror and disbelief at his reflection swimming in the dark pools of Ada's glasses. His drool-soaked chin glistened beneath a snarl. Purple veins twitched between his brows.

"NO."

He tore himself away from Kevin, from the fire red, the dark purple bruise, he filled his mind with a blanket of falling snow — pure, white, and sparkling clean.

"Raymond —"

"I don't want it!" he hissed.

She reached for him, cupping his cheek with her soft palm. "But you *need* it."

Ada stood and offered him her hand. He took it, letting her guide him back up to standing. Raymond kept one hand on the wall, just in case, but the stomach-churning dizziness was gone. The stabbing pain in his gut had softened to a dull ache. Not exactly fun, but bearable. He nearly laughed with relief. But there was nothing funny about any of this.

"How are you?"

"What's wrong with me, Ada?"

"Not one thing. You're perfect."

"I don't get it. Any of it."

"You will. I'll explain more next time. For now, get some rest." Ada turned away from him and started down the hall. "And remember your promise."

Veiling. He'd already forgotten it. "I will."

Raymond watched Ada as she headed down the dark hallway. He couldn't help but see her colors. They radiated, like never before, encircling her, glowing bright, like the silver corona of a pale full moon in a starless sky.

He sensed a world of neon color beyond that ghostly, luminescent, absence of color. He *wanted* it.

Imagined diving into it, drinking it down in big gulps, like a waterfall of sweet nectar. But he stayed put. He *veiled*.

It was *her* choice, and he would let her have it.

For now.

Chapter Eighteen

ANOTHER PICK-UP DAY. Raymond had come to hate them.

But tonight's goodbye party was different. He was going to enjoy this one *big* time. Kevin was leaving, and Raymond couldn't stop smiling.

After a great night's sleep — the first one in a long time — he'd gone to breakfast feeling hungry for a change. Everyone was buzzing about Kevin's "good news." And the non-stop chatter had kicked his day in to high gear. He'd practically *skipped* down the gloomy hall to his session with Ada.

Raymond rapped his knuckles on Ada's door in a quick-fire triplet. He didn't need to knock — she always knew he was there — but it felt good to make a loud, happy noise.

"I'm blind, Raymond, not deaf," Ada's muffled voice, even through the closed door, was light and happy, "come on in."

He stepped into the office and gasped. Ada looked … *fresh*. Years younger, and strong, like she'd chugged a protein shake for breakfast and hiked Mount Katahdin.

"Wow, Ada."

"Wow, yourself. How are you feeling?"

"Kevin's leaving."

"Is he?"

She already knew — Raymond could feel it. "Did you do that?"

She flashed him a smile. "Anamnesis. Do you know the meaning?"

He repeated the word, but it sounded like gibberish. "No."

"It's Greek. One of the best known of all Platonic themes. The theory of anamnesis says that there are certain concepts, or knowledge, in the mind before birth. Innate ideas that are already ours before we're born. Therefore, much learning is simply a matter of recollection. Do you understand?"

"Sort of. That's why you hate when I say, 'I don't know,' right?"

"Right. And you *do* know, don't you?"

"I guess. I mean, the weird things you tell me about. I don't know them with my brain, but I know they're true."

"Of course, you do. And always have."

"We're born just *knowing* things but don't remember? Until someone reminds us?"

"Correct."

A tingle of excitement ran through him. "So, other people know this stuff too?" This was great news. Maybe he wasn't such a freak after all.

"No. Very few ever remember. Even when reminded. *Very* few. But you do."

"Me? *Why?*"

"Because, Ray, you are *rare.*"

Irritation snapped in him like a dry twig. "I don't *want* to be rare. I told you, I just want to be normal."

"Fuck normal."

Raymond froze, shocked by her language.

"You are not *normal.*" She wrinkled her nose, like the word smelled bad. "You are —"

"A freak. I know. How could I forget?" His little-baby voice. He hated it. He shrunk into his chair, scratching shapes into the fabric of his corduroy pants.

Ada sighed, deep and heavy, and covered his hand with hers. "If *they* are flowers, then *you* are the Gardens of Babylon. If *they* are words, then *you* are a Shakespearean play. If *they* are raindrops, then, *you,* Raymond, are the *storm.*"

His heartbeat drummed in his ears. When he spoke, his mouth was paper-dry and his voice was barely a whisper. "What do I do with that?"

Ada leaned in closer. "Never let them know."

"Why?"

Ada smiled and sat back. "You're asking the wrong question."

"It's the one in my head."

"Look deeper."

Raymond shifted in his seat. He took a breath, but the air was hot and heavy, and his chest too tight to receive it. He didn't want to look deeper. He hated this. Hated the whole crazy idea of *anamnesis*. He didn't *want* to know. He wanted to be a regular flower like everyone else. Not … not …

"Just tell me. What am I?"

Ada dipped her chin. When she spoke, her voice was hushed and full of air. "Do you know hummingbirds see colors humans can't even *imagine*?"

Another twig of irritation snapped inside of him. He wanted answers while she spoke of birds!

"Can you just —"

"Humans, and most primates, are trichromatic. Their eyes have three types of color receptors — cones — that receive blue, green and red. So, they see the spectral hues — red, orange, yellow, green, blue, indigo, and violet. And one non-spectral, purple, because it stimulates red and blue simultaneously. About a million colors. But hummingbirds have *four* cones — "

"Ada, why are we talking about birds and —"

"Hummingbirds see colors *outside* the rainbow. Tetra-chromatic. That's the word for it. The word for *you*."

Raymond's heart stopped. *Everything* inside of him stopped. "There's something wrong with me? With my eyes?"

"Not something *wrong*, Raymond. Something remarkable, extraordinary, super-human. Tetras see over one-hundred million colors. *That* is a gift."

His head, his entire body, began to buzz with confusion. Raymond felt like he was bobbing across a dark lake, a thousand tiny realizations bubbling up and breaking the surface around him. Was this possible?

"You're saying other people don't see what I see?"

"They're physiologically incapable. Pebbles in the school yard — dull grey to others, but for you, they shine like rare jewels. How may blues in your sky? How many yellows, greens, pinks, reds in a field of grass?"

"But why don't I *know* this? Why hasn't anyone ever *told me*?"

"They don't know. How *could* they? You're seeing what they can't! They'll never understand. The closest they can get is through your art. That's why you do it."

"I make art because I'm ... I'm ..."

"A Tetra. You can say it."

He didn't want to say it. To make it *real*.

"It's a gift, Ray."

"Some gift. To be a freak? A *thing* that nobody will ever understand?"

The loneliness of it bored a hole through Raymond's heart. Then it struck him,

Nobody else knew.

How could they? But Ada knew.

"How do *you* know about ... Tetras?" The word was so strange on his tongue.

Ada chuckled. "You think you're the only one?"

Relief gusted through him like a cool breeze. He

sensed a tiny flicker of hope, finally, in all Ada had told him. "There are more? Like me?"

"Yes and no. You're a very special breed of Tetra. Rarest of the rare."

"But you *do* know other Tetras like me?"

"I have known others. But not like you."

"What's different about me?"

"You'll see. One step at a time. There's something else you need to know."

Raymond tensed. Ada's tone, the darkness of it, frightened him. "Something bad?"

She nodded, pausing a moment to gather her words carefully. "Your gift is very powerful. And power needs to be fed."

A vicious cramp ripped through Raymond's stomach. Anamnesis. His body *knew* before his mind would admit that Ada was about to tell him something terrible.

"What does it eat?" His voice trembled.

"Energy."

"What kind of energy?"

"What are colors?"

Raymond groaned. "Just tell me, *please*, I don't want to —"

"*What* are colors?" she snapped. "C'mon now."

Ada irritated so easily.

"Vibrations … emotions, feelings, secrets, flowing from everywhere." He parroted her, unable to hide his own irritation.

"Information."

Thoughts slid through Raymond's mind like

puzzle pieces, slowly shifting, clicking into place. He whispered, "Information is power."

"Power. *Energy*. Grief, fear, *pain*. The greater the suffering, the greater the energy that is released."

"But this isn't possible."

"Of course, it is. You proved it yourself, yesterday. With Kevin."

Raymond went cold. Questions flooded his mind, but he feared Ada's answers. "No. No, that's … *crazy*."

"Energy is being exchanged and absorbed all around us, all the time. This isn't magic."

"You're saying I eat … *suffering*?"

Ada took his hand. "I'm saying *you* will suffer if you don't. You're suffering now, aren't you?"

Raymond pulled his hand from hers and turned away. He couldn't bear to look at her.

"That's only going to get worse."

The scene outside of Father Galen's office replayed in his mind. Kevin's anxious, breathless, whining. His fear. His suffering.

Then the cool relief that washed through Raymond's belly with "just a taste."

"No way."

"You need to feed."

"*Feed?*" He sputtered a laugh.

"Yes, *feed*. And quickly. Tomorrow. Yesterday's nibble will burn fast. Your hunger pains — your *deterioration* — will return. The longer you let it go on, the harder it is to come back from."

Raymond's head swam. It was true, he hadn't felt

this good in months. But already, a hollow pocket in his stomach had returned. "B-but, *how* do I do it?"

"Just as you did yesterday. Use the skills I've taught you."

"On *who*?"

"Isn't it obvious? Keisha! You're half-way there with her already."

Raymond felt sick. Repulsed. This was a *horror* story. Worse than any moment in the cellar with Benny.

"No, this isn't real."

Ada pounded her fist on the arm of her chair. "*Stop* that! You *know* it's real."

"It's not real for *me*! It's horrible. I'm not some … cannibal! I won't do it."

"Then you will starve. And you will die."

Ada stood, crossed the room, then opened the door.

"Ada, please … "

"GET OUT!"

Her scream terrified him. He'd never seen her so angry.

Raymond snatched his bag then ran, choking on the knot in his throat.

She slammed the office door behind him.

He stood in the cold gloom of the hallway, letting his tears flow. His thin body cast a long, gray shadow that flashed with tiny, blurry diamonds of azure, magenta, sienna, and periwinkle. An endless display of rich, beautiful, ever-changing color dancing across his slight, shadow body. *His* colors. His energy. His essence.

He hated them — every shade, hue, pastel, and jewel-tone.

Every single one.

Chapter Nineteen

"FAITH. It is your turn at the board." Sister Connie's nasal bark filled the classroom, "You will write large and legibly."

Faith's desk was across the aisle from Raymond's. Her best friend, Chloe, sat behind her. They were always whispering and giggling about something, often about him.

"Yes, Sister Connie." Her sing-song voice was sickly sweet as she popped up from her desk.

Chloe snorted and covered her mouth.

"What is 4/6 x 3/5?" Sister barked, "you have two minutes."

Sister Connie liked to sit at the back of the class when she called out math drills. Normally, that made Raymond anxious. He could feel her stare scanning the backs of their heads, like a heat-seeking missile. Not that he was dumb enough to get caught doing something he shouldn't — not in *Sister Connie's* class.

He just didn't like the feeling of her gaze on his back. But right now, he was glad she couldn't see his face.

Raymond closed his eyes and squeezed his hands together beneath the desk. He dug his fingernails into the soft space between each knuckle, welcoming the sting of pain. Just for a moment, it took his mind away from the gnawing hunger inside of him.

He prayed. *Jophiel. Fill me with your creative light. Fill me up. Please. Please.*

Raymond tried to picture Jophiel's gentle expression as she floated above the pulpit, seeming to offer pure love and infinite kindness to all who would but look up to meet her gaze. He imagined her colors, brilliant marigold yellow and rose pink, radiating from her wings, flowing over him, inside of him, filling his dark, hungry emptiness with soothing light.

But it didn't help. *Nothing* helped.

Except one thing — a little taste?

No! He didn't want to think about it. He wouldn't.

Raymond watched Faith's back, concentrated on the squeak of chalk as she faltered at the board. She wasn't going to get it. Faith *never* got it.

"Time's up. You failed."

Faith turned around, grinned, and shrugged comically. Chloe giggled, but not loud enough for Sister to hear. They were dumb but not stupid.

Raymond shook his head. What was it like to be so simple? So easy. Unafraid. So … free from pain. He burned with resentment.

"Keisha, you're up. Let's go. Maybe you can show Faith how fractions work."

When Keisha's chair scraped behind him, Raymond's shoulders tensed. She still hadn't said a word to him since Ada kicked her out of the infirmary. She must have blamed him, of course. Maybe she was right to.

Faith smiled as she held out the chalk to Keisha, but Raymond caught Faith's little wink to Chloe. As Keisha reached out take it, Faith let the chalk fall on the floor. "Oops!" she said, with big, innocent eyes. Muffled giggling erupted around him.

Raymond had a view of Keisha's profile, but it was enough to see the lifted chin, and the death glare she shot at Faith, refusing to look away until Faith did. Then Keisha retrieved the chalk, before stepping up to the board with the cool serenity of a queen. But Raymond felt Keisha's truth. He *saw* the jagged green spiral of her fury. And more, beyond that. A vast, rippling lake of Keisha's pale blue sorrow.

Before Raymond knew what was happening, the churning hunger, the starved coiled animal inside of him, sprouted razor claws and snatched at Keisha. He caught a *taste*.

Just a taste … but it was enough.

Raymond went *savage*. There was no other word for it.

His hunger — because surely it could not be *him* — lunged at her. It tore through her outer field, digging deeper and deeper, down into the depths of her sorrow, where the pale blue pool darkened with oily streaks of blood red. Where Mommy waited, reaching up with bloated arms of rotting gray flesh, to hug her little girl.

Anamnesis. He just knew how to do it. Like he'd *always* known.

He could feel Keisha straining, struggling to stuff the nightmare back down into the darkness where it couldn't hurt her. But Raymond wouldn't let her. No, he *pushed* her, deeper and deeper, toward the agony of her loss, *dragged* her along the razor-sharp edge of her horrible grief.

And when Keisha was full to bursting — when she was *ripe* — Raymond fed. He raked in her suffering, gulping it down. He *gorged* himself like the animal he was.

When he was done, when he was *full*, Raymond smiled, closed his eyes, and floated in the cool bliss of non-pain. Weightless, radiant … sated. He didn't want to open his eyes. Meet her gaze. Ever. He wanted to stay in that joyful place of fullness, that *state*, for all eternity.

Rapture.

There was no other word for that, either. It was unlike anything he'd ever known.

But … Keisha. He opened his eyes.

She was staring right at him from across the class-room. Shocked. Tearless. A broken doll, lifeless and hollow-eyed. No horror, no anger, no accusation at his greedy betrayal.

Keisha was looking at him for help. *Help.*

A twenty-ton rock fell from the sky and crushed his chest. The guilt, the *shame*, was unbearable. Her sorrow was now his sorrow. And he knew — he just *knew* — he would carry her sorrow, along with his own, for the rest of his life.

He would never, *ever* do this again. He would rather starve. Waste away to nothing!

Raymond held Keisha's gaze as best he could and conjured a picture. Pink and cream, swirling like a peppermint candy. A shape in the center. A unicorn. Two unicorns, then many, running, jumping, dancing on two legs, over and over against a sea of pink.

A pattern. He knew what it was. The wallpaper in Keisha's old room. A birthday surprise from her not-yet-dead mom. The last happy moment of Keisha's *before*-life.

Raymond would draw that for her. He would. A small thing to give back. *Nothing* compared to what he'd stolen from her.

But it was all he had to offer in return.

Chapter Twenty

LIFE WAS ABOUT to get to get easier.

In a few minutes, Kevin would lug his suitcase downstairs to the foyer, say goodbye to them all, then walk out of the Haven's front door with his new family.

The knot of anxiety that had lived in Raymond's chest since Kevin's first attack so long ago, was already starting to loosen. And for the first time in months, the stabbing pain in his belly had dwindled to a dull ache, like a fading bruise.

At dinner, Raymond had waited until nobody was looking, then slid his uneaten pizza in the trash. He didn't want it, but this time, not because he was sick. He was still full, thanks to Keisha.

The shame of his attack on her — because that was the only word for it — still burned, but in so many ways, this was a *good* day. Years of bullying, of fear, were about to end. Raymond wanted, *needed*, to focus on that.

He headed out to the foyer. Most everyone was already there, lined up against the walls and up the stairway, waiting for Kevin to have his last moments with Father Galen before they came down the stairs together. Raymond searched the faces in the crowd until he spotted Keisha near the foot of the stairway.

Raymond pasted a smile on his face and headed straight toward her before he could chicken out. Ignoring the dirty looks from the girls crowded around her, he wedged himself in beside her. "I had to feed my pizza to the trash barrel this time. Would have rather given it to you."

"Huh? Oh. Yeah. I wasn't that hungry, anyway." Keisha slouched against the wall and sighed.

"What's the matter?"

She shrugged, staring straight ahead at nothing.

"Something wrong?"

"I don't know."

"You mad at me?"

"No. I don't know. I have to pee." Keisha squeezed out of her space, then walked away from him.

Raymond watched her weave through the jumble of kids. His heart ached to chase after her. To try to explain, tell her something — anything — that would make it all right. But what could he say? She knew he'd done something he shouldn't, even if she didn't understand what it was. Even if he could find a way to explain, what he did was unforgivable. She'd hate him forever. And he wouldn't blame her.

They all turned when Sister Ann stepped into the

foyer, then held the door open behind her. "Right this way."

Everyone craned their necks to get a look at Kevin's new family. Raymond peered through the throng of heads and shoulders until he caught sight of the couple who'd stepped into the hall.

His stomach cramped, like he'd been punched in the gut.

James and Debbie Devlin.

Of course, they chose *Kevin* over him. Good-looking, athletic, *likable* — all the things Raymond wasn't. Things would *always* be easy for the Kevins of the world, whether they deserved it or not. That's just the way it was.

Sister Melinda and Sister Connie joined the Devlins, fussing around them, all big smiles and handshakes. While the women chattered, James Devlin had the look of someone who felt out of place. His gaze was restless, drifting around the room without taking anything in, until it landed on Raymond and froze. Their gazes locked, his expression nervous but defiant, demanding that Raymond turn away first. But Raymond couldn't. James Devlin's colors wouldn't let him.

Mushroom truffle, dusty dark, midnight sky, charcoal-purple, swirled together like oil and ink. Just like the day they'd met. But then, Raymond didn't understand.

Charcoal-purple? There isn't a charcoal purple.

There's more. There's more, there's more.

Raymond went cold.

Ada's voice filled his head. *And what is charcoal purple? You know. You KNOW.*

"Violence," Raymond whispered.

James Devlin was still staring, his lip curled into a street-dog sneer. *That's right, asshole. I bite.*

Raymond gripped his hands together to keep them from shaking and squeezed his eyes shut tight. Shifting his entire focus inward, he pried himself away from James Devlin. It was like climbing out of a sewer.

The room erupted into applause. Raymond looked up to see Kevin at the top of the stairs, holding his arms up in a big V-sign, like he'd just scored the winning goal. But as Kevin came down the steps, Raymond could almost taste the thin, green ribbons of anxiety trailing behind him.

Raymond sneaked a look at the Devlins and immediately wished he hadn't. Debbie was clapping along with everyone else, her eyes shiny with happy tears. James stood beside her, arms crossed over his chest, rocking slightly on his heels. As he watched Kevin hug and handshake his way down the stairs, James flexed and gripped his upper arms so tightly, his knuckles went white. And just for an instant, he flicked the tip of his tongue, snake-like, through his thick, wet lips, and quick-sucked it back in again.

Just a taste.

A searing, acid bloom of charcoal-purple burst in Raymond's inner vision. His stomach lurched, like he'd swallowed something rotten. His heart began to pound, and then race, as adrenaline flushed through his veins.

This man meant harm. *Pain.* He *enjoyed* it.

Kevin had made it to the end of the stairs and was two kids away. Raymond's forehead was slick with sweat. He wiped it away with his sleeve, careful not to press too hard on the lump that Kevin's ice ball had given him. It was smaller now, and more yellow than blue. But it still hurt.

Raymond had to warn him about Devlin. Didn't he? The guy was first class jerk, but it was still the right thing to do. He looked around the room, hoping to spot Ada. She'd know what to do. But Ada was nowhere to be seen.

It was Raymond's turn to say goodbye. Kevin stood there, smirking at him, just like the afternoon he'd whopped Raymond in the belly during dodgeball. Just like the day he'd given Raymond a "swirly" by stuffing his head in the toilet bowl and flushing. Just like the first time he'd tied Raymond up and left him in the cellar for Twenty with Benny.

Raymond *had* to tell him. He had to say something. But his mouth wouldn't move.

Kevin shrugged, then held out his hand for a shake. Raymond hesitated. His eyes flicked toward the front door. James Devlin was watching them with narrow eyes. Raymond reached out slowly to shake Kevin's hand.

"Psych!" Kevin yanked his hand away and ran through his flop of golden blond hair. "You're such a douche." He laughed.

Raymond's eyes flicked to James Devlin. His lip was curled in an ugly smile that sent a chill up

Raymond's spine. He leaned in close to Kevin and whispered, "Don't go with them Kevin. It's not safe."

"Yeah, right. Good one. I'm *so* scared."

"That man's going to hurt you."

"Shut up, weirdo. You're just jealous because nobody's ever going to want a freak like you." He sneered and turned away, but Raymond saw the lime green, lightning flash of fear that shot through Kevin's color field.

Kevin moved on to the next group of kids, not looking at Raymond on purpose. But he didn't have to see Kevin's face to know he was more scared than ever. And as much as it sickened Raymond to admit it, part of him was pulled toward that fear. It smelled *good*.

He flushed with shame and forced his thoughts back to Devlin. The cold hunger in his eyes. The horrible flick of his tongue when Kevin appeared at the top of the stairs. Like a snake tasting the air for *prey*.

What should he do? The sisters wouldn't believe him. They'd think he was jealous, just like Kevin did, and send him to Father Galen's office. And Father would probably punish him for "making nonsense." Starting trouble.

It was pointless.

His *gift*, as Ada called it, the *information* it brought him, was pointless. *He* was pointless. Worse than useless. He was *cursed*.

Sadness and guilt hung like a wet blanket over his shoulders as Raymond climbed the stairs to his room.

His head, like it did so often lately when he was upset, flooded with strange, disturbing pictures. As if his darkest thoughts, his heaviest feeling, were fighting to take shape. Begging to jump from the shadows of his mind onto his sketchpad. To live in the outside world. A thing to be seen. To be *mourned*.

This time, he was adrift in a coal-black river. It rushed all around him, carrying others in its wake, sucking them under, spitting them back up to gulp and suck for air to fill their water-logged lungs. He recognized some faces — Kevin, Keisha, even Mrs. Devlin — thrashing and gasping as the cold water dragged them, on and on, wherever it felt like going.

Raymond realized, with a start, that he hadn't actually told Kevin goodbye. He could turn back, but what did it matter? They *hated* each other. *That* was the truth of it.

Besides, he didn't need to say goodbye to Kevin.

They would see each other again. Raymond was sure of it.

Chapter Twenty-One

RAYMOND HAD the dorm to himself. Everyone else was in the rec room watching a movie. They always did that after Pick-Up parties. But he had something on his mind.

He had no words for Keisha — nothing he could *say* that might bring back her friendship. But Raymond had her pictures in his head. Things that Keisha loved in her "before" life. And he could bring them into this world for her to see. To hold. To keep forever. He wanted to do that for her.

Sitting cross-legged on the floor, he studied his collection of pencils. Ballet slipper pink — that would work. Raymond began to draw unicorns. Keisha's unicorns. He took his time, carefully outlining, shading, pulling the image from his memory in minute detail. He wanted it to be just as she remembered. The *best* thing he'd ever done.

The air seemed to shift around him. He looked up from his work.

Ada was coming.

She stepped into his room without asking and took a seat at the foot of his bed.

"Sulking?"

Raymond kept drawing. He wasn't in the mood for Ada talk. Not at all.

"What *is* the point, Ray?" she snapped.

"I'm just … sad! That's all. Can't I be sad?"

"What good will it do you? It changes nothing."

"I can't help it —"

"It's a choice you're making. A *stupid* one."

"That man, Devlin? He's going to do something bad to Kevin. I know it."

"And?"

"I tried to tell him!"

"How did that work out for you?"

"He laughed at me. Said I was just jealous. But … he got really scared. I could feel it."

"Well, then. At least you got something out of it. Right?"

Raymond didn't answer. But the memory of Kevin's fear, the *smell* of it, set a little hungry flame burning in his belly.

"Raymond?"

"No."

"Why not?"

"Because it's … it's not a good thing. I don't want to be *that*."

"Well, you *are* that!" Ada stood up, "You missed a good opportunity. An *easy* one."

"I don't care!"

"You will." She tapped her way across the room, then paused at the door. "I'm disappointed in you."

He waited until the click of her cane faded to let his tears flow.

Later, after he'd dried his eyes and finished his work, Raymond stepped into the hall and listened. Movie night would be over soon, but he had time. He slipped into the darkness of the girls' dorm without turning on the light and found Keisha's neatly made bed in the corner. Something about its precise, tidy lines made him sad.

Raymond slid the unicorn picture out from under his sweater. He glanced over his shoulder — nobody there — before placing a light kiss on the bright, pink image in the middle of his drawing. He slipped it under Keisha's pillow.

He padded back down the hallway to his room, as all around him, shadows crawled up the walls and across the ceiling, reaching for one another. They formed pictures. Keisha's upturned face, glowing with happiness. Her mother's smooth, coffee-colored cheek pressed against hers. Laughing and smiling, like a happiness was a given. Something they could count on. Forever and ever. No sorrow, no blood, no death.

But they were wrong.

And Ada was wrong. Knowledge wasn't power.

It was *pain*.

Chapter Twenty-Two

SINCE MAMA DIED, this was the hardest part of Keisha's day. She hated bedtime. Not so much the sleeping part — she liked to dream. Especially of Mama, who came to her, sometimes, all pretty and happy, like she was before Ronnie moved in.

It was the getting *in* bed part that she hated.

She used to love those last few moments, snug in her warm, soft bed at the end of the day, right before sleep time.

But now, it was just so, so … *lonely*. Nobody to ask if she remembered to brush her teeth, which she *always* did anyway. Nobody to smooth the covers over her shoulder and say, "Ten more minutes with your book, then lights out, okay sweets?" And, for sure, there would be no kiss on the top of her head and a whisper — *angels on your pillow*! That always made her giggle.

Keisha didn't giggle anymore. Things were different now. *She* was different now.

At bedtime, she crowded the bathroom with the rest of the girls, watching as they elbowed for room to brush their teeth and wash their faces. She always went last, so she could take her time and do a good job. The way Mama taught her.

By the time she was done, most of the girls were already sleeping. Her sheets were always cold, and the mattress of her narrow bed was so thin, she could feel the springs beneath it. She'd try hard not to think, to *not* go back to the day she found Mama, sick and scared, on the kitchen floor. But in the quiet darkness of her dorm room, the bad thoughts were *so* loud. She'd yank the covers over her head, shut her eyes tight, wrap her arms around her flat pillow, and *force* herself to sleep, as quickly as she could.

But after movie night, after the usual brushing, washing, and lights-out, when Keisha curled up on her side and reached for her pillow, something *crinkled*.

She slid her hands underneath it and felt something smooth and dry.

Paper.

Keisha pushed her pillow aside. It was a drawing. But of what? It was too dark to tell.

As the dorm room breathed the sounds of sleep, Keisha pinched one corner of the paper, careful not to rattle it, then pushed off her covers. The floor was icy on her bare feet as she padded to the bathroom.

Shivering in the darkness, she fumbled for the light switch. The white glare forced her eyes to squeeze shut. Keisha fought it, blinking them into a watery squint. She stared down at the picture in her hands, taking it in, making sense of it. And as her mind understood what she was looking at, a warm tingle spread from her heart outward.

Keisha's mouth dropped open, then, slowly, formed a wide smile.

Her unicorns! Dancing, without a care, against the ballerina pink wallpaper of her room! The last birthday present she ever got. There they were, in her hands, like someone had plucked them right out of her memory.

And then Mama was there. All around her. Wrapping her in a cocoon of joy and the sense of ... of ... *home*.

Keisha's giggle bounced off the bathroom tiles. Happy tears spilled down her cheeks.

Magic. This was pure, real magic.

And she knew — she just *knew* — that strange, weird, wonderful, Raymond was the magician.

Chapter Twenty-Three

RAYMOND RESTED his hands behind his head, as the shadows moved across the ceiling above his bed. They undulated in shimmery waves, of pink and gold iridescence. Keisha. He could *feel* her.

Delight, surprise, the warmth of her smile — it filled him, right to his core. Her happy tears dampened his face. Joy. Mama. Home. Love, love, love!

He smiled and whispered to himself in the darkness. Just a single word.

Magic.

Then soft, downy-feathered wings wrapped around Raymond and carried him off to sleep.

He woke early, rested, happy, and sneaked into the shower before anyone else could get there first. He combed his thick mop of curls off his forehead while it was wet, hoping it would stay there when it dried. Pinpoints of gold flashed in his dark eyes and his skin glowed. He barely recognized himself.

As he headed downstairs to breakfast, butterflies

played in his belly. He'd be the first one there. And he'd save the seat next to him for Keisha.

Raymond swung round the corner banister of the staircase and jumped the last two steps to the floor, Kevin style. He pushed through the doorway heading to the dining room and ran right into Sister Ann. She stumbled back a step but, luckily, held her ground.

"Raymond! Watch yourself!"

"Sorry, Sister Ann. I didn't see you."

"I guess not." Sister Ann squinted, tilting her head to one side. It reminded Raymond of Mr. Gregg's crow stare. "There's something different about you."

Raymond shrugged. "What's wrong?"

"Nothing. In fact, you look … well. Like you're eating. That's it. Full cheeks."

"Oh. Umm, yeah. I'm just heading to breakfast now."

"No, you're heading to Father Galen's office."

Raymond's heart sank. What did he do now?

Sister read it on his face. "You're not in trouble. For once."

"Can I go after?"

"No, you may not. He's waiting."

Raymond looked past Sister's shoulder through the windows of the dining room door. It was still empty. Maybe it was early enough that he could see Father Galen and be back before Keisha came down. He turned and took off running.

"Raymond! WALK!" Sister called after him.

He slowed down until he was through the doorway, then picked up his run down the hall. He was out of breath when he knocked on Father's door.

"Come."

When Raymond stepped into the office, a thin jolt of surprise ran through him. Ada sat at Father's desk. She turned her face toward him and smiled.

Father waved him in. "Sit, sit, my boy."

He was in a good mood.

"Morning, Raymond." Ada was still smiling.

His nerves jangled. What could *possibly* be up?

Raymond sat next to Ada. He took a breath, dragging it deep into his lungs, then blew it out slowly, silently.

"Miss Ada brought us some good news."

Ada smiled and nodded, obviously pleased with herself. "There is a young couple." She lifted her chin high but did not turn toward him. "Lovely people. They are very anxious to meet you, Raymond."

Another Meet and Greet? Big deal. "Oh."

Father Galen's eyebrows popped up then settled into a frown. "*Oh?* That's all you have to say?"

"He's just nervous." Ada's hand found Raymond's shoulder. "You've been down this road before." She leaned toward him. "This time, it's different."

"Different how?"

Ada shrugged. "It just … feels right. A good fit."

Raymond's nerves jangled again. Something in Ada's manner told him something new was happening.

This time it's different.

His brain went fuzzy, jumping from one thought to

another, but always landing on the image of Keisha's smiling face. *Magic.*

"You'll meet them this morning for a nice breakfast. If all goes to plan, you'll be on your way to a new home this afternoon!" Father Galen tapped his desk like he'd just won a hundred dollars, "Isn't that exciting?"

"So — so fast?" His heart thumped hard in his chest.

"It's a quicker process than normal, yes. Of course, it would be just a foster arrangement to start. But Ada has vetted them carefully." Father nodded at Ada like she could see him. "*Very* carefully, yes? Soooo … lucky you!"

He'd never seen Father Galen smile so much.

"But, um," Raymond chose his words carefully, "What if I *don't* like them. Is that okay?"

Father Galen sighed, and the smile dropped from his face. "Don't be difficult, Raymond. Of course, you'll like them. Ada just told you. They're wonderful."

"I know but —"

"Raymond will give it a chance, no matter what." A cold edge slipped into Ada's voice. "Right, Raymond?" She tilted her face upward and waited for him to agree.

Raymond chewed his lower lip. He was being ungrateful. Making her look bad. But that wasn't it. Ada didn't give a rat's butt what Father Galen thought. No, she'd made up her mind about this. And so had Father Galen. Any talk to the contrary was just an annoyance to them both.

"Right," Raymond said quietly.

Wasn't this what he'd been waiting for? A home, a *real* home at last? Would it really happen this time?

Ada seemed sure of it. And she loved him, didn't she?

Maybe they would actually *like* him. Maybe they *were* wonderful, like Ada said. *A good fit.*

Or maybe …

The tender spot in Raymond's stomach began to throb.

Maybe they would cast shadows of charcoal purple.

Maybe they would smile with thin, wet lips, and their red tongues would flicker, searching for just a moment — just a taste — of delicious pain.

His pain.

Either way, Raymond would meet them. Give them a chance. Right?

Sure, he would.

What choice did he have?

Chapter Twenty-Four

In all his years at Haven, Raymond had never been in this room. He never even knew it existed. Now that he did, he felt like an idiot. He'd never once seen Father Galen in the dining hall. But it never crossed his mind that Father had to eat *somewhere*.

Father's private kitchen was small. But it was bright, cozy, and smelled like warm pancakes. It had a window seat overlooking the garden that was filled with leafy plants and jars of colored sea glass. They flashed like jewels in the morning sun.

Raymond sat with Ada at the kitchen table. It was old — antique, probably — with thick, wooden legs carved with trailing vines and leaves. The table was set with four snow white plates, cloth napkins, and silverware. In the center was a mason jar filled with daffodils that looked so fresh and perfect, they could have been fake.

Raymond leaned forward and trailed his finger over the soft yellow petals. "Real flowers."

"How nice."

"Yeah. But it's *weird*. Father Galen's idea, I bet."

Ada ignored his comment. "What time is it?"

"Ten past ten."

"Late." She sniffed. "That's not particularly impressive."

"Maybe they're not coming."

"Don't worry. They're coming."

"Why aren't we at the regular room?"

"Father Galen thought this would be better. He'd like it to go well for you."

"I bet."

Ada had nothing to say to that, either. They waited in silence until they heard the clack of footsteps in the courtyard.

"Sit up straight," Ada said calmly, "and smile."

Raymond sat upright in his chair. Ada cleared her throat when Father Galen appeared in the doorway.

"Here we are."

He had that phony cheerful tone that got on Raymond's nerves.

Father stepped into the kitchen and moved to one side. Behind him stood a tall, thin woman with long brown hair and eyes like Bambi. She peered into the kitchen. Her eyes found Raymond, and a shy smile spread across her face.

Raymond smiled back. Wow, she was pretty. But sad.

She took two steps into the kitchen before a tall, muscular man followed. He looked like he used to play football, or maybe hockey.

"This is Lisa and Matt Narron." Father Galen's voice was too loud in the small room. "Say hello to Raymond. And you already know Miss Ada."

"Hi, Raymond. I'm Lisa. Oh, wait." Lisa giggled. "Father just said that." She rolled her eyes, then tucked a lock of hair behind her ear with long, thin fingers. Her hand trembled.

Raymond felt sorry for her, though he wasn't sure why. Ada nudged him under the table. "Oh. Um, hi."

"Hey, Raymond." Matt waved at him.

Raymond waved back.

"Have a seat. Get comfortable," Father Galen said. "The sisters will be in shortly with breakfast."

Lisa and Matt took the last two seats at the table. Father Galen left, whistling his way down the courtyard walk.

"So," Ada said, "Lisa is a history teacher. Raymond is fascinated with history. He's a straight-A student."

Lisa opened her eyes extra big. Warm, honey brown, Raymond thought, like a shaft of sunlight through a bottle of root beer.

"Impressive." Lisa smiled. "Handsome *and* smart."

Raymond knew she was just being nice. But still, his face went hot, and he couldn't look at her for a moment.

"Jeez, Lees." Matt laughed. "She does that to me, too, Raymond. Embarrassing, right?"

"Well, he must get that all the time," Lisa said.

Raymond snorted. He didn't know what to say — nobody had ever called him handsome. He was relieved when one of dinner ladies shuffled in with a tray of pancakes and coffee.

Ada, Lisa, and Matt slipped into conversation about Haven's school curriculum. Raymond half-followed the conversation, stealing looks at them when he could, nodding when he was supposed to. But his mind was full of color. *Their* colors.

Lisa was cool cream, like rose petals, against a deep, verdant green — the good kind. Rain drops on fresh ferns, moss on white birch, grassy hills on the first warm day of spring. But through the middle of that rich green field cut a midnight blue shaft, like a pointy icicle. It speared, dead-center through her thin, fragile-looking body, pulsing consistently, like a second heart.

Matt was bright yellow, a field of corn under a cloudless sky. They paired well. They sat close, their sides pressed together, his muscled arm wrapped around the back of her chair, her fingers wrapped loosely around his hand as it dangled over her narrow shoulder. They looked easy and relaxed. He was hers. She was his. Confident. Normal.

But Raymond felt a twinge.

There's more.

Matt was *shielding* Lisa. But from what?

And then, something Raymond had never seen before. The dark, sharp icicle was there, in Matt's chest too. Like Lisa's, except it didn't pulse. It was still. Solid and silent.

It troubled Raymond, those dark, frozen spears through their chests. But they were not charcoal-purple, and whatever he felt, it wasn't fear. In fact, he could tell that they wanted him, and that felt good. It was as if it had all been worked out before he'd even met them. Ada must have arranged it, somehow, just as she promised. But at least they hadn't changed after seeing him in person.

Maybe Keisha could visit someday.

If she ever wanted to.

IT WOULDN'T TAKE Raymond long to pack — he didn't have much — but he rushed, anyway. The Narrons were waiting downstairs, ready to take him away to his new life. His head spun, it was happening so fast. No last day of classes. But he was so far ahead of everyone else, it didn't matter anyway. No Pick-Up party. And *that* was okay. The thought of all those awkward goodbyes made him shudder. He was glad to be spared all of it. But his heart ached when he thought of Keisha. She was still in class, and Father Galen wanted this over quickly ... quietly. It felt strange. Ada promised to tell her goodbye for him, and that he'd send her another picture when he was settled in.

Raymond had just finished rolling up his sheets and blankets for the laundry — see ya, Benny — when Ada walked into his room She sat on his bare mattress and patted the spot next to her.

He sat.

"Are you scared?"

"A little."

"What if I said I'll visit you every week?"

"Really? Is that allowed?"

"I've gotten the okay from Father Galen to continue our behavioral therapy. The Narrons are happy for the help. It all works out. Do you like them?"

"I think so. But they have something weird. A sharp ... *block* shape. Dark blue."

"And what is dark blue?"

"Theirs? Grief. But ... not *just* that."

"Channeling."

"What?"

"It's called channeling. You need to channel that blue block. *Mine* it."

"For what?"

Ada laid her hand on his. "Ray, you must *eat*."

He pulled his hand away. "I don't want to talk about this. Not now."

"Well, guess what. We can talk about it whenever you want." Ada reached into the pocket of her jacket and pulled out a phone and a charger, wrapped in a plastic bag. "This is for you."

Raymond stared at the shiny black rectangle in Ada's palm. He'd never had a cell phone. He barely knew how to *use* one. It wasn't like Haven just handed them out to all the orphans. Who would they call, anyway?

"I can't take that, Ada. It's ... too expensive."

Ada picked up his hand and pressed the phone

into it. "It's yours. And it's a *secret*. Between you and me."

"Why?"

"Because I want you to call me. Every day. *Every single day*. At least once."

A lump swelled up in Raymond's throat. She *loved* him. She really did.

"My number is in there. *Our* secret. Once a day. You promise?"

Raymond nodded and stuffed the phone into his pocket. He didn't want to cry, but it was all just ... so much.

"I love you, Ada." He sniffled.

"And I love you. Now give me a hug. And let's get you out of this shithole."

Raymond wrapped his arms around Ada's shoulders, laughing through his tears. "Thank you. For *everything*."

Ada and Father Galen stood together on the front porch of the Haven as Raymond slid into the back seat of Lisa and Matt's Jeep. As they rolled down the long driveway, he waved from the back window. He watched them grow smaller and smaller, until the road curved and the Haven for Tender Souls disappeared into the tree line.

Lisa looked back at him from the front seat and winked. Even in the semi-darkness of early night, she was glowing. "Going to be a lot of girls at your new school wondering who *you* are."

Matt groaned and shook his head. "Sorry, bud,"

he said over his shoulder. "Just going to have to get used to it."

Bud.

The treetops swayed against the night sky, flying past his window as they drove, mile by mile, further from Haven and toward his new life. With a real family. *His* family.

Sorry, bud. Just going to have to get used to it.

The engine hummed and the tires rumbled over the gravelly potholes that scarred the winding road out of Brunswick. Raymond laid his head back on the seat and smiled up at the first stars poking through the velvet sky.

Maybe he *was* handsome, just a little.

Chapter Twenty-Five

"WAKEY, WAKEY, SUNSHINE. WE'RE HOME."

Raymond opened his eyes to see Lisa's smiling face floating above him. She stepped back and held the car door open for him.

We're home.

Raymond rubbed the stiffness out of his neck as he slid from the back seat. He gazed up at the elegant, two-storey brick house that was now his home.

"Wow."

Glowing lanterns edged the driveway, a short flight of stone steps, and a neat, curved walkway leading to a set of tall, white, double doors. Matt came around from the back of the car holding his suitcase. "What do you think?"

"It's ... it's so big. How many people live here?"

Lisa and Matt laughed.

"Just us," Lisa said. "And now you, too." Her smile was nervous but full of kindness. "Let's get you settled in."

Raymond reached for his suitcase, but Matt pulled it away.

"Nah, I got it." He started up the stairs to the front door.

Lisa waived Raymond forward, then followed.

As they stepped through the front door, Raymond gasped. They stood in a massive living room of pure white — walls, carpet, furniture. The ceiling soared to a second storey, reached by a sweeping staircase. A modern-looking chandelier hung from its center, glowing above a grand piano. Beyond that, a set of glass doors lead to a huge patio lit by more glowing lanterns.

Raymond had seen rich people's houses on TV. But he never expected to see one in person, never mind *live* in one!

A man and a woman walked in from the patio. The man was big, like Matt, with the same muscled arms and sandy hair. The woman was small and wore glasses. Her dark hair glistened with thin streaks of silver. They each held a beer and smiled wide.

"There he is!" Matt said. "Raymond, this is my goony brother, David, and his sweet wife, Jean, who he doesn't deserve."

David held out his hand. "Hey, Raymond."

As Raymond stepped forward and shook David's hand, a vibration — instant pins and needles — coursed through his arm. It traveled upward, leaving him light-headed. David's colors rushed around him like a muddy brook. Murky brown, like it had torn through the roots of a shore tree and taken the earth with it.

Raymond fought a flush of panic. It reminded him of meeting Keisha for the first time. And he could *not* have that happen now. Not here, on the first night, in the middle of this fancy living room.

Raymond felt a hand on his back and turned to see Lisa staring at him with concern. "Are you okay? You look a little peaky."

"Uh, yeah. Yeah. Just … still waking up, I guess."

"The poor guy must be starving," Matt said. "I know I am. C'mon, bud, let's see what we got in the kitchen."

They all bustled into the kitchen. Like the living room, it was huge, with a square center island wrapped around a shiny stove that looked like it was never used. They all took a stool at the counter, while Lisa started pulling items from an enormous refrigerator. She slid bottles of beer and soda on the countertop, then set a pan on the stove.

David clapped his hands together once, sharp and loud. "Please tell me you're making grilled cheese, Lees."

"Yup. My specialty. And the only thing I know how to make." She giggled.

"Yeah, but you're *good* at it." David elbowed Raymond, "I don't know what she does with a couple pieces of bread and a slice of cheese, but — "

"Oh stop. A monkey could make a grilled cheese." Lisa laughed again, but her cheeks bloomed like roses and flashes of red popped, like tiny fireworks, across her normal field of green.

Something was strange here. Something private that Raymond didn't want to know about. Not now. Not ever. He drew energy from deep in his center and formed a veil, thick and complete, over all of them.

Raymond drank his soda, though the bubbles hurt his stomach. He chatted with his new family, answered their questions, nodded with interest when they talked about themselves. He laughed when he felt like he was supposed to and did his best to just be *normal*.

But while he smiled and nodded and chattered with these strangers, the discomfort in the back of his mind crept toward sadness. If this was normal, then normal felt strange. *Very* strange.

Maybe he belonged in the place he'd just left behind.

And what if *his* place there was gone for good? Father Galen was in an awful hurry to get him out.

The thought made him shiver with anxiety. But worse, the tender spot in the pit of his stomach that had been cool and quiet ever since his moment with Keisha, gurgled like an unclogged drain. Raymond knew what was coming next.

Please, no.

He took in breath, dropped his shoulders, softened his limbs, and released the air slowly through his nostrils.

But no, it was coming. The hated, familiar *heat* of his hunger.

It rose, gathered, found its center. The burn, like a

quarter dipped in acid and lodged in his gut, was back. He'd kidded himself that it was gone for good.

Gone for good. He nearly laughed out loud at that thought. Pathetic.

So far, in his short life, only the *good* things ever fell in that category.

The bad things?

They always found their way home.

Chapter Twenty-Six

RAYMOND LAID his head back against the sofa and allowed his eyes to close just for a moment. But it was long enough for Lisa to catch him. "Raymond, you look sleepy."

"I'm not sleepy." Raymond said, faster and louder than he needed to. He pushed himself upright and widened his eyes. He wasn't lying. He didn't want to sleep and doubted he could. What he wanted — *needed* — was a rest. He wasn't used to all this talking.

After eating, they'd moved from the kitchen counter to a sitting area of extra-long, extra soft, couches and chairs. Thankfully, the conversation had moved on from all-things-Raymond, to sports, the weather, and gossip about people he didn't know. He had Lisa to thank for that. She seemed to sense the spotlight was too intense for him and steered the others away. But even so, the effort of veiling four people at once for so long was exhausting. He felt like a battery that was nearly out of juice.

"Okay, not sleepy. Got it." Lisa grinned at Raymond, but in a nice way. "Do want to see your room, anyway? Get settled in?"

"Yeah, bud," Matt said. "We four will sit here and yap all night." He pointed at his brother and winked at Raymond. "Especially *him*. Might want to escape while you can."

Raymond laughed at the mock-hurt look on David's face. "Guess I am a little tired."

Lisa stood and held her hand out to him. Raymond took it, and she pulled him up to standing. "It's upstairs. Matt brought up your bag already."

Raymond turned toward Matt but was too shy to make eye contact. "Thanks, Matt," he said softly. "For everything."

"Nooo problem." Matt smiled. "Good to have you on board."

David held up his palm for a high five, and Raymond slapped it lightly. "We'll be seeing you soon, Raymond. We're regulars."

Raymond waved goodnight to Jean as he followed Lisa back to the living room.

He paused at the pearly white piano, admiring a row of abstract paintings that hung on the wall behind it. Imagine, having actual art in your own living room. The top of the piano was covered with photos in carved frames of every size. Images of people — family, Raymond assumed. A silver-haired man and woman, in fancy clothes, dancing together. A younger David and Matt in deck chairs on a boat, all floppy-haired and tanned. Lisa in a cap and gown, posing under a willow tree by a lake. A little girl with dark, curly hair, dressed as a cupcake, winking at the camera.

Raymond ran his fingertip lightly along the keys. "Wow. This is beautiful. Do you play?"

Lisa slowed a moment but didn't stop. "I used to. C'mon. You're just at the top the hall."

She led him up the sweeping staircase, past a wall of windows that reached nearly to the ceiling. They looked out over a sprawling yard that was softly lit with the same glowing lanterns he'd seen everywhere else. In the center was a large built-in pool, edged by neatly trimmed shrubs and trees. It was sealed with a green plastic covering.

Lisa stopped at door mid-way down the hall and threw it open.

"Well, what do you think?"

The room was bigger than his entire dorm at Haven — and he had shared that with *seven* others. The bed had two layers of big, fluffy pillows and was large enough for three people. His suitcase and jacket were placed neatly on a bench at the end.

Like the rest of the house, the walls were mostly windows, including a skylight above the bed. Underneath the largest window was a sleek wooden desk surrounded by shelves. They were filled with what looked like a brand-new set of encyclopedias.

"Whoa! Are those for *me*?"

"Yup. You like them?"

"I love them."

"That is *so* cool. Most kids have their noses stuck to computer screens these days."

"Well, we only had two computers. But lots of encyclopedias. I never had to wait for those."

"Ada told me you spent a lot of time in the library."

Ada! Shoot. He remembered the phone in his jacket pocket.

"Um, what time is it?"

"Oh, yeah. You're pooped. I'll leave you to it." Lisa pointed at a door in the corner, "The left door is your closet. Not to be confused with your bathroom, which is the door on the right." She laughed.

"*My* bathroom?"

Her smile was kind. "Uh-huh. I know it's all … a bit much. But it won't seem strange for long."

"No, it's all … amazing. Like a dream come true."

"Well, *you're* a dream come true for me. For *us*."

Raymond didn't know what to say. All he had for her was a nod and a moment of awkward silence.

Lisa filled it with a quick hug before she turned to leave. "If you can't sleep, just knock. We're two doors down. I'll probably be awake."

She closed the door softly behind her.

Raymond listened to her footsteps fade, then grabbed the phone from his jacket. After he managed to get Ada's name to pop up on the screen, he pressed "call." She answered on the second ring.

"I thought you'd forgotten about me."

"Sorry Ada, they had a little welcome home thing for me."

"A *welcome home thing*? What did that entail?"

"Matt's brother, David. And his wife, Jean. They wanted to meet me. They talked a lot, for a long time." Raymond laid down on the bed. It was like falling into a cloud. He pressed a fist into the sore spot in his belly and rubbed it gently.

"You sound tired."

"Yeah. I'm on my bed. It's weird —"

"It's not weird," Ada snapped. "It's unfamiliar. That will pass."

"No, I mean … these people. The colors are …" Raymond didn't want to say weird again. She'd think he was being an ungrateful baby. "Anyway, I'm taking care of it."

"You're what?"

"I'm veiling them. And it's fine. It just made me tired, that's all. And my stomach is —"

"No, Raymond. No. No. No. Are you *actually* a fool, or just doing a very good impression of one?"

"Don't be mad, Ada."

"Why not? Why shouldn't I be? You're risking your health."

"I'm not! I just didn't want to see … I wanted to feel normal. Just once."

"You are NOT *normal*, Raymond. I don't know how to make you understand that."

Raymond's stomach churned. He pulled his knees up toward his chest and stifled a groan.

"Are you in pain?"

He didn't answer. She knew.

Ada sighed. "Never compromise your health for a

veil. Do you understand? Certainly not a whole group of people."

But I veil you, Ada. You make me.

He wouldn't dare say it. But he wondered; why veil *her* but nobody else?

"Drop them. All of them. You will not veil *anyone* in that house. Or anywhere, for that matter."

"All right." He was too tired, too sore to argue.

"Promise."

"I promise."

"Honestly, Raymond. When will you learn to use your wits?"

"I'm sorry, Ada. I wasn't thinking."

"Well, it's time you started thinking. I can't do it for you. Not forever."

"I know."

"Get some rest," Ada's voice softened, just a little, "I'll visit soon."

"Okay. Goodnight."

"Call me tomorrow. Don't forget."

"I won't."

Ada ended the call without saying goodbye.

Raymond kicked off his shoes, then crawled under the covers. The bed sheets were soft, and the blankets heavy and warm. It was like being hugged by a giant teddy bear.

But it didn't matter. Lisa, Matt, the fancy house, the soft sheets, the cushy pillow — they didn't change anything. The loneliness of Haven house had followed him here.

Because he carried it inside of him. It lived in the burning hole deep in his belly.

It slept, sometimes — Raymond was beginning to understand that much, at least. But no matter what, this ugly, burning thing would wake up, again and again. For sure it would.

And it woke up hungry.

Chapter Twenty-Seven

RAYMOND WAS FLOATING in the dark. He was still in his room — the skylight above his bed was nearly close enough to touch. But below, his body was curled up, breathing softly, under the covers. He sensed the warmth there and longed to sink back down to his bed. But no, he — or some part of him — drifted, caught in an invisible current.

It pulled him toward, and then *through*, the wall of his room. The current picked up speed, dragging him down the sweeping staircase. It slowed to a near stop, leaving him hovering above the piano.

Somebody was playing. Not an actual song, but a string of soft, random notes, one key at a time, with no noticeable rhythm. He squinted through the darkness but could see no person, no form, seated at the keys. Yet the piano's black and white teeth moved down and up, their uneven, random *plink* floating upward through the shadows of Lisa and Matt's enormous living room.

And then — *whoosh* — Raymond dropped to the bench. His hands moved over the keys, picking one, then another, in whatever direction pleased him. The picture frames on the piano rumbled gently as he plunked one key after another. The dark-haired little girl in the cupcake costume jiggled, like she was dancing. It was so funny! He laughed, but it wasn't his voice. It was a high-pitched giggle. Playful, silly, carefree. When he looked down at his hands, he didn't recognize the tiny pink fingers tapping out the rhythmless tune.

He blinked as a bright ray of sun cut across the piano. It was daylight — a golden, bright morning. Outside, the trees in the backyard swayed gently in the breeze, and bright blue water in the pool rippled. A pink flamingo floated on the water's surface. Its smiling face — so silly! — bobbed up and down, saying, "Yes, yes, yes."

The hands that were not his clapped with delight.

"He wants to play with me!" It was not his voice that whispered happily.

And then he was moving, running through the kitchen, the living room, then out through the sliding doors into the warm sunshine. The damp grass on his bare feet was cool, and it tickled. It made him laugh, again, in that happy, carefree giggle-voice.

"I'm coming, Mr. Mingo!" the voice sang.

The smell of chlorine filled his nostrils as the little fingers gripped the edge of the pool. The hand stretched out over the sparkling water, reaching for the pool toy as it drifted nearby. The fingertips managed to graze the sun-warmed plastic, only to push it further away.

"Come here, Mingo. *Here*!"

The knees scooted forward until they were half-over the pool edge. A reflection … a face, *her* face, rippled in the water. Dark, round eyes matched a mop of shiny, dark hair.

The cupcake girl.

Grunting with effort, she reached out again, both hands now, stretching closer, closer, then — yes! The little palms landed on the neck of the float. But … oh, no! He — she — was tilting forward. Fingers gripped the plastic. Slipped, then clawed, trying to push upright, back to the safety of the pool edge.

Oh, no! Oh, NO!

Squeak went damp palms against the plastic pool toy, followed by a splash. The shock of cold water made him cry out. But his mouth filled with water. His nose stung. He tried again to call for help. But all he managed was an "mmmm" sound before the rush of water slapped the back of his throat and filled his lungs.

Mommy, mommy, mommy!

The word crowded his brain, lodged in his heart. And down, down, down he went. Above him, Mingo's belly, a rippling pink oval, got smaller and smaller, and farther away.

The little arms flapped. The tiny legs kicked. But it didn't matter. Nothing worked! His chest burned! No breath — not even enough air to cry.

The water around him began to bleed with color.

Slick, oily iridescent rainbow shades flowed from his body. Currents of shock, panic, *terror*.

Mommy, mommy, MOMMY!

"Raymond! Wake up. Wake up, honey!"

Raymond snapped upright. He was in his bed, his face wet with tears. His chest burned, heaving up and down, as he sobbed.

"Hey. Hey, it's okay."

Mommy was rubbing his back. He stared at her, blinking his eyes into focus.

No. Lisa. *Lisa* was beside him, her eyes wide and shiny with concern. She brushed back his damp hair. "Just breathe. Take a nice, deep breath."

Raymond swallowed a sob and dragged a stream of air through his nostrils. He held it, then puffed it out through pursed lips, just as Ada taught him. "I … I had a nightmare."

"Sure did. Sounded like a doozy."

"It was … it was *bad*." He wiped the dampness from his cheeks and nose. His hair flopped back down over his eyes.

Lisa brushed it back again. Her hand was ice cold. "You were yelling."

"I was?"

She nodded. "You want to talk about it?"

A shadow blocked the light streaming in from the hallway. Matt stood in the doorway, rubbing his left eye. "What the hell's going on?"

"Raymond had a bad dream."

"Jesus. Sounded like someone was being murdered."

"It was a *bad* dream, Matt," Lisa snapped, "Very bad."

"Yeah, all right. Bad dream, got it." Matt shuffled a little closer and squinted at Raymond, "You're all right now, right, bud?

Raymond sat up straighter and shrugged, like Kevin would. "Yeah, I'm cool."

"See, he's good."

"Go back to bed. I'll be there in a minute."

"It's okay, Lisa," Raymond's croaked. "I'm fine."

"See, Lees. He's fine. I got an early meeting, so —
"

"So *go to bed*, Matt."

Lisa and Matt locked eyes. Matt said nothing, just stood there in the dimly lit room, his jaw muscle twitching. Raymond remembered his promise to Ada and let the veil slip away.

The cool, yellow flow around Matt's body rippled in halting, uneven waves. Bright red, jagged lines flashed across its surface. And the dark blue ice block in his center seemed to hum, like an angry hornet trapped between the windowpanes.

Something about that hum made Raymond nauseous. A sharp cramp stabbed his left side, and he clenched his teeth to keep from grunting in pain. He was relieved when Matt turned on his heel, without saying anything, then stalked back to his room.

Raymond held his breath, waiting for bedroom door to slam. But it did not. Just a quiet, sad click from down the hall.

Lisa exhaled a sigh — she'd been waiting for that,

too. She turned back to him. "He's a bear when he's woken up."

"Sorry I woke him."

She waved the thought away, "Doesn't matter. How are you feeling now?"

"I'm totally cool."

"You don't have to say that. I have bad dreams all the time, and sometimes ... well, they feel so real."

"Yeah. But it's just dreams, right?"

"Mostly. Sometimes memories. Were you dreaming about your mother?"

"Not mine."

Lisa frowned in confusion. She leaned in closer and whispered, "Then whose?"

Something clenched tight in Raymond's chest. Lisa's dark round eyes, her shiny dark hair ...

"Just a dumb dream." He slid down into his bed and yawned. "I'm pretty tired."

Lisa stared at him for a moment, then sat back. "Okay." She pulled the blanket up over Raymond's shoulder. "Ada will be here early, so ... better get some rest."

"I can't believe it's been a week already."

"Right? Starting to feel like home yet?"

"I'm not sure what home feels like. But it sure is nice here."

Lisa's face was a mix of sad and happy. She leaned down and kissed Raymond's forehead. A yellow daisy bloomed in his mind, then melted, spreading, like warm honey, down to his heart.

But in the back of his mind, the dark place where the bad things hid themselves, a tiny, terrified voice bubbled up, like the cry of a broken-winged bird caught down a well.

Mommy, mommy, mommy...

Chapter Twenty-Eight

"RAYMOND! SHE'S HERE!"

Lisa's voice rang out in the downstairs hall. She sounded more nervous than he was.

Raymond quickly slipped his charcoals into the case, then slid his sketch pad into the desk drawer. He stopped in the bathroom for a mirror check and sighed. His hair was a mess of waves that trailed from the top of his head to just down below his collar. It was shiny but seemed to be growing faster and thicker every day. His shoulders, too, were wider, making his sleeves too short, and even his height had changed. Pants that were fine just a week ago had now crept up to his ankles.

Lisa called it a "growth spurt" and proclaimed it time for new clothes.

"I'm on it!" She'd grinned like he'd given her a present. Raymond liked to see her happy and loved being the reason. Even if it was something he had no control over.

He wet a comb and dragged it through his hair, then yanked down his sleeves, stretching them over his wrists. There wasn't much he could do about the dark circles under his eyes. Raymond hadn't slept much after his nightmare.

It wouldn't matter, anyway. Ada couldn't see, yet she would know. She always did. Still, he was excited to see her.

Ada was standing at the kitchen counter when Raymond walked in. She looked a bit tired but brightened instantly when he said hello. She held out her arms to him and the candle — *Ada's* candle — ignited in his chest. He went to her, and she hugged him, pressing her cheek against his, like she hadn't seen him for months.

He had missed her *so* much. but never knew, until now, that she felt the same.

Lisa, in a cornflower blue summer dress, looked even prettier than usual. She was busy opening and closing cabinets, pulling out dishes and things from the fridge. "I was thinking you might like to sit outside. It's such a beautiful day."

"That sounds very nice," Ada said. "If that's good for you, Ray."

"Oh, you *do* go by Ray," Lisa's smile was as bright as the sun streaming through the kitchen windows, "Great. I didn't want to just assume —"

"*I* call him Ray. He goes by Raymond."

Lisa's expression went dark, like a cloud had passed between them. "Okay." Her smile looked strained. "I'll bring out some breakfast in a little bit."

"I'm a light eater. But tea would be nice." Ada held out a hand.

Raymond tucked it into his bent elbow, just as she'd taught him. As he guided her through the living room and out the sliding doors, images from his nightmare elbowed their way to the front of his mind.

Ada paused at the piano. "Who's the player?"

Raymond hadn't mentioned there was a piano in the room. "Lisa used to. But not anymore."

"Interesting. Don't you think?"

"I guess." He hadn't thought about it. He didn't want to think about the piano at all. Not after his nightmare.

Raymond led Ada down the steps carefully, then toward the outdoor table that Lisa had already set for brunch. When they passed by the pool, Ada froze in place. She lifted her chin upward and sniffed, like a dog reading the wind at a park. She turned toward the pool and smiled.

"Ahhh, yes," she murmured. "A good fit."

A chill rushed up Raymond's spine. He didn't want to think about the pool, either. He gently tugged Ada forward. "We're over here."

He brought Ada to the table and waited for her to sit, before taking the seat beside her.

"Is David a large man, like his brother?"

The question was so odd, Raymond wasn't sure if he'd hear her right. "I'm not sure what you —"

"It's a simple question."

"I guess they look alike. But David's not as neat and tidy."

"And his wife, Jean. Did she seem happy?"

"She was nice."

"That's not what I asked."

"I just met her."

"Lisa and Matt, do they laugh together? I mean, at home. When no one is else around."

"Why do you —"

"Don't be tedious. Do. They. Laugh?"

"Not a lot, I guess. But they're nice."

"Who goes to bed first, Lisa or Matt?"

A spark of anger caught Raymond by surprise. Why was she asking these stupid questions? She hadn't asked once how *he* was doing. "I'm fine, thanks for asking," Raymond snapped.

"Do you think I need to *ask* if you're fine?"

"You *could* ask. Why do you need to know all these … *personal* things about them?"

"You ungrateful brat."

"I just don't understand —"

"No. You don't. And you won't, without me. You'd be wasting away with a burning hole in your belly instead of lounging poolside at this vulgar McMansion. So perhaps you should just say, 'Thank you, Ada,' and answer my goddamned questions!"

Raymond was shocked. *Hurt.* Just minutes ago, she seemed so happy to see him.

They sat in stony silence for what felt like ages. Raymond sneaked glances at Ada from the corner of his eye, not wanting her to feel him looking at her. *He* wasn't going to talk first. Not this time. For the first time since she arrived, he noticed she looked tired.

Smaller, somehow, than when he'd said goodbye to her at Haven. Her shoulders rounded forward slightly, as if it were too much effort to square them. Her face was pale, almost gray, and her lips were chapped and flaky. She kept sucking them in, trying to moisten them, but Ada seemed to have no moisture in her. She wasn't feeling well — he could see that now. And she'd come all this way to see him.

She was right. He *was* an ungrateful brat.

He touched her hand gently. "I'm sorry, Ada. I didn't sleep well last night. I … I'm a bear when I'm woken up." He hoped he sounded as convincing as Lisa did.

"No, you're not. You're never a *bear*. You're just hungry."

"I am?"

"Your belly hurts."

It wasn't a question, but Raymond nodded.

"It was the veiling. I told you. It uses up too much, too fast."

"I understand. I'll … get some rest."

"It's not a matter of rest. You need to follow where the colors lead. Through that channel. Mining, remember? The secrets, the painful reasons *behind* the secrets."

"I know. You told me. Like what I did with Keisha." He ached with guilt at the mention of her name but didn't dare ask if Ada had told her goodbye for him.

"Keisha was a start. But to thrive, to even *survive* in this house, you must go further."

"But I *am* thriving. Lisa says I'm having a growth spurt. She says I need —"

"Lisa doesn't understand the first *thing* about what you *need*. And neither do you. But you must. Goading. It's time you learned how to do it."

"*Goading?*" Raymond didn't want to hear this. He didn't know, exactly, what Ada was about to tell him, but he knew it would be terrible.

"There's only so much you'll find at the surface. People are good at deluding themselves. As you grow, you'll need more. You'll need to be creative. Assertive. Push them. Pull things from them. That is goading."

"Push them where?"

"Past their walls. You draw the secrets up, pulling from their darkest wells, until there is a … cataclysmic burst, a *detonation*. A release of energy for you to absorb. To feed on. To fill you."

"You're saying to survive, I have to hurt people?"

"In a sense, yes."

Carefree clouds billowed across the deep blue, early summer sky, unaware, unconcerned with the ugliness of the world beneath them. It made his heart ache.

A tear slid down Raymond's cheek and he swiped it away. "Ada, if I absorb all that … hurt, then their secrets, their *pain*? It all becomes *my* pain too, right? I carry it, with my own, forever. Don't I?"

Ada turned her face to one side. Raymond watched her mouth working, chewing the bone dryness of her lip as if it were an itch she couldn't scratch. She swallowed, like she was forcing a piece of stale bread down her throat. When she finally answered him, there was a crack in her voice. "You do. And I *am* sorry about that." She cleared her throat. "But things are as they are. Channel, goad, then feed. You must do it. And you must start now." Ada nodded toward the house. "With them."

Disgust, shame, and bitter sadness slithered and twisted in his stomach like a nest of snakes. She couldn't mean it. Lisa and Matt were so good to him. So kind. They had good intentions, good *hearts*.

And yes, a secret. A very painful secret, and Ada had known all along.

A good fit.

"No. It's not fair. There has to be another way. We have to figure it out. All this ... it's not for me."

"It's not *fair*?" Ada's laugh was ugly, mocking and resigned. "It's not *for* you. It *is* you. You're a Tetra. Like the sky is blue. Like water is wet. And that, my boy, is that."

"Tea time!" Lisa crossed the lawn holding a tray, her summer dress billowing in the breeze, "I brought some toast too, just in case you felt like a little something." She winked at Raymond and carefully slid the tray onto the table. Her smile was radiant, and she glowed, a flower in her own garden.

He suddenly understood that this simple gesture, serving tea in the garden in a pretty summer dress, was something she loved. And something she missed very badly. Drinking beer with David and Jean wasn't the same thing. No, this was ... *girlier*.

"That's very kind," Ada said. "Now, tell me about

this pool. Why on earth is it *still* covered up with this beautiful weather?"

Lisa looked toward the pool and the smile fell from her face. "Oh, we just … well Matt and I haven't talked about it."

"But wouldn't it be wonderful, Raymond? Did you ever think you'd get so lucky?"

Ada tilted her face upward, in that way she had, just waiting for him to agree. To *comply*. Her black glasses, reflected the brilliant summer sky, turning the pure white clouds a dismal, somber gray.

It's not for you. It IS you.

"Raymond? Wouldn't the pool be wonderful?" Ada said again with just a tinge of edge to her pleasant tone.

"Yes," Raymond murmured. "Wonderful."

And even the in bright, warm sunlight, in the vibrant green of Lisa's beautiful garden, Raymond had never felt so cold.

Chapter Twenty-Nine

"WHAT DO I WEAR?"

"To a ballgame?" Matt frowned in exaggerated confusion, then sputtered with laughter.

Raymond felt the heat in his face. Would he ever grow out of blushing like an idiot every time he was embarrassed?

"Matt, stop." Lisa cuffed him on the shoulder. "He's probably never been. How's he supposed to know?"

Matt quieted. The surprise on his face melted into pity. "That true, kid? They never took to you guys to see some baseball?"

Raymond wanted to laugh at Matt. But he didn't. The last thing he wanted to do was embarrass him. "Nope."

"Well, that's just plain wrong. Every kid needs to see the Sox up close. And David's seats are about as close as you can get without being on the field."

"We got four field trips a year, once you were old

enough. They pretty much had to be free things. And we always had to wear our church clothes off-grounds. That's why I asked."

"Well." Lisa threw up her hands and smiled. "You can wear whatever you want now. Just grab a pair of the new jeans I got you. And a sweatshirt in case it gets cold."

"*Cold?* Lees really?"

"It's a night game, Matt. Plus, Raymond feels the cold like I do. Right?"

Raymond shrugged. He didn't want to disagree with Lisa, but he didn't want Matt to think he was a wimp.

"Okay, fine. Grab the sweatshirt, and make it quick, bud. David's on his way."

"Why didn't you just meet him at the park?" Lisa asked. "We're out of his way."

Matt shrugged. "I offered, but you know him. Once he's made up his mind … Hey, tick-tock, Raymond!"

Raymond ran to his room, taking the stairs two at a time. He pulled off his shorts, then yanked on the new jeans Lisa had gotten him. The fit was perfect. After putting on a fresh t-shirt and grabbing a sweat-shirt from his closet, he dashed to the bathroom, where he wet a comb and ran it through his hair, careful to smooth down the stubborn, wild clumps on the sides.

The crunch of tires on gravel filtered through the window. He looked out to see David's black truck rolling into the driveway. Soon, he heard the front door open and Matt's voice drifted up the stairs.

"Whoa. Watch that friggin' tank, asshole." Matt laughed. "You're chewing up my gravel."

David jumped out of the driver's seat, then gave Matt the finger. "Sorry, didn't mean to hurt your little rocks." He wore a paint-stained Red Sox shirt. It was sloppy, but just tight enough to show off his muscled shoulders and chiseled biceps. His gray chinos were wrinkled and loose, but in a cool way. Even his beat-up baseball cap, with his hair poking through it in random clumps, looked just right.

"You're early."

"Nice to see you, too. Hoping to snag a beer."

"There's a shocker."

The men disappeared into the house.

Raymond looked in the mirror at his crisp new t-shirt and his damp hair plastered to his scalp like it was made of wax. Kevin's voice invaded his head.

Look at this fucking dork. Look up pussy in the dictionary and there's a picture of GAY-mond.

Raymond snatched a towel off the railing and attacked his hair, rubbing the damp neatness out of it as best he could. He peeled off the fresh t-shirt and put the dirty one back on. He threw his sweatshirt back in the closet on his way down to the kitchen.

Lisa was packing up a bag of snacks while Matt and David sat at the counter drinking beers.

"There he is!" David held up his hand for a high five.

Raymond tapped David's palm before taking a seat at the counter.

David snorted, "That all you got? C'mon, kid."

His palm went up again. Raymond slapped as hard as could.

"Yow!" David grimaced and shook his hand.

Lise laughed, "Serves you right!"

David held up his beer in a toast to Raymond, then swigged it.

Raymond smirked but hid his hands under the counter, rubbing the sting out of his palm.

"So, I hear this is your first ball game, huh?"

"Yup. Played a little, but first real game."

"Oh, man. By the time I was your age, I seen a hundred. Pop used to take us every weekend."

Out of the corner of his eye, Raymond caught Lisa giving David a look and a tiny shake of her head. Was he trying to be mean? Or what?

Raymond let the veil on David drop, just a bit, just enough to… check. What he saw was a field of simple, basic blue, cool-toned and flat. Raymond took it in, quickly, a shallow scan, then shut it down. If there was more to it, he'd worry about it later. David was smiling at him, and it seemed real enough.

"Well, Ray, it's never too late to become a Sox fan. Here, I got something for you." He reached under his seat and pulled out a rumpled plastic bag. He slid it down the counter to Raymond.

"Hey, where's my present?" Matt said.

"Got it for you right here." David made a show of

reaching into his pocket and pulling out his middle finger. He and Matt cracked up.

Raymond grinned — must be nice to have a brother. He opened the bag. "Wow! Sox hat! Awesome!" He pulled out the hat and tugged it down over his messy hair. "Thanks, David!"

"No problem. Can't show up at Fenway without a cap."

Lisa folded her arms and raised her eyebrows at David. "Well, well." Her smile was wide and happy.

David shrugged and said nothing, but he grinned like he'd just scored a run himself.

"All right, sports fans." Matt stood, pulled a ball cap from his back pocket, then tugged the brim low over his eyes. "We're going to miss the first inning if we don't get our asses in gear."

Lisa leaned over the counter and kissed Matt on the cheek, then returned David's fist bump. "Have a good time, boys. And no beer for Raymond, David. I mean it."

David turned around, raised his hands palms-up as he shrugged, grinned, then winked at Lisa before heading out the door behind Matt.

Lisa laughed and shook her head. She stepped around the counter and gave Raymond a hug. "Have fun, sweetie."

Raymond felt her gaze on his back as he walked out with the guys. A warm, sweet thrill ran down his spine. This was what family felt like. *His* family.

The good feeling stayed with him as he hopped in the rear seat of David's truck. Matt snapped on the radio as they pulled out. The chime of a dirty sounding guitar riff rattled the speaker near Raymond's head.

"Yes! Aerosmith, the Bo-Sox, and a night out with the guys." Matt cranked the volume, then smiled back at Raymond. "Doesn't get any better than this."

David and Matt, elbows hanging out their open windows, nodded their heads in time with the music. The warm night breeze blew through the truck like a welcome guest.

A night out with the guys.

Raymond smiled.

Me. Just one of the guys. No, it doesn't get any better than this.

And it wouldn't.

Not long after they arrived at Fenway Park, something changed.

No, *someone* changed.

Armed with beers and hotdogs, they threaded through the chattering throng of people that packed the concourse. Their excitement, their *energy*, seeped into Raymond bones — a pleasant buzz that lit up his whole body. He followed Matt through the short hall that led to their section, with David following behind.

Matt turned around and grinned at him. "Packed house!"

Raymond couldn't stop smiling.

When they finally stepped out into the stands, it hit him. A sledgehammer in the chest. The brilliant white lights of Fenway Park shone, clear and bright as day, on the perfect green grass of the outfield.

The colors and sounds of the crowd, as they rumbled, like one giant happy voice, the glowing windows of the surrounding buildings — they all clashed and blurred in a constantly shifting kaleidoscope of images. Thousands of shades and hues, rippling and flowing, like a Pollock painting come to life.

Raymond stopped short and gaped, stunned, *awestruck* — he couldn't help it. David bumped him, hard, from behind.

"Fuck me! What the hell, Raymond?"

David's beer breath was hot on the back of Raymond's neck.

Raymond turned around, still dazed. David must have walked into him beer-first. His paper cup was half-empty, and the front of his chinos looked like he'd peed himself.

"Whoa. Sorry, David. It's just so … lovely."

"The fuck?" David snarled. "*Lovely?*"

Matt turned around and laughed. "C'mon Dave. He's never seen it before."

"It's fucking *lovely?*"

"He's an artist."

"Right." David snorted. He gave Raymond a sour look but let it go.

A dark feeling crept over Raymond, ugly and familiar, like the stink of a musty blanket. He shook it off, turned back to the thrilling scene around him, then followed Matt down the steps, closer and closer to the field. They squeezed past the long row of knees and took their seats, Matt on one side of him and

David on the other. They were right in the center of the action, just four rows back on the first base line.

Matt elbowed him and grinned. "What'd I tell ya? Great seats, huh?"

"Killer." Raymond instantly felt stupid. He'd never used that word before, and it showed.

"Season tickets. Big bucks. David won them in a poker game. Nearly cost him his marriage." Matt sniggered.

David gave Matt a sour look, then took a sip of what was left of his beer.

They fell quiet as they watched the ads and crowd shots on the jumbo-tron.

Raymond noticed the seat on the other side of David was empty. Desperate to find something to talk to David about, he pointed at it. "That your seat too?"

"That's supposed to be Jean's."

"Oh, is she coming?" Raymond forced a brightness into his voice, hoping it would warm David up.

David repeated in a mocking tone, "Oh, is she coming?" He pointedly avoided eye contact, turning away to stare across the field. "No, Jean's not fucking coming."

A fissure cracked inside Raymond's chest as he stared at David, shocked by the venom in his tone, the anger in his expression. He dropped the veil.

Gray clouds, like he'd seen in Ada's glasses, rushed across David's block of simple blue. They piled together in a threatening storm, and from the center, like a lightening flash, was Jean's face — angry, bitter, snarling, her cheeks hot red and slick with fresh tears.

David's head snapped round, "Take a picture, you little prick. It'll last longer."

"Hey!" Matt's voice was angry. "What the hell, Dave?"

"He's staring at me," David growled. "Gives me the creeps."

And there it was, sudden and clear.

The mean, musty familiarity that seeped from David like a leaky cesspool. David was Kevin. Older, larger, more experienced. But no less bitter, no less devious, no less angry.

And *certainly* no less dangerous.

Chapter Thirty

RAYMOND SLID three plates slowly from the cabinet, grabbed a trio of knives and forks, then walked quickly and quietly to the dining table. He arranged the place settings carefully, making as little noise as possible. The atmosphere in the kitchen was as brittle as frozen glass. The slightest vibration could crack it, and who knew what would spill out?

The sounds and smells floating into the dining room from the kitchen — Lisa frying chicken, Matt washing pans — seemed too loud, too ... *crisp*. There was no conversation to pad them.

A rush of guilt made the sore spot in Raymond's stomach throb. Matt was mad at Lisa, and it was *his* fault.

Ada's, too.

After her talk with Ada, Lisa had pushed Matt to open the pool. When Matt refused, she'd put her foot down and said she'd ask David to do it. That did the trick. Matt took care of it without another word. But they'd barely spoken since.

While Lisa and Matt finished cooking dinner in silence, Raymond took a seat at the table closest to the window. The pool did look beautiful without its green blanket of industrial plastic. He watched the water shimmer blue-gold, catching the last rays of the sun, as it sank below the tree line. Serene and peaceful. It made him sleepy.

A sudden breeze blew a ripple across the surface. Raymond's breath hitched in his chest. In the deep end, an arm's reach from the edge, the water churned, turning in on itself, forming a slow-moving whirlpool alive with iridescent color. Just below the surface, tendrils of dark hair twitched and slithered like baby snakes, freshly born.

It was *her*. The rainbow girl from his dream.

Raymond's heart slammed in his chest. He held his breath, waiting for the crown of her head to break the surface, sopping wet. Her pink face would contort, her little mouth would stretch into a blue-lipped oval, and the watery scream that had died in her chest when she did would finally break free.

Mommy, mommy, mommy!

No, no, no. She's not there. Not there!

Raymond dug his knuckles into his eyes. He rubbed hard, desperate to erase the image from his mind, terrified that when he opened his eyes again, Rainbow Girl would still be there, clawing the edge of the pool, heaving her sopping body, bloated and gray, from the bubbling water.

"No, no, not there," Raymond whimpered.

"What's not there?"

Raymond opened his eyes.

Matt stood across from the table holding a bowl of steaming mashed potatoes, his brows drawn together in irritated concern. "You okay?"

"Yeah, yeah. I just … lost something, and I'm trying to remember where I put it."

Matt sighed and placed the bowl on the table. "Always in the last place you look," he mumbled as he took his seat at the head of the table.

Lisa came in from the kitchen with a plate of chicken and some extra napkins. "Here you go. Probably going to be a messy one."

Matt huffed and rolled his eyes.

Lisa glared at him. "Something funny?"

"Nope." He reached for a piece of chicken.

Lisa sighed and dished out the potatoes. They ate in cold silence, each lost their own troubled thoughts. But Raymond caught Lisa's gaze once or twice, her expression nervous, concerned, apologetic.

Raymond was relieved when Lisa reached across the table to squeeze Matt's hand. "Hey, why don't you take tomorrow off, huh? We can hang out by the pool, all together, order some pizza. Have some fun. What do you think?"

Matt sat back in his seat and rubbed his eyes with his free hand. "What do I think? I think NO. I don't want to get in the damned pool. I don't want Raymond in it, either."

"C'mon, Matt. That's not helping anything."

"It's no big deal," Raymond said, "I don't need the pool. I don't even have any trunks. It's totally fine."

"It's not fine." Lisa's voice trembled. "Matt, you're … why can't you just give it a chance?"

"I don't want to give it a chance!" Matt threw his fork down. It clattered on the plate. He pushed back from the table. "What I *want*, Lisa, is to fill the thing with fucking cement!" He stormed out of the room.

A few moments later, the front door slammed, then Matt's car engine rumbled to life.

Lisa jumped up. "Matt! Wait!"

The squeal of tires vibrated off the windows as Matt tore out of the driveway.

Raymond's belly gurgled with acid and anxiety. He got up and started to clear the table. The sooner it was done, the sooner he could sneak off to his room. He needed to talk to Ada.

He was scraping off the last dinner plate when Lisa came back and took a seat at the counter. Raymond could tell she'd been crying, and it made his heart ache.

"Hey, Ray, you don't have to do that. Oh, sorry, Ray*mond*."

"You can call me Ray."

"You don't mind?"

"I like it." He took a bottle of water from the fridge, then placed it in front of her.

"Thanks." Her smile was full of sorrow. "I'm sorry about all that."

"Oh, it's fine. I'm … I'm fine."

"No, it's not. We're *all* adjusting, trying to be a family here. And it's hard. For *all* of us."

Raymond chewed his lip, unsure if he should say what he was thinking. Lisa must have read his mind.

"What? Go ahead, you can tell me."

"Maybe Matt doesn't … I mean, maybe I'm not the right —"

"No. Stop right there. You are wonderful and we are *so* grateful to have you. We both are, really. It's just … Matt's damned temper!"

Raymond sat down beside her. "Does he get mad a lot?"

"Not … no. Don't get the wrong idea. He's a *good* man. He has his reasons, I guess. He'll cool off and be back soon. It'll be fine, you'll see."

"Okay." He stood. "I'm kind of tired. I'll just head up early. If you're okay."

"I'm fine, really."

"I'm … sorry you're sad, Lisa." He didn't know what else to say.

"You're sweet, Ray." She smiled at him, but he could tell she didn't really want to. "Sleep tight."

Once he reached his room, he closed the door, dug his phone from its hiding place under the mattress, then dialed Ada. As always, she answered immediately.

"You're early. What's going on?"

"They're fighting, Ada. It's awful."

"Fighting about what?"

"The pool. Matt hates it."

"Why is that?"

"I don't know." But he had a good idea, why.

"He wouldn't open it up?"

"No, he did. Lisa made him."

"How did she do that?"

"She said if he wouldn't, she'd get David to help her."

"And what did Matt say to that?"

"I don't know, Ada. What difference does it make? I'm ... a *problem* here."

"So, Matt opened it. Then what?"

Raymond sighed. He didn't want to answer Ada's endless questions. He wanted her to tell him that everything would be all right. "He doesn't want to swim in it. And he doesn't want me in it, either."

"Why not?"

"I don't know, Ada."

"Well, find out," she snapped. "You know how."

"I'm tired now. I don't feel too good. I'll talk to you tomorrow."

Raymond ended the call then powered the phone down. He'd *hung up* on her. She'd be mad at him for that.

He'd apologize tomorrow. When he wasn't so ... *worn out*.

He pulled off his clothes, then climbed into bed without brushing his teeth. The stars twinkling through the skylight above him seemed cold and distant. Like Ada. Like his mother, his father, and Matt.

But not Lisa. Not at all.

Raymond thought of her curled up on the dining

room chair, hugging her knees to her chest. Her sad eyes when she smiled and said goodnight. It was probably the last thing she felt like doing, but she'd done it for *him*.

Lisa deserved to smile for real. She deserved happiness, and love, and all good things.

But in this world, that didn't mean she'd get them. Did it?

Chapter Thirty-One

RAYMOND WOKE to the sound of a rustling bag. Then a giggle.

"Good morning, sleepy head."

Lisa was sitting on the edge of his bed.

"What time is it?"

"It's almost noon. You were conked *out*." She pushed the bag toward him. "I got you something."

Raymond sat up and rubbed the sleep from his eyes. He opened the bag and pulled out two pairs of swimming trunks, a snorkel, a diving mask, and pair of blue plastic flippers.

"I didn't know what color you would like. So, I got a couple."

"They're great. It's all great. But do you think Matt —"

"Don't worry about Matt. We talked it out last night."

"He's okay? With the pool and everything?"

She ruffled his hair. "Don't worry so much."

Raymond picked up the snorkel and turned it every which way. "I've never snorkeled before."

"It's easy, I'll show you. You'll love it. Eat your breakfast so we can go for a swim." Lisa stood. She was wearing a terry robe over a bathing suit. "C'mon, slow poke!" She walked out of the room humming.

Raymond sighed. Lisa seemed happy again — he didn't want to screw that up. But the thought of swimming in that pool made his skin crawl. He stepped into the new trunks, and his heart sank. Of course they fit him perfectly — she was good at shopping.

There was no getting out of it.

Raymond pulled on a t-shirt, grabbed the new snorkeling gear, then went down to breakfast. Matt was at the table, mopping up the last of an egg with a piece of toast.

"Hey, bud. How's it going?" Matt's gaze flicked to Raymond's swimming trunks, then away.

Raymond felt embarrassed, like he was somehow letting Matt down. He mumbled, "Morning."

Matt got up from the table before Raymond could sit. "Heading to work. You have a good day."

"You, too."

Matt stopped at the door, keys jingling, "Raymond. Be careful, huh?"

The fear in Matt's eyes tapped into his own. His stomach fluttered with nerves. "Definitely." He hoped he sounded reassuring.

Raymond watched Matt through the window as he walked quickly past the pool, head down. He let

Matt's colors come through — he barely had enough energy to veil, anyway. Matt's normal, cool yellow had paled, and that mysterious icy center had taken on a greenish tint. Just looking at it made Raymond woozy.

Be careful.

Great idea. But how was he supposed to do *that*?

"You ready?" Lisa stood in the kitchen doorway with an armful of towels.

No, he *wasn't*. But he nodded and followed her out to the pool.

Lisa dropped the towels onto a lounge chair and looked upward, shading her eyes. "What a day!"

A warm breeze played in the treetops. They swayed, gentle and lazy, against a cloudless sky. The sun warmed Raymond's back and cast diamond flashes across the pool's crystal blue surface. The knot in his chest loosened.

It had been a dream — a *terrible* dream — but nothing more.

Lisa tapped the snorkeling gear in Raymond's hands. "You ready to give that a try?"

They sat on the first step, in the shallow end, while Raymond fastened the flippers onto his heels. Lisa adjusted his mask, then showed him how to hold the tube in his mouth and kept it straight above the water.

"Looks easy enough," Raymond said.

"It is. Someday I'll take you to Mexico for *real* snorkeling. That'll blow your mind."

"I'd love that."

"Me, too." Her smile was as warm as the sun on his back. "Okay, give it a try."

Raymond dipped his face into the water and stretched his arms wide, like Lisa had shown him. He pushed off, then doggy-paddled to the middle, careful to keep the tube upright. Beneath him, the blue liner of the pool rippled with his movements, and shafts of sunlight shimmered in the bubbles. He relaxed his body and gave his weight to the water. His head filled with the slow, hollow rush of breath and the distant, rhythmic thud of his flippers. He was floating in another world. One of peace and ease. It was beautiful.

He ventured to the deep end, circled around and around, enjoying the silky touch of the warm water across his skin. Below him, the sun flashed in shifting beams on the pool's floor.

Then something ... strange.

Way down at the bottom, the water curled, forming a swirl. It was tiny at first, but with each rotation, it grew bigger, expanding outward. The swirling took on an oily sheen, as if the drain had spit up some backwash from a clogged pipe. Raymond circled above it, fascinated, hypnotized, as colors appeared, rippling through it like a rainbow, twisting in and around itself. They radiated in the sunbeams, growing brighter, flashing like lightning, as the whirlpool gained speed.

Even as his heartbeat began to race, pounding in his ears, he couldn't look away.

Somewhere inside of him, but far away, a voice, the woman, was screaming.

Get out. Get out, get out, get out!

But Raymond did not. He *could* not. The pull beneath him, that oily swirl of magnificent color, was too strong.

It spun even faster, a blur, ever-expanding, until it was wide as the pool itself. A dark center point emerged, like an eye of a volcano, or an underwater cave, black and infinite. Raymond was drawn to it, something in him reached downward, wanting to swim deep into the vortex.

Raymond's breathing tube flooded, filling his mouth with bleach-y water. He pulled it out — he had no need of it. Not where he was going. He kicked downward, arms reaching out for the dark center that reached for him.

Then it erupted, a jet-black geyser, spraying out and upward, shooting oily ribbons of darkness all around him. And from its core, a shape emerged. Oval, like the top of a white balloon. It took on features, shadows and lines that wriggled together to form a face, staring up at him through the water.

He knew the face. *Of course* he did. He *knew* she was down there … waiting for him.

The cupcake girl smiled up at him through the mess of color and oil, though Raymond knew that was impossible.

She was impossible.

Raymond tasted blood and realized he'd bitten his tongue. There was sound, far above him, high-pitched but blurry. Someone was calling his name.

But down below … that was all that mattered.

The face grew pale, pudgy, shoulders with little

dents in the soft spot at the top. Then round, fleshy arms grew from those shoulders. They stretched upward, reaching for him.

Her mouth opened and closed, like a fish gulping for air. She was speaking, two words, over and over, but Raymond couldn't make them out in the cloud of black ink surrounding her.

Raymond shook his head. *I don't understand.*

Her face crumbled in sadness and frustration. She reached for him, harder than ever, stretching out through each fingertip. Now, she was shouting, though no sound reached Raymond's ears. Her blue lips pouted and stretched in frustration.

Then her words hit him. He *felt*, more than understood, what she wanted.

Come down.

Come down. Come down. Come DOWN.

She was frightened. A little girl, abandoned. So alone. So *lonely*. Raymond knew what that was like

She wanted company.

She wanted *him*. Down there — *drowned* down there — with her, in the watery darkness. *Forever.*

No. He shook his head, firmer this time. NO.

COME DOWN!

NO! NO!

Her sad, hopeful, innocent expression fell and darkened, becoming an angry glower. The blue lips spread into a snarl, stretching wider and wider, as she bared her tiny white teeth.

Cupcake girl began to rise upward in the water, hands like claws, outstretched to snag him, to hook him like prey. Her body jerked grotesquely, side to side, as she tried to kick herself upward. She snapped at the water around her, glaring up at him, gnashing her teeth in fury as she rose.

She kicked and jerked, moving upward, closer, closer. Soon, she would pull him down through that murky black where he would never breathe again.

A scream roiling in Raymond's gut broke through, bursting from his mouth like sewage from a busted pipe. It rattled his ear drums, shook him awake.

Panic shot through his chest and out through his limbs. Above him, the sun rippled, a messy golden orb in a blanket of blue. Raymond reached for it, kicked his flippers as hard as he could, but his legs barely moved. He had nothing. He was weak, feeble, half-drowned already. *Waterlogged.*

She called to him — *screamed* — her little girl voice cutting through the water, mutated, now, into a ragged, furious screech. A spike through his forehead, piercing his ear drums.

Raymond wanted to kick, to fight, to thrash furiously upward for the golden warmth of the sun above his head. But he was sinking. Down, down, down, farther from the shimmering surface where there was light, air, and life.

Soon, Raymond would feel her baby claws. Her tiny, soft fingernails digging into his skin, raking across his heels until she found her grip. And there was nothing he could do about it.

He quit fighting — he was *so* tired. He let go. *Soft-*

ened. Every muscle in his body went limp and loose, like a dead squid, and he sank.

Raymond closed his eyes. He didn't want to see her up close.

Maybe he could fall asleep. Yes, that was possible.

He was half-way there, already.

Chapter Thirty-Two

RAYMOND FELT the splash before he heard it. A slow-motion impact above his head. Then a rush of water that made his ears pop. A rhythmic motion rippled downward, shunting his body side to side, like a seaweed in a changing tide, rousing him from his dark, sleepy haze.

Something warm wrapped around his chest and gripped his shoulder. It bucked, powerful and strong, against his back. He was *rising*. Something was *yanking* him upward.

He peered through the murky water beneath him. She was still down there, floating just above the floor of the pool, as if anchored. Her pale form undulated in the murky shafts of sunlight stabbing the water. Her arms stretched upward, the little fingers frantically bending and stretching in a gesture Raymond had seen a thousand times with the little ones at Haven.

Pick me up! Pick me up! Pick me up!

She was getting smaller and smaller, far below him

now, though Raymond could still see, still feel, her fury. Her mouth opened and closed in that guppy-like movement that Raymond now understood was not a gasping for breath. It was a one word — she never had time to learn much more — and it was her *last* word.

Mommy! Mommy! Mommy!

Raymond's heart ached with hers. His had once broken *like* hers, his tiny arms had reached in that same, horrified desperation.

Hungry ghosts. She and he, the same.

I'm sorry. I'm sorry. I'm sorry. I'm sorry. Raymond prayed she could hear his thoughts. She *deserved* an apology from someone.

At last, her pitiful face, frozen in a mask of anger and grief, blue lips stretched wide in one, final silent scream, sunk down into the black, inky eye from where it came.

The water lightened around him then cleared. Raymond could see through it easily now.

No, he realized, he wasn't seeing through it. He was out of it.

The air was cool on his skin, the sun warm on his face. There was sound, the drip of water, the rustle of the branches overhead. Solid ground, rough and hot beneath his back. And his name, over and over.

Lisa was shouting.

"Raymond! Raymond! Raymond, wake up! Oh, my God! Can you hear me? C'mon, Raymond *Please*!"

She was frantic. Terrified. He took a breath to answer her, to *reassure* her, but an explosion of wet and bile poured from his nose and throat. Her hands gripped his shoulder, dragging him onto his side. Then her soft fists thudded hard against his back, over and over, as she sobbed and prayed.

"Oh, please, dear God, not again. Please, please. Oh, God. Dear God, not again. Please …"

A sharp pain cramped Raymond's chest. He convulsed and snorted out more water. It tasted of blood. He gulped air into his lungs, and his body spasmed again. The sputtering coughs went on and on, until his chest and belly burned. Slowly, they eased, then his breath began to flow.

Lisa quit pounding on his back and squeezed his shoulder so hard it ached. Her voice became a blurred whisper of sobbing and prayers of thanks.

"Oh, thank God. Thank you. Thank you, God. Thank you, Jesus. Thank you." Her trembling hands stroked his face and smoothed the sopping hair back from his eyes. "You're okay, Raymond. You're okay. Can you hear me?"

He managed a nod.

"C'mon, sit up now. Try to take some deep breaths." She pulled him up to sitting.

"I'm sorry," he sputtered.

"You're *sorry*?" Her breathless laugh was half-sob. "*You're* sorry?"

"I said I'd be careful. I promised Matt."

"Are you kidding me?" Lisa pulled him to her in a bear hug.

Raymond turned to his side to spit out the taste of chlorine and blood. "Sorry."

"Stop saying that." She grabbed a towel and

handed it to him. "What happened? Did you get water in the snorkel and just … panic?"

"No … it was *her*."

"What?"

"You didn't see?"

Lisa frowned. Her throat moved in a hard swallow.

"At the bottom of the pool."

She shook her head, sending drops of water from the ends of her hair onto her heaving chest. "There's nothing at the bottom of the pool."

Lisa wrapped her arms around herself, gripping her shoulders tightly. She was shaking hard, but he could see she was trying to stop. Raymond had never seen her so bare. Her collarbones protruded from her thin skin like matching kitchen knives. Her skeleton was designed for more flesh. Without it, she was so frail. *Breakable.*

"Did you hear me, Raymond? There's nothing at the bottom of the pool." She repeated herself, but this time, there was more pleading, a question mark in her statement, that stung.

Sorrow? What good will that do you? It changes nothing.

Ada's voice. So loud, she might have been right there beside them.

"It's like you said. I sucked in water and panicked. Maybe I passed out."

Lisa studied him a moment. "No." She looked toward the pool, then back at him. "Tell me what you meant. What you saw."

"It's like you said."

"No, it isn't," she snapped. "I *want* to know."

"It was just, colors. A whirlpool of shiny colors. It made me dizzy, like, hypnotized —"

"You said *her*."

"No, I didn't."

"You said, *her*, Raymond!"

"You'll think I'm a freak," Raymond croaked. He couldn't look at her.

Lisa took his hand and squeezed hard. "Never. You can always talk to me. We need to learn to trust each other. That's love. That's what family is all about, right?"

"You won't like it."

"Maybe not. I'll just have to deal with it. Who is *her*?"

"The cupcake girl. She tried to pull me down."

Lisa's face darkened. "What?"

"I don't blame her," Raymond stammered. "She's only small. And so ... *lonely*."

"Cupcake girl?

Raymond nodded. He couldn't bring himself to say any more — it would only upset her. Besides, he didn't need to. She'd figure it out.

He watched Lisa's expression change, could practically see her mind working through the cloud of confusion. He knew she'd found it — that she'd remembered the little girl's photo on the piano — when her hand went to her chest like she'd been shot with an arrow.

Her eyes trailed from his face to the glassy surface of the pool, as the terrible meaning of his words became clear. The water was dark blue and shadowed from a blanket of thick clouds that had smothered the sun. There was no breeze. The trees and plants in the yard were still, as if they were listening.

When Lisa finally spoke, her voice trembled, "Sh-sh-she's *still* down there?"

Raymond felt the black wave of horror that crashed over her. When Lisa got up and ran, hand over her mouth to stifle a scream, he didn't follow. He didn't need to see her collapse, crippled by grief and guilt. He knew it would happen. *Had* to happen. There was nothing he could do but wait until she was drained of tears, too exhausted to sob.

Raymond wrapped the towel around him like a blanket and kept his eye on the water. He wondered if she was really down there, waiting for her mama to pull her up. Or maybe he'd channeled Lisa's memory without meaning to, like a replay of a scary movie. Whatever it was, he never wanted to see the little girl, or anything like it, ever again.

The shadows of the trees were long and thin by the time Lisa appeared at the kitchen door, red-eyed and sniffling. She waved him in. "Come inside, now. I'm okay."

She waited for him at the door but couldn't tear her eyes away from the pool behind him. When he approached, she managed a weak smile and pulled him in close for a long hug, but her hands were ice-cold.

Later, after they'd put on dry clothes, they huddled in the den. It was small and cozy, much less fancy than the living room. Raymond preferred it. Despite the warm evening, Lisa built a fire. Then she curled up on the sofa with a glass of wine and a blanket. She looked so small, so tired. It made his heart ache.

"Can I get you anything, Lisa?" Raymond asked, his voice barely above a whisper.

Her smile was weak, but it was a relief. "No, I'm good, thanks. Can I ask you something?"

Raymond's stomach clenched with anxiety, but he nodded.

"How did you know my daughter drowned in the pool? Did Ada tell you?"

"Ada?"

"She wasn't supposed to."

"Ada didn't tell me anything."

"I understand that you want to protect her. But she was wrong to do that. It was part of our agreement."

"I'm not protecting her. Honest."

"Then who told you about Ivy?"

"Is that her name?"

"Was."

"I saw Ivy's photo on the piano. But I didn't know who she was."

"I know Matt didn't tell you what happened. He hasn't so much as spoken her name since … " She shook her head and took a long sip of wine. "David … wouldn't have told you. I know that."

"*Nobody* told me. I had a dream about her. And I don't know what happened today. Or why. It's just how I am."

"What do you mean?"

"I'm … different."

"Are you saying you're *psychic*?"

Raymond couldn't look at her. He felt angry, embarrassed. Why did everything always end up like this? It wasn't fair.

"Look, Ray, I'm not really a believer in, ah, supernatural things. If that's the word for it —"

"Me neither!" A lump cramped Raymond's throat. "I hate it! I hate that I'm like this!" He tried to swallow the lump, but it wouldn't budge. Tears stung his eyes. He took in one deep breath after another, but it didn't matter.

Lisa put down her glass and squeezed his shoulder. "Like what?"

"A freak! A weirdo! Ada didn't tell you because then you wouldn't want me!" Raymond hid his face in his hands. He didn't want Lisa to see him cry.

But she pulled his hands away, then gently gripped his chin with one hand and wiped his tears with the other. "Listen to me. You are not a weirdo. You're a sweet, intelligent, sensitive boy. And anyone would be lucky to have you. Got it? Now take a breath. We're okay."

Raymond took a breath and tried to relax. They sat together, watching the fire in silence for a while, until he felt better. He didn't want to talk about Ada or the girl or anything else. But something Lisa had said was bugging him, and he couldn't let it go. "What was the agreement?"

"Huh?"

"With Ada. You said you made an agreement."

She sighed and picked up her wine again. "The

house was just so empty without Ivy. I — *we* — wanted to adopt a child so badly. I'm not able to have any more. Ivy's delivery was … complicated." Lisa swallowed a gulp of wine. "We applied to a dozen places, but nobody approved us."

"Why not?"

"Because we … I … " Lisa took a breath and started again. "It was determined that there was negligence. That *I* was … at fault."

"For what?"

"For Ivy's death." Lisa began to cry.

Raymond took her hand. "That's not right. It wasn't your fault. I just know it wasn't."

"No, it was," Lisa muttered. "I … wasn't there. And should have been."

"Ada let you have me, anyway? That was the agreement?"

"Yeah. She said it was a good fit."

Lisa's phone buzzed, and they both jumped. She picked it up and peered at the screen. "Matt's going to be home late. Figures." She tossed the phone on the table and sighed. "I'm sorry, Raymond. You deserve better."

"I'm not. I'm *glad* nobody else wanted me. Or you."

Lisa chuckled softly, sadly. "Yeah. Me, too. Thanks, Ada." She wrapped her hand around his. "How about hot fudge sundaes for dinner and the dumbest movie we can find?"

Ada's face floated in Raymond's mind. He'd hung

up on her last night. She'd want an explanation. An apology.

But Lisa was looking at him, hollow and sad, yet trying to brave. Trying to be *worthy* — like he deserved *that*. Mostly, she looked like she needed a friend. Needed him. *Him*.

This time, Ada would just have to wait.

Chapter Thirty-Three

RAYMOND KNEW HE WAS DREAMING. And, for once, it was a good one.

He was a baby again, sitting on the shoulders of a broad-shouldered man. Raymond never saw his face, just the top of his head. His small fingers were sunk deep into the man's thick brown hair, clutching tightly, as they strolled through snow-covered trees. The man chattered away, and though Raymond couldn't understand the words, his deep voice was gentle and pleasing. Suddenly, the man tightened his grip on Raymond's legs and began to trot like a pony. Raymond bounced and giggled, as the man's laughter rang through the woods around them.

Somewhere in the middle of this simple, happy dream, an iron fist gripped Raymond's stomach and squeezed. He bolted upright. "Gah!"

"Raymond?"

Raymond looked around, confused by his surroundings. A fire was burning. Above it, images flickered on a television screen. He was in the den, stretched out on a chaise lounge, with Lisa curled up on the sofa beside him. He had no idea how long he'd been sleeping.

She leaned over the arm rest and brushed his hair out of his eyes. "Are you okay?"

"Yeah. Just a stomach cramp."

"Guess ice cream for dinner wasn't such a great idea, huh?"

"I have a weird stomach. It just … hurts sometimes."

"Anxiety, maybe? What happened in the pool must have been scary for you. I'm sorry I ran off and left you alone."

"That's okay."

"No, it isn't. That's not how a mom is supposed to behave."

A mom?

A tiny candle, just like Ada's, sparked in Raymond's chest. "It *really* is okay. Some moms run away and *never* come back."

"That must hurt. Do you remember her?"

"Not really. I dream of a woman sometimes that I think might be her. But I'm not sure."

"What about your dad? Do you know anything about him?"

Raymond shrugged. "They're not allowed to tell us."

"Nothing? Not even their names?"

"I think his name was Ray, too. It was on a note pinned to my sweater. She left me in the hall at Haven and ran away. But I guess she wanted to leave me a name, at least. That's all I know."

"That's not fair."

"Father Galen says life isn't fair. That today it's not fair to you, and tomorrow it won't be fair to someone else."

Lisa's face darkened. "Easy for *him* to say. We all have a right to know where we come from, at the very least. Wouldn't you like to know, at least a little bit, about who you are?"

Before he could answer, another cramp ripped through Raymond's abdomen. He sucked in his breath and waited for it to pass.

"Wow. Are you sure you're not sick?" Lisa felt his forehead. "No fever. Can I get you something?" She frowned as she studied his face. Her eyes really were huge. And they were filled with warmth and concern. For *him*.

"You're a really good mom, Lisa."

"What?" she asked, softly. Then a smile spread slowly across her face. It was so beautiful — joyful, sad, *grateful* — Raymond wished he could freeze her, right there, and paint her portrait. "I love you, Ray."

The heat rose in his cheeks. His whole *face* burned. He couldn't look her in the eye, but there was no way to hide his smile. He mumbled, "I love you too."

"How would you feel about calling us Mom and Dad?"

"Weird." Raymond grinned. "But really cool."

Lisa laughed. "Cool."

"Hey, bud. You up?" Matt stood in the doorway holding a beer and a glass of wine.

"Ray woke up with a stomachache."

Raymond shook his hair out of his eyes and sat up taller. "It's not bad. Just a little cramp."

"You were out cold when I got home. Wild day?"

Lisa made eye contact with him but looked away quickly. She pointed to the wine glass in Matt's hand. "That for me?"

"Yup." Matt handed Lisa the glass. He frowned, shifting his eyes between her and Raymond. "You sure you're feeling okay, Ray? Your face is kind of red."

"Yeah, I'm good. I'm going to head up to bed." Raymond gave Lisa a hug and stood up.

Matt put his hand on Raymond's shoulder. "We'll hang out tomorrow, yeah? Want to help me with a little work around the house?"

"Sure."

"Deal." Matt leaned in for an awkward half-hug, then ruffled his hair. "Night."

Raymond looked at Lisa. Her happy smile made him feel brave. "Night, Dad."

Matt's eyelids fluttered shut.

Just before Raymond turned to go, he caught Matt's colors. His usual field of cool yellow had become a golden glow. Bright blue sparks, like little shooting stars, shot across it. Surprise. *Pride.*

Raymond flushed with happiness. They cared for him. They *really* did.

But in Matt's golden center, an icy silver spike broke the surface, like a fish flicking its tail. A sharp, cold flash of pure grief. There and then gone. As if Matt had flicked off a light switch and shut the door to a room he never wanted to enter again. As if he could keep whatever was in there locked away, hidden from sight, and forget it had ever existed.

But Raymond could have told him pain didn't work that way.

Whatever was in that room wasn't going anywhere. It *lived*. It breathed. It waited, lonely and restless, for Matt to visit.

Sooner or later, it would get tired of waiting. It would push through the door, snap on the lights.

And it would come looking for him.

Chapter Thirty-Four

"SON OF A BITCH! C'mon, you piece of junk!" Matt whacked the side the of pool pump, then threw his wrench down on the patio. After pulling a rag from his pocket, he wiped the sweat from the back of his neck. "I tell ya, Ray, if it were up to me, this would be a basketball court."

"That would be cool," Raymond said, and stooped to pick up the wrench.

"Yeah? Would you mention that to my wife?" Matt laughed. "And where the hell is David? He's the mechanic." Matt turned toward the house and cupped his hands around his mouth. "Hey, smartass!" he yelled. "You going to help me or what?"

David's face appeared in the kitchen window. He put on a big goofy grin and waved.

Matt laughed again. "Asshole."

A moment later, David came around corner of the house, shirtless, his chiseled chest and shoulders glistening with tanning lotion. He sauntered past the pool toward them, taking his time. "S'up, ladies?"

"Pump's acting up. Or the filter. I don't know. Can't get it open. Will you take a look?"

"It's hot as hell out here. I thought we were invited for a pool party. Not a pool-fixing party."

"Not my idea of fun, either, brother. It's been working fine. Can't figure it out."

David squinted at the trickle of gray water dribbling through the filter hose. He sighed and shook his head, "Dry your tears. The master is here."

"Give him that thing, will you, Ray? Before I knock him over the head with it."

Raymond handed the wrench to David.

"How 'bout you grab us a couple beers, Ray?" David said.

"No problem."

Ray jogged up the path to the house feeling light-hearted and happy.

Grab us a couple of beers.

Nobody had ever said that, or anything like it, to him before. It was just so … *normal.* Like he was a regular kid with a regular Dad.

Lisa and Jean, already dressed for the pool, were in the kitchen making sandwiches when he ran through the door. Lisa took one look at him and rolled her eyes. "Don't tell me. David sent you to fetch, right?"

Raymond laughed. "Yup."

She took two bottles of beer from the fridge, then handed them to him. "Pool time in ten minutes. Tell Matt, okay?"

"And tell *David*," Jean snapped, "that if he wants someone to fetch, he can get himself a dog."

"Woof!" Raymond said.

Lisa and Jean's laughter rang through the kitchen as he headed out the door for the path.

Just as he reached the corner of the house, Raymond heard his name and froze. David was talking. About *him*.

"For *Raymond*?"

Eavesdropping was a sin, according to the sisters. At the very least, it was sneaky and rude. But something about David's tone, the way he spat out Raymond's name like a mouthful of sour milk, put a nervous twitch in his gut.

Raymond pressed himself flat against the side of the house, careful not to clink the beer bottles together, and listened.

"Yup. I told her if I had my way, I'd fill in the damn pool and cement over it. But she wants to play happy family, so …" Matt's voice trailed off.

The conversation stopped and, for a minute or so, there was nothing but the metallic clink of tools and the occasional curse word as the men worked. Raymond was about to step back onto the path when David spoke again.

"About Raymond. Hate to say it, but me and Jean were worried you two were rushing into this too soon."

"We had to do *something*, man. Lisa was just … broken."

"Uh-huh. What about you?"

"What do you think? It's fucking …" Matt lowered his voice, "I never stop seeing her on that gurney. Completely still. The life and color just drained out. Her face, her hands, bloated and *gray* …"

"I know, man. It's fucking rough. For both of you. But keep an eye on that *kid*, Matt."

"What you mean?"

"Something's *off* with him."

"Oh c'mon. We all know how much you *love* kids, dude."

"Yeah, yeah. This ain't that. Have you noticed how cozy him and Lisa have gotten?"

"So? Isn't that the point of adopting a kid?"

"Bit fast, wouldn't you say? And all this 'Mom and Dad' shit?"

"It's a little awkward. But what do you expect? His own mom and dad dumped him. Poor kid's bound to have issues."

"It's more than *issues*. I'm telling you. He gives me the fucking creeps."

Raymond's heart slammed in his chest.

"What the hell are you talking about?"

"You ever notice the way he looks at you?"

"Again, what are you talking about?"

"That intense fucking *staring* thing. Like he's trying get inside of you. Like he's digging around for —"

No, no, *no*. He's going to ruin *everything*!

Raymond jumped onto the path and jogged around corner toward the pool house. "Who's thirsty?" he yelled. It was too bright, too eager, but they didn't seem to notice.

"Me," Matt said. He took a beer from Raymond and mussed up his hair. "Thanks."

Matt grinned at him, and the knot in Raymond's stomach loosened a bit.

He turned to David and held out the second beer. He took it, silently. Fixing Raymond with a hard stare, he cracked it open, tossed the cap into a shrub, then drained it. He held the empty bottle out to Raymond. "Encore." He jutted his chin toward the house.

In that second, Raymond saw the kind of man Kevin would become. *And* the kind of kid David was. Bullies. Both of them. Ugly, ignorant, and angry. Violent toward anything they couldn't understand. Couldn't *control*. It was all there in David's cold, shark-eyes. And you didn't have to be a Tetra to see it.

Raymond seethed inside, but he forced a smile on his face. "Jean says if you want to play fetch, you should get a dog."

Matt cracked up laughing. "Good for you, Ray."

David's nostrils flared, and his face flushed with anger. He nodded slowly at Raymond, saying nothing. But Raymond heard him loud and clear. *Game on, fucker.*

David turned his attention to the filter, working in silence, while Matt and Ray watched over his shoulder. With a deep grunt, he leaned his full weight into the heavy wrench. The pump belched, then gurgled.

"C'mon you son of a bitch!" David gave the pipe a hard whack and was rewarded with the sound of rushing water blasting through the pump.

"Hey!" Matt threw up his hands. "You are good for something, after all."

"Fuck you very much," David said. "Let's eat."

Lisa and Jean were waiting for them by the pool. David spun the wrench around his finger like a gun slinger, blew imaginary smoke off the end, then flipped it into his pocket. "Summer is saved."

Jean rolled her eyes, but Lisa laughed. "Awesome! It's all ready. Let's sit."

Raymond took a seat at the table, which was set with trays of sandwiches and salads. Just looking at them made him want to vomit.

"Finally." Jean settled into her chair. "I'm starving."

"Of course, you are." David muttered.

She gave him a sharp look, then turned to Lisa. "He thinks I'm fat."

"Oh, stop!" Lisa laughed, but Raymond felt her uneasiness.

David snagged a beer from the cooler. He tugged the wrench from his pocket, set it on the table, then dropped into his chair. "Pool's looking good. Nice to see it open again."

Matt gave David a look. He shrugged and cracked his beer.

"Get that greasy tool off the table, will ya, David? We're trying to eat here."

David ignored Jean, took another swig of beer, then sneered. "How about you, Ray? Enjoying your pool?"

"It's really nice." Raymond murmured.

"Right?" David waved his arm wide. "It's *all* really nice. You sure landed on your feet. I wouldn't mind being an orphan myself." His eyes flashed with menace and amusement. He was really enjoying this.

Raymond's hands curled into fists under the table.

Lisa passed a tray of sandwiches to David "C'mon, everyone. Tuck in." She filled their glasses with water, chatting non-stop about the food, the weather, the plants in the garden. Filling up every quiet space on purpose.

Space is dangerous, Raymond thought.

You're dangerous.

The woman's voice. He'd almost forgotten about her, it had been so long.

But she was right. When he looked at David's sneering smile, he *felt* dangerous.

He watched David, caught up in his conversation with Lisa, making her laugh. He was good at that when he wanted to be. Lisa didn't know — she was too nice. Too *generous*. She couldn't see him for real.

But Raymond could. He studied David's field of murky brown. Once again, the image of a tree clinging to an eroding shoreline, gnarled roots, mud-clumped and twisted, half-exposed, half-buried in the earth.

Raymond dove in further. He *channeled*, the way Ada taught him. He *dug around*, as David would say, reaching into David's brown muck until he brought something up.

A secret.

Raymond sensed there was more, deeper and darker, but this one would do.

Game on, asshole.

"Been to see the Sox this week, David?" Raymond chirped. "Your seats are really awesome."

"No kidding," Matt said around a mouthful of sandwich.

"Nope, not this week." David reached for another beer. "You're not eating, Ray? Trying to lose a few pounds?"

They all laughed, but only David sounded mean.

"Why not?" Raymond pressed.

"Why not what?"

"Why aren't you going to the game this week?"

"Yeah, man," Matt said. "And why aren't you taking *me*? It's the Yankees."

"I know it's the Yankees."

"You're going to miss a Yankees game?" Raymond raised his eyebrows in exaggerated shock. It made Matt laugh again.

"What do you know about it?" David snapped.

"The kid learns fast." Matt frowned. "You're sitting out a Yankees game? Who are you and what have you done with my real brother?"

"Yeah, David," Jean said. "I wouldn't mind going."

"Oh, *now* you want to go." He glared at his wife.

"Fine. Forget it."

Matt was still staring at David, confused, concerned. "Seriously, what's up?"

David held his sandwich halfway to his mouth

and stared down at his plate like he was trying to bore a hole through it with his mind. The muscles in his jaw twitched. His gaze flicked to Raymond. His eyes were filled with hatred. And something else. Panic.

Deeply satisfying panic.

A track of prickly heat crawled up Raymond's spine and spread to his forehead. His entire brain seemed to pulse and hum with energy. It was exciting … thrilling.

It was *power*.

Ada's words came back to him, and he finally understood what they meant.

He looked at David and couldn't help but smile. Then, with hardly any effort at all, like flicking a ladybug from the page of a book, he *pushed*.

David eyes squeezed shut in a grimace, like he'd just swallowed an icy drink too fast. He opened them slowly, dropped his half-eaten sandwich onto his plate, then turned toward his wife.

"I lost the seats to my bookie. And nighty-eight grand."

Everything, *everyone*, froze. Even Raymond, shocked at how easy it had been, like he'd done it a thousand times, held his breath.

Finally, Jean spoke. "If this is a joke, David, it's not —"

"It's not a joke. I screwed up."

Jean's mouth dropped open and stayed there.

"David," Matt said, "tell me you didn't."

"I had a lock on this game, Mattie. I mean, a

fucking *lock*. Nobody could have guessed they would
—"

"Shut up!" Jean screamed, "SHUT UP! You
pathetic … You … you ruined us!" She covered her
face with both hands and broke down in harsh, angry
sobs that shook her whole body.

"C'mon Jeannie. We'll figure it out," David
pleaded. "We can re-mortgage the house."

"We've already re-mortgaged the house! TWICE,
you fucking idiot!"

"We'll figure it out!" David screamed.

"YOU'LL figure it out, asshole! I'm done! I'm
more than done!"

"Yeah? Good. Fuck off, then!"

Jean snatched the wrench from the table and
threw it at David's head. He ducked, but it caught his
right temple, then clattered down onto David's plate.

"FUCK!" David hands flew to his head.

Lisa jumped up. "Raymond, let's go. NOW."

Raymond stood, and David glared at him with
boiling hatred. Lisa wrapped a protective arm
around his shoulders and pulled him away from the
table.

As they walked quickly toward the house,
Raymond looked back to see David still glowering at
him. A thin trail of blood trickled down the side of his
head, and his eyes flashed with shock and fury.

Lisa took him through the kitchen and into the
den. Her hands shook as she shut the door behind
them. "Let's just sit and … and just … calm down."

Raymond's heart was racing too, and his stomach

burned like he'd swallowed a bottle of acid. "He's going to blame me."

Lisa looked at him, her eyes glossy with unshed tears. He could see that she was struggling to calm her breath, but her expression was defiant. "Let him try."

It was awful to see Lisa so upset. He knew it was his fault, but he wasn't sorry he did it. Not one bit. In fact, it felt good to fight back, for once.

But as they caught their breath, the adrenaline drained from Raymond's body, leaving him weak and empty. His nausea returned, as bad as it ever was at Haven. Maybe worse.

"Are you okay, Raymond?"

"I don't know," he whispered.

The kitchen door banged open, and they both jumped. Lisa held a finger to her lips, her gaze darting around the room, as they listened. It was Jean, sobbing. It sounded like she was gathering her things.

Soon, the front door opened, then slammed shut. It was followed by the rumble of the truck in the driveway and the screech of tires, telling them Jean was gone.

Lisa exhaled. "Oh, my God." She flopped back against the couch. "Looks like we have a house guest."

Raymond went cold. He pictured David's bloody face, the hate radiating off him like fumes from a burning tire.

He whispered a prayer to his favorite angel, hoping she'd hear him all the way from the Haven.

Please, Jophiel. Let the lock on my bedroom door be a strong one.

Chapter Thirty-Five

RAYMOND SLID the phone from underneath his pillow and tapped Ada's number. For the fourth time that night, the call rang and rang, but she didn't pick up. The fear that he'd lost her for good ate at him. He'd disrespected her. He'd broken his promise to call her every day. He'd hung up on her! He wasn't going to win her back with something as simple as an apology. Not Ada.

His stomach twisted in knots, writhing inside of him like a wounded animal. The worst cramps were so vicious, he had to stuff his face in his pillow to keep from crying. But Lisa would come running if she heard him, and he'd caused her enough trouble today.

And what if David, sleeping in the guest room *right next door*, heard him first?

Raymond focused on his breathing, just as Ada had taught him. He wondered if she could feel him, somehow. If she knew he was suffering but didn't care anymore.

No. Don't think about that. Don't think at all. Just breathe. Slow, slower, in and out.

Eventually, he drifted off for a while.

He woke to the sound of whispering. It was still dark. He couldn't have been asleep for long. It was coming from the room next door. David's room. Even through the wall, Raymond recognized that one of those muffled voices belonged to Lisa.

"Shh. You'll wake him."

"Three shots and four beers? I don't think so?"

"You had nearly *twice* that."

"Yeah. But *he's* a lightweight. Always was."

"Whatever. I'm heading to bed."

"We need to talk about this."

"No, we don't."

"C'mon Lees. You're not happy. *He's* not happy."

"We're working on it."

"How? By taking in some freak kid? His own mother didn't want him!"

"That's very cruel, David."

"You're right. I'm sorry. I'm just upset. In fact, I'm at my wit's end here."

"I know it's difficult."

"I love you, Lisa. I want to be with you. I *have* to. And I think you want me, too. So, let's do it. Let's just *go*. Get the hell out of here, you and me."

Raymond sat up, blinking into the darkness. He was shocked — *horrified* — by what he was hearing. She was going to leave him. *He* was going to take her away!

"David, that's impossible —"

"Why?"

"What happened was a mistake —"

"Don't say that. Please, don't say that —"

"A horrible mistake! Haven't I paid enough for it? Hasn't Matt? Just … let it go!"

"I can't. I just can't."

There was a rustling sound and muffled words that Raymond couldn't make out. Someone was sobbing. It didn't sound like Lisa — he'd heard her cry before.

"Shh. C'mon, now. Don't …" Lisa murmured.

Raymond imagined Lisa's arms wrapped around David, soothing and comforting, as he sobbed against her. Raymond looked down at his hands gripping the end of his blanket. He realized he was shaking. Not in fear, though he was afraid, and not because of the pain, though he was in agony. It was anger. *Rage.*

"We have to tell him."

"No. Absolutely not. Never. We agreed."

"I don't care what we agreed!" David's voice was louder now. And more desperate.

"Shh! Jesus, David."

That horrible, lying bully, was trying to destroy the only family Raymond had ever known. Tear her away — the first person who ever really *saw* him. Ever really *loved* him.

A cold dread, like Raymond had never known before, raced through his veins like ice water.

"We'll tell him together, Lisa. You and me."

"No! *Please*, David." Lisa begged, her voice bristled with panic. "I love him. I can't lose him. Not him, *too.*"

"What about losing ME?" David's voice through the wall grew louder. And more frantic.

Lisa said something, but it was too low, too muffled for Raymond to make out.

A moment later, David's door creaked open, and he heard the shuffle of footsteps on the carpet.

They were going downstairs!

Let's just go. Get the hell out of here, you and me.

Was she leaving? She promised she would never do that.

But the world was full of broken things, wasn't it?

Raymond's heart pounded in full blown panic. Dizzy with grief and confusion, he slipped out of bed. His legs shook as he quietly unlocked his bedroom door, and slowly cracked it open. The hallway was dark and empty. Raymond crept halfway down the stairs, then dropped to a crouch. Peering under the banister, he had a clear view through the open doors to the kitchen.

David was at the center island, gripping a kitchen stool with one hand. Lisa had her back to Raymond in the center of the room, as if she were blocking David's path back up the stairs.

They were still here. For now.

"I'm his brother." David swayed when talked. "He'd *want* me to be happy. He'll *understand*."

Without the door to muffle David's voice, Raymond could hear, now, that he was slurring badly. He was drunk.

"He'll *understand*?" Lisa laughed — an awful, bitter sound. "Are you insane? Matt will *hate* you,

David. You'd be out in the street *tonight*. DEAD to him."

"I don't care!" David yelled.

"Shh!" Lisa flapped her hands at David and looked over her shoulder, in Raymond's direction. He ducked low under the banister. "*Please.*"

A door in the hall above him creaked open.

"Lees?" Matt's groggy voice echoed in the hall upstairs. "Hey? Lisa?"

An idea, a *realization*, clicked in Raymond's mind, like a lifeline thrown to a drowning man. Raymond suddenly understood what had to happen.

David was right. Matt needed to know the truth. And Lisa was right, too. Matt would send David away if he knew what his brother was trying to do. He'd forgive Lisa. He *loved* her, that was obvious. It was a stupid mistake, she *said* so. But David was trying to steal Lisa. To take her away from him forever.

Once Matt found *that* out, David would be gone for good. Raymond was sure of it.

Then everything would be just fine. Just like it was.

"Down here, Matt," Raymond whispered.

"Ray?" Matt appeared at the top of the staircase, then squinted down at him. "What are you doing there?"

"Lisa's in the kitchen. With David. He sounds upset."

Matt sighed and rubbed the stubble on his face. "What the fuck is his problem *now* ..." he grumbled as he stomped down the stairs.

Raymond squeezed to one side to let Matt pass,

then trailed behind him, slowly, hovering in the shadows of the hallway.

Matt crossed the hall. "Hey. What the hell's going on?"

Lisa turned around, then stepped toward Matt. "What are you doing up?" Her nervous smile flickered on and off, but her eyes widened with fear.

"I heard something. Ray told me you were fighting."

Her gaze slipped past Matt and found Raymond in the dark hall. "Ray?"

"That fucking kid," David slurred. "I fucking told you —"

"Give it a rest, Dave!" Matt snapped.

"Fuck you. You know I'm right —"

Matt pushed past Lisa toward David. "I'm sick of your shit!"

"Matt!" Lisa grabbed Matt's arm. "We're just talking. Go back to bed. I'll be right up."

"We're fucking talking, Mattie." David's blurry, belligerent voice rang through the kitchen.

"About what? What the fuck is going on, Lisa?"

"Yeah, what the fuck's going on, Lisa?" David sneered. "Why don't you tell him?"

Matt turned around and glared at her. "Tell me *what*?"

Lisa wrapped her arms around herself, frozen, mute. Like a frightened deer cornered by wolves. It filled Raymond with rage.

It was *time*.

He took in air, drawing it deep into his chest, then

released it slowly. Ada's voice filled his mind, the rhythmic cadence of her breath. *Inhale. Exhale.*

Raymond turned inward, feeling his inner body expand in all directions. Then, like drawing heavy curtains across a wall of windows, one by one, he closed off the searing pain in his belly, his anxiety, his fear, his anger. Until he barely felt himself at all.

And there was only Lisa.

He reached out, his focus a pinpoint laser, aimed deep into her center.

She turned away from her husband and stared at Raymond, confused, fearful. Her color field dripped with bubbling streaks of piss-yellow. The icy block in her center flashed and crackled with energy, like she'd swallowed a hurricane.

Raymond dove in.

He channeled deep down, swimming through ice and lights that flashed around him like knife blades. Until he was there, dead center in the tar-pitch darkness of Lisa's shame. Her agony. Her deepest, most *terrible* secret.

Lisa eyes went wild with horror. She *felt* him there. He knew because, in that moment, he knew *everything* about her. He felt her terror like it was his own.

Raymond wished he could explain that he was there to help. To *rescue* her. That she didn't need to be afraid. Not of *him*. That no secrets meant no pain. And he was about to take it all away.

Later. He would tell her all that later, and she would understand. She'd forgive him, like Matt would forgive her. That's what love meant.

He gathered her secret, spun it, like a fire devil on a stark plain, stoking it until it burned white hot. Lisa's gaze locked on his. She shook her head just once. A weak, hopeless gesture that saddened him. But Raymond *had* to do it.

He pushed her.

In an instant, her terror evaporated. She blinked as her eyes filled with tears, though she did not cry. Then, with an expression of cool clarity, Lisa turned toward Matt. Tears now streamed down her cheeks, but she didn't seem to notice.

She spoke calmly and quickly, like she was delivering bad news to a sick patient.

"I killed Ivy."

"What?"

"She's dead because of me."

"Lisa, no. We've been through this —"

"She woke from her nap. I'd left the sliding doors wide open. She wandered out. Then fell into the pool. She *must* have called for me. But I didn't hear her. I couldn't. Because I was upstairs. In our bed. With your brother."

Matt's mouth dropped open. His eyes, wide with shock, shifted left to right. He stayed that way, wide-eyed, shocked, a man leaning out over a cliff, in the first breathless moment of his fall, searching for something to grab.

If David had just kept his mouth shut, just for a few breaths, things may have been different.

But David *never* knew when to shut the fuck up.

"I love her, Mattie," David slurred. "And that's fucking *that*."

Matt snapped. "MOTHERFUCKER!" He charged at his brother, spitting and grunting like a frenzied bull. He slammed his shoulder into David's chest, sending him sprawling over the kitchen island. They crashed into the counter, still stacked with the afternoon's dirty dishes, and slammed David's head into a glass cabinet door. He fell to the floor in a shower of glass shards, busted plates, and cutlery.

Lisa screamed.

Matt dove on top of him. He clawed up a fistful of David's t-shirt, lifted him half off the floor, then pounded his fist into David's face, over and over.

Lisa jumped on Matt's back, flailing at his shoulders, trying to drag him off. He swept his arm backward, trying to push her off. It was just enough time for David to snatch a shard of broken plate. He slashed at Matt's face, ripping a jagged gash down his cheek and across his neck. Blood sprayed across David's chest, his mouth, his eyes.

Matt roared, as his hands flew to his face.

Lisa clutched at his shoulders, trying to yank him backward. "GET OUT, DAVID!"

David scrambled to his feet, then yanked open the kitchen door.

Matt jabbed an elbow back at Lisa, trying to shake her off. He caught her on the nose.

She shrieked in pain and fell backward, onto the floor.

"Lisa!" Raymond screamed. He tore across the kitchen to help her up, get her away from them!

But David saw him coming. Before crossing the threshold, he turned, lunged toward him, and swung, throwing his full weight into his hard, meaty fist. It slammed into the center of Raymond's forehead.

Just before his legs buckled, an image of a snowball, *Kevin's* snowball, flashed in his mind.

Stay awake this time.

It was her. The woman. The *she* voice.

Raymond crumpled into a heap on the floor. But he didn't pass out. Not this time. Fuck you, David.

He spied a kitchen knife in his reach. If his brain was still operating at full capacity, he could have grabbed it, or at least kicked it out of the way. But he was too dopey, too slow.

Matt's mind was working just fine. Maybe even faster than normal. He snatched up the blade then threw himself at his brother. They toppled through the open kitchen door, spilling into the yard.

"STOP!" Lisa screamed. She jumped to her feet, then ran outside. "MATT, STOP!"

Raymond pushed himself up to a sitting position. His brain sloshed against his skull. He threw up before he could stop himself. When Lisa screamed again, that got him going. He groped for anything to help him, found the seat of the kitchen stool, then hauled himself up. Dizzy and still nauseated, he wobbled through the open door and followed them into the back yard.

Lisa, Matt, and David had reached the pool deck.

Raymond tried to run toward them, but his legs gave way again, leaving him sitting upright on the grass. "Lisa!"

She was there, in between David and Matt, as they punched and tore at each other. A tangle of humans, fists flying, turning in circles, caught up in a drunken, three-person dance of violence and hatred.

Raymond could only stare, terrified, at the horrid scene before him. Woozy and sick from the blow David had given him, he was helpless. *Useless.*

Under the glowing lanterns, the blood pouring from the gash on Matt's face looked like black ink.

The pool water shimmered, pale blue and serene, illuminated from the bottom. Though there was no breeze, a ripple ran across the surface, from one end to the other. Raymond shivered, watching in cold horror, as the water slowly began to churn. A shimmering swirl of iridescent color bloomed in its center.

"LISA!" Raymond screamed, again. "GET AWAY!"

Matt lunged at David, but Lisa slammed her hands against his chest, desperately trying to keep them apart.

"I'LL FUCKING KILL YOU!" Matt screamed.

"YOU DON'T HAVE THE GUTS, PUSSY!" David's speech was thick and garbled, "NO WONDER SHE'D RATHER FUCK ME!"

"NO!" Lisa sobbed.

Matt cocked his arm back. The knife flashed in his hand. He threw his weight into it, slashing downward, losing his balance.

David jerked back, pushing Lisa forward at the same time.

Raymond screamed.

This time, Lisa heard him. She looked in his direction, her eyebrows lifted in surprise. Blood dripped down the knife handle protruding from her throat. She reached up, touching the handle lightly with the fingertips of one hand. Then, *impossibly*, Lisa smiled at him. She waggled her bloody fingertips in a soft wave. Her mouth moved.

I'm sorry, Raymond.

She fell backward, over the edge of the pool, into its shimmering, rainbow iridescence. The water churned and swirled around her. *Receiving* her. Raymond watched in mute horror as two pudgy, pale gray arms broke the surface, wrapped around Lisa's bloody neck, then pulled her under.

Raymond dissolved. He tipped backward, like Lisa, and slammed into the ground. A scream rattled in his chest but wouldn't come out. He couldn't breathe, couldn't move. Could only listen to the wind rustling in the trees. To his heart pounding like thunder in his ears. To Matt's horrific screaming, *wailing* his wife's name, over and over and over.

Pain, pain, pain. So much agony. A waterfall, gushing and flowing all around him.

Raymond knew he was in shock. He'd read about it. His body was ice cold, but his mind was calm. He knew that later, grief would come for him, with sharp teeth and razor claws, foaming at the mouth like a rabid tiger.

But right now, his belly hurt.

He was hungry. *Starving*.

Raymond settled deep into the damp grass of Lisa's perfect garden and gazed up at the stars winking in the infinity of the velvet summer sky.

He fed.

Chapter Thirty-Six

SOMEONE DRAPED A BLANKET OVER HIM. That was nice. But he didn't need it. Raymond didn't need anything. He was floating in a tranquil mist, warm honey sliding through his veins, loose-limbed, pain-free ... *full*.

Thoughts glinted in his mind like sunspots on a still lake. For some reason, he thought of Keisha's beautiful mama and her bent spoon full of brown liquid. Suddenly, he understood how *it* was able to pull her away from everything. Her little girl. Even life itself.

Electric blue pulsed in the trees like the beating of an anemic heart. There were only a few police cars left now. The first to arrive had taken Matt and David away. The torrent of shouting and scrabbling, David's raging profanity, Matt's broken wailing, was a faraway blur. Thunderclouds rumbling over distant mountains.

An ambulance came for Lisa's body. *Just* her body, though. *Lisa* was in the pool with Ivy. Raymond could hear them, splashing and giggling, though he couldn't see them anymore. Soon, he wouldn't hear them, either. True death was slow.

Someone was speaking. Someone close.

Raymond forced his eyes open. He didn't want to — he was happy where he was. A policeman, no police*woman*, knelt beside him. "What?"

"I'm Officer Allen."

"Okay." His mouth felt mushy.

"What's your name, honey?"

"I don't really know. I'm an orphan." Raymond giggled.

He knew what she'd meant. Why did he say that?

Officer Allen laid her hand on his shoulder.

They probably taught them to do that.

"Is there someone we can call?" she asked.

Ah, she was trying to get rid of him. That made sense. He was coming out if it now. Or coming down? Whatever the word was for the *high* wearing off. There was, probably, a word for it. And only one person could tell him what it was.

"You could call Ada. But she might not answer."

"We'll make sure she does."

Officer Allen brought him into the house. Raymond chose to wait in the den. He liked this room best, though it didn't matter now. He stared at the empty fireplace and tried not to think of Lisa.

"Knock, knock." Officer Allen stood in the doorway. "She's here."

"Who?"

"Your caseworker. Ada."

"Already?"

"She said you called her." Officer Allen frowned, like a suspicious TV cop. "Did you?"

"Yeah. I guess I forgot."

"Okay." She nodded, but the suspicious look remained. "She's waiting for you in the car."

Officer Allen helped Raymond pack. He took his art supplies and the new clothes Lisa had given him — his old ones didn't fit anymore — then stepped out the front door onto the steps.

A shiny black car idled in the driveway. Ada stood beside it, resting her hand on a cane. Not the white cane she used to scan her surroundings. A walking cane.

Raymond started down the steps toward her, then froze. She looked like an alien life form.

Everything about her seemed, somehow, *diminished*. Her familiar outfit — black pants, black shirt, gray jacket — swamped her thin frame. Ada's dark, shiny hair had paled. Dry, wispy strands floated around a face that reminded Raymond of a dehydrated apple. Thin, chalky skin stretched across the blades of her cheekbones. And beneath them, hollowed-out pockets had formed, as if her face was about to collapse. Even her shadow seemed translucent, like it had been washed with bleach.

But still, with her black glasses gleaming in the porch light, Ada held her chin high and waited for him to speak first.

"Ada?" Raymond breathed.

"Who else?" she replied with a little smile. Even her smooth, glossy voice was now thin and gritty.

A hard lump rose in Raymond's throat. "Are you okay?" His eyes burned with tears.

She held out her arms, and Raymond ran to her. He dropped his bag and embraced Ada carefully, as if she were made of glass. Her body was all angles and edges.

"You're sick." Raymond sobbed softly into her shoulder. "I didn't know."

Ada stepped back and skimmed his shoulders and arms lightly with her palms. "You've grown." She slid her fingertips down his cheeks and across his jaw line. "A boy becomes a man when a man is needed," she murmured.

"I didn't think you'd come. I thought you were fed up with me."

"Maybe I am. We'll see."

She tapped on the driver's side window. A man got out, picked up Raymond's bag, then opened the back door. Ada slid in and settled her cane on her lap. Raymond followed her.

As they pulled out of Lisa and Matt's driveway, she sighed. "Don't look back."

"I wasn't."

"Good. Now tell me everything."

"I don't feel like talking. I need to —"

"Yes, it's all about what *you* need, isn't it? That's really all you care about." She turned away. "I don't know why I came," she mumbled, staring out the window, as if she could see the fine lawns and fancy houses passing by.

"I'm sorry." He reached for her hand, but Ada yanked it away.

"I don't feel like talking," she snapped, but her voice trailed off into a raspy grunt. Ada sucked in a breath, then broke into a wet, hacking cough that rattled her whole frame.

Raymond gripped her thin shoulder. "Ada!"

She waved him away, dug a tissue from her pocket, then pressed it against her mouth. It went on and on, until the cough became a wheeze. Finally, it eased off.

Raymond bit down on his panic, sick with worry about her but afraid to upset her again. He waited until she had wiped her mouth and nose and eased her body back into her seat. "Can I ... *do* anything for you?"

She didn't answer.

"I'll talk about what happened. Will that help?"

"No need," she whispered, and offered her upturned palm. "Just breathe with me."

Raymond took her hand. Her skin was cool and papery.

Ada started the count, then trailed off, as Raymond joined her, breathing in synch with the faint, rhythmic pulse of her fragile hand squeezing his. A sense of peacefulness arose in him almost immediately. He'd missed this!

As always, Raymond expanded from the inside out, until he was floating in vast, endless space.

"Now, Raymond," she murmured, "remember.

Play it all for me. Just as it happened. Every. Detail."

He did it, just as Ada wanted, his eyes streaming hot, salty tears. Like clicking play on a video, he saw it all again. *Lived* it all again. He stepped inside a home movie, in full-color detail, of Lisa, Matt, David, Jean, and, of course, the little cupcake girl. Poor, gray-skinned Ivy, lost and alone at the bottom of her pool. The anger, the grief, the violence, the blood, the *pain*. And, finally, Lisa's last wave of goodbye as her husband screamed in horror while the tiny arms pulled her down, down, down to the bottom. Mama and Ivy, together again.

When he was done, Ada slid her hand away and pulled another tissue from her pocket. She handed it to Raymond.

They were on the highway now, on their journey back to Haven. The streetlights whizzing past lit up the back seat with silvery light as the first red streaks of dawn stained the pearly sky. Ada laid her head back against the leather seat and sighed. She was smiling. *Glowing*.

A chill ran up Raymond's back. He stared, trembling, as Ada *changed*. Slowly, she filled out, plumped up, like a sponge taking on water. The shadowed hollows under her cheeks were gone, and her wrists had lost their bony frailty.

She lifted her head up and laughed — that warm liquid gold laugh that Raymond found so beautiful.

She was back. *All there*. She was Ada again.

But who was that?

He really had no idea, did he?

Chapter Thirty-Seven

THEY PULLED into the driveway of the Haven in the full light of morning.

"Just in time for breakfast," Ada chirped.

"I'm not hungry," Raymond said.

"Me, neither!" She chuckled, like they were sharing a private joke. "But *you* need to get back into the routine. The sooner the better."

The routine.

The word landed like a rock on Raymond's chest.

He stared at the front entrance to Haven, the steps his mother had carried him up, the front door she had pushed him through, just before she ran. "What's my name, Ada? My real name."

"Go to breakfast."

"You came to Haven looking for *me*, didn't you?"

The front door creaked open. Raymond's stomach flipped when he turned to see Keisha stepping out onto the porch.

"Raymond!" she squealed.

He realized, with a sting of guilt, that he hadn't thought about Keisha much, if at all, in the last few months. But now, seeing her bright smile, as she waved at him from the porch, his heart melted.

He jumped out of the car, then ran up the steps. She threw her arms around him and did a little dance. "You're back! Sisters said you were coming!"

"I'm here."

"You are! I can't believe it!" She stepped back and looked him up and down with wide eyes. "You look different."

"Bad?"

Her smile was shy. "Uh-uh. Definitely not."

She looked different too. Taller, rounder, like the doll she was had become a real person. And even more beautiful than he remembered.

"Weird to be back," Raymond said.

"What happened? Was it bad?"

He'd forgotten the clear, pure blue of Keisha's eyes. Her blunt sincerity. "Yeah," Raymond whispered, his throat tightening. He didn't dare say more.

She nodded, then hugged him again. "You can tell me later. Want breakfast?"

"Let me get my bag."

Ada stood beside the car with Raymond's bag at her feet. She'd been listening to them, he could tell. Raymond jogged back and picked up his bag. "Thanks for coming to get me."

"We have a session this afternoon."

"Already?"

"You have other plans?"

Raymond stole a look at Keisha waiting on the porch. "I guess not."

"I'll see you just after lunch. I suggest you get some sleep."

"Where?"

"Your bed, of course. In your old room."

"Nobody moved in?"

"I wouldn't allow it. I saved it for you."

Raymond chest tightened. "You ... what?"

"You'll find it just as you left it."

"How did you know I'd be back?"

A smile played on Ada's lips, but she didn't respond.

Heat flushed through Raymond's body. No. No, she couldn't have planned it all. It wasn't possible. His heartbeat pounded in his ears. She *wouldn't*. Ada loved him. Didn't she?

But her sly smile, the glow on her filled-out cheeks, the discarded cane ... he turned away from her and started up the walkway.

"Raymond ..."

He didn't stop. He couldn't look at her.

"Don't get sloppy," she snapped.

Raymond bit down, grinding his teeth so hard it hurt.

"Come on, slow poke!" Keisha dropped her chin to her chest, like she was falling asleep, then looked up at him and laughed.

Raymond studied Keisha's happy face. Focus on that, and nothing else. No *one* else.

He walked, then ran, up the pathway to Haven's

porch, away from Ada as fast as he could.

HEADS TURNED when he and Keisha walked into the dining hall. Raymond was used to that. But now, it felt different. The dining hall was the same as it ever was. There were a few new faces, but he recognized most everyone else. But it was like they didn't recognize *him*.

"Look at you." Sister Ann beamed. "You filled out, boy."

She hadn't. Just a skinny as ever.

"Mel!" Sister Ann waved Sister Melinda over. "Look at what remains of this boy."

Sister Melinda waddled over, popping her eyes wide. "Raymond! Shew! You must have sprouted up half a foot! Got yourself some muscles."

The sisters laughed, and Keisha sputtered out an embarrassed giggle. When they walked away, she whispered in a sing-song voice, "Awkward!"

Raymond laughed, but he caught Keisha looking at his arms. He hoped she didn't notice him blushing.

They slid plates of eggs and toast onto their trays, though Raymond didn't want them. His stomach felt sour. Not quite an ache ... yet. But the sweet relief he felt lying in Lisa's garden was fading fast.

"Where do you want to sit?" Keisha asked.

Raymond scanned the dining hall, then walked to a table in the middle of the room — far away from his old spot on the end. His days in the corner were over.

"So?" Keisha crunched through her toast, raising her eyebrows at him.

"So ... what?"

"Why are you back? What happened?"

An image of Lisa filled his head, her shocked expression, blood oozing from her throat, a slick crimson bloom soaking her white cotton dress. Raymond shook his head, suddenly too choked up to talk.

"Really bad, huh?"

He nodded, swallowing hard.

"Did you like them?"

"I loved them."

"I'm sorry," Keisha said softly.

Raymond watched Keisha eat and listened while she filled him in on what he missed while he was gone. But soon, lack of sleep crept up on him. His head ached, and his eyes felt scratchy and heavy. When Keisha had nearly finished her food, he slid his uneaten toast onto her plate. She giggled.

"You look tired."

"Yeah. I should sleep." Raymond yawned.

"Go ahead. I'll clear your tray. But you'll tell me about it later, right?"

The warm concern on her face reminded Raymond of Lisa. He looked away and stood. "Thanks. It's really good to see you."

"Same."

Raymond climbed the stairs to his old bedroom. It was strange, as if he were a ghost reliving a memory of another life. When he opened the door, his body tensed.

His bed was already made up for him, ready for his nap, like he was a toddler.

Ada. *So* certain he would do as he was told.

Raymond dropped his bag on the floor, then fell onto the bed with his sneakers on, suddenly flat-out *exhausted*. But as much as he tried to sleep, the mattress seemed so much smaller than he remembered, and the frame let out a rusty squeal with every movement. Eventually, he gave up and lay on his back, staring at the ceiling, counting down the minutes until his session with Ada.

When the time came, he walked the familiar hallway to her office, tired and hot, with his stomach in knots. The door was open when he arrived.

Ada stood at the window, her face lifted toward the sun. She had changed into a cream-colored dress and restyled her hair into a thick, glossy braid. The walking cane was nowhere to be seen.

Raymond took his usual seat and waited. She sighed, walked toward him slowly, then eased into her chair. She leaned back and rested her interlaced fingers on her belly.

"Cat got your tongue?" she said.

"You lied to me."

"Did I?"

"You knew what would happen."

"And you didn't?"

"No!"

"Huh." She smirked. "Who's lying now?"

"You sent me there! *A good fit.* That's what you said!"

"And I was exactly right."

"You're supposed to help me … to look *after* me."

"Yes. You're welcome."

"He killed her! Lisa's dead and … and I *loved* her!"

"Well, that will teach you for being foolish!"

Anger coiled inside Raymond like a snake ready to strike. In that moment, he didn't care about Ada's love. He didn't care about his promise. Like flipping a switch, he dropped the veil on Ada.

An image hit him in the gut like an iron fist.

Shiny black shoes dangling below a pair of khaki pants, with razor sharp creases. They swayed, slowly, in a shaft of dusty sun light. Back and forth, back, and forth. A creaking sound, rhythmic, almost hypnotic, filled his ears. His gaze followed the sound — up, up, up, along the path of that creaky whine — and landed on a rectangular patch of olive gray. Stamped into the center, in chunky black print, was his own name: RAY.

A scream ripped through Raymond's head. Frantic, high-pitched, like a thousand glasses shattering at once.

He's dead!

"Stop!" Ada jumped out of her chair and slapped him across the face.

Raymond's cheeked burned, and his heart slammed in his chest. "Who are you, Ada?"

She laughed.

"You came to Haven looking for me, didn't you?"

Raymond swiped the tears from his eyes, "You found me at the art museum. I *felt* you."

Ada leaned toward him, her voice dark and menacing. "You're getting ahead of yourself, boy. Get out."

"You've been using me. What happened to Lisa — it was *your* fault."

Ada lunged toward him, landing a claw-like hand on one shoulder, and a savage grip on his other arm. She yanked Raymond out of his chair with a strength that shocked him. "You GET OUT!" Ada screamed.

She shoved him from behind, slamming her palms into his back. Raymond landed on his knees in the hallway as the office door crashed shut behind him. Raymond pounded the door, as hard as he could.

"YOU KILLED HER! YOU DID IT! I HATE YOU!'

Down the hallway, an office door down swung open.

Raymond ran.

He charged down the hallway, burst through the side door, then tore across the yard toward the tree line. When he reached the wooded edge of Haven's grounds, he dropped to the ground, sucking air into his heaving chest. Searing pain, brutal and horribly familiar, stabbed at his belly, over and over.

Raymond curled into a ball, pressing his knees against his chest, like it was the only thing keeping his guts from spilling out onto the dirt and leaves beneath him.

He — everything he thought of himself as being

— was disappearing. No skin, no bones, no dreams, no thoughts. No Raymond.

Just a writhing organ, empty, but for sadness upon sadness.

And hunger. *Insane* hunger that would drive him, *force* him, to feed.

It could be anyone. Anyone at all.

And it was beyond his control.

Because Ada would choose. Soon.

Chapter Thirty-Eight

"I'll never understand it." Keisha shook her head, then tossed a handful of popcorn in her mouth.

"Understand what?" Raymond mumbled, still watching the TV screen, though his head ached so much he could barely focus.

"Why that girl would go back to that old Kansas." She swept her arm wide. "Nothing but dust when she could have stayed with her friends and been, like, *Queen* of Magic Land."

Raymond pulled his blanket tighter around his shoulders. A soft, steady rain was falling, but the breeze drifting through the rec room windows was soft and humid. Still, Raymond could not get warm. His stomach felt like an open sore. "I don't know," he said, trying not to sound grouchy, "guess Oz wasn't home."

"But home was shitty."

"Oz was shitty, too, in its own way."

Raymond felt Keisha's gaze on him but pretended he didn't. He didn't want to explain. Not here.

He and Keisha sat on the floor against the back wall, while all round them, kids sprawled on sofas and bean bags, crunching popcorn and slurping on lemonade. Raymond had seen this movie a few times — they all had. It was old but still a popular choice for movie night. Maybe because, for a little while, Dorothy was an orphan, like them. But one who made it back to her family. Her *real* family, who actually *wanted* her.

Keisha was still staring at him when the door swung open. Everyone turned to see Ada step into the room. A chill ran up Raymond's spine. He hadn't seen her in three days, not since their argument.

But she wasn't there for him.

A collective gasp rippled through the rec room when Ada moved to one side, and a tall, thin boy walked in. It took Raymond a moment to realize that the boy was Kevin. Not the Kevin he remembered, but a pale, whittled-down version of an almost-Kevin.

His wide, straight shoulders had narrowed. They dipped toward each other, as if guarding the sunken cavity that was once his broad chest. The cocky arrogance had been replaced with a nervous-animal twitchiness. He looked ... *wrung out.*

With his chin dipped low, as Kevin's gaze darted around the room. They found Raymond and stopped.

Kevin's colors burst outward, like juice from a brown, rotting orange. They flashed in shaky, uneven patterns, like random thoughts too dark to finish. Hundreds of tiny, black, crab-creatures scuttled across Kevin's muddy brown field. They scrambled over one another, claws snapping. It hurt to look at them, but Raymond was mesmerized.

Kevin's eyes filled with tears. Raymond felt him pulling, trying to wrench his attention away, but he couldn't. With barely an effort, Raymond was stopping him. It felt *good* to be the strong one.

"C'mon now." Ada gripped Kevin's shoulder. "Make some room for Kevin."

Like he was slow-pulling a bandage from a cut that was still bleeding, Kevin tore his focus away from Raymond. He scanned the room until he found Derek, who was on a bean bag on the floor. Derek nodded, got up, and squeezed onto the couch next to Joey. They both stared, mute and wide-eyed, as Kevin crossed the room toward them, then dropped onto the bean bag. Kevin turned toward the TV, hugged his knees to his chest, then watched the screen, dead-eyed, like a zombie.

"Whoa," Keisha whispered, "does *everyone* come back here?"

Raymond barely heard her. His belly writhed and twisted inside of him like a severed worm. His mouth was full of spit. He swallowed, but it filled up again instantly. He couldn't stop staring at Kevin. The sight of him — thin, breakable, maybe even broken — sent black waves of sadness crashing through Raymond's chest. But the ache in his gut was unbearable.

Raymond felt Ada's frosty, gray tendrils curling toward him like winter fog. He looked at her, standing by the door, lips pursed. She nodded at him — quick, curt, and as *in control* as ever.

"Goodnight, all," Ada said, then she was gone.

Raymond turned back to Kevin, transfixed. He *reeked* of pain. A huddled ball of anguish. *Ripe*.

Deep down inside of him, in a sunless, desolate place Raymond never knew existed, a door began to swing open. He knew what was behind it. Ancient, writhing, greedy, creatures that smelled like Benny. They wanted to be fed. *Now*.

Raymond fought it. He tried. For a blink, one brief flash of human resistance, he turned away. From the door, from Kevin, from the black hole of Ada's savage manipulation. He buried his head in his hands and tried to breathe. But his fingertips found the sore, swollen lump from David's punch. There, in the center of his forehead. His *third eye*.

For a moment, Raymond could do nothing but *remember*. The mocking nicknames, the mortifying taunts. How Kevin's eyes would sparkle with excitement before he tripped, slapped, punched, or pummeled Raymond with an icy-packed snowball to the head.

He saw David, soaked in his brother's blood, shove Lisa straight into the arc of Matt's blade.

Raymond yanked the internal door open wide. And what lived in that black, putrid space, slithered out. They wormed through his veins, into his brain, screeching like starving bats over a twilight field.

"Hey, Kevin," Raymond sneered. "They kicked you out, huh?"

"Shut up," Kevin mumbled into his knees.

Kevin didn't look him. *Wouldn't* look at him. Raymond felt his fear and was warmed by it. Delighted *in* it.

He wanted more. *So* much more.

"Devlin did it to you, didn't he?" Raymond laughed, "I *told* you he would."

"Shut up!" Kevin yelled.

"Who's the pussy now, huh?"

Raymond watched the faces around him turn his way, then to Kevin, confused, shocked that Raymond would dare risk a beating, like so many times before.

But *they* didn't know, did they? They had no idea. Things had changed.

"What's he taking about, Kev?" Derek asked.

"Nothing," Kevin mumbled. "He's just being a freak asshole, like always."

"Am I?" Raymond laughed again. "Maybe I should tell them."

"Shut the fuck up!" Kevin yelled.

Everyone looked around, waiting for one of the sisters to storm in and drag Kevin out by the ear for swearing. But nobody came.

"Admit it, and I'll shut up," Raymond offered, like he was the most reasonable person in the world.

"Raymond, stop it!" Keshia hissed, laying her hand on his arm.

Raymond shrugged it off.

"Just tell us what happened," Joey said. "What are you *doing* back here?"

"Yeah, just tell them, Kevin," Raymond echoed.

"Yeah, tell us, Kevin!" George, another favorite victim of Kevin's, yelled out in high-pitched squeak.

That got all the kids laughing, nervously at first, but it caught on like a viral fever. Soon they were all laughing and shrieking like a pack of monkeys, slapping their thighs in rhythm. "Tell us! Tell us! Tell us!"

"SHUT UP!" Kevin screamed.

That just made them laugh more. Too many of them had been at Kevin's mercy when he had none to give. They chanted louder, stomping their feet now to a chorus of, "TELL US, KEVIN! TELL US, KEVIN! TELL US, KEVIN!"

Kevin screamed again — a wordless, enraged howl. He glared at Raymond like he wished him dead. His Adam's apple juddered in his throat as tears filled his eyes., then he jumped up, yanked open the door, and ran.

Raymond tossed off his blanket and tore after him, a ravenous wolf running down its prey. He chased Kevin down the hall and into the boy's bathroom. Kevin dove into a stall.

"Gotcha!" Raymond breathed. He paused a moment, caught his breath, then quietly locked the bathroom door behind him. He walked to Kevin's stall, pressed his back against the door, then slid to the floor. He braced his feet hard on the opposite stall.

Kevin was trapped.

"Fuck off!" he growled.

"Nope."

The door rattled.

"Open the fucking door," Kevin snarled, "NOW."
His attempt to sound menacing came out as desperate.

Raymond almost felt sorry for him. "No," he replied calmly.

"Let me OUT!" The door jumped violently against Raymond's back as Kevin pounded and kicked from his side.

But it was no use. Raymond had him. "I tried to warn you. But you wouldn't listen. Now, I want to know what Devlin did to you."

Kevin howled in frustration, slamming what must have been both feet in one explosive kick. But the door — and Raymond — held fast.

"He hurt me, okay!" he screeched. "That what you want to hear?"

Kevin's wrenching sob echoed off the bathroom walls.

With a coolness to rival Ada, Raymond smiled. "It's a start."

"I don't want to talk about it," Kevin sputtered between sobs.

Raymond nodded to himself. He knew how *that* felt. "Give me your hand."

"What? Fuck no!"

"You don't have to say a word. But I need your hand."

"Why?"

"You know about me. What I am. Well." Raymond chuckled. "Sort of."

"You're a fucking freak!" Kevin spat.

"I *am* a fucking freak. And I'm going to get what I want from you, one way or another. And you know I can. Don't you?"

Kevin quieted. His breath was heavy and stuttering.

Raymond felt his fear. The *taste* of it flooded his mouth, filled his nostrils. It was *delicious*. "Give me your hand," he said calmly, "under the door. Palm up."

Moments passed. Raymond waited in silence.

Finally, the sound of scuffling.

"Don't do anything," Kevin whimpered, "okay?"

Kevin's hand emerged from beneath the door, shaking and glistening with sweat and tears. Raymond laid his palm on top and pressed downward, pinning Kevin's hand beneath his own. "Take a breath, Kevin," he whispered, "a deep one."

He pressed his ear against the door. Kevin sucked in noisily, then sputtered out a breath.

"Again."

He listened to Kevin breath. His hand trembled, hot, and sweaty, beneath Raymond's.

"Good," Raymond said, "now remember what he did —"

"No," Kevin whined.

"The worst of it. In detail. Play it your mind like a movie. I can help."

"I don't want to!"

Raymond reached out for Kevin's memories, diving down fast and deep. It was like sinking into a bottomless pit of muddy quicksand.

Kevin cried softly, pitifully on the other side of the door. "Don't …"

The black crab-creatures were everywhere, scuttling through the wet, murky brown in a frenzy of panic. Their claws tore at one another — *click click click click click!*

Raymond pushed the door to Kevin's memory open, and the murky mud-brown seeped out and turned black. With a click, a single, dirty bulb shone in a deep, cold darkness.

The musty wet smell of a basement, just like Benny's, was all around them. A mattress on a concrete floor. No sheet, no blanket.

"Not a sound this time, ya here me?"

Raymond knew the cold, brutal voice of James Devlin. He knew this memory before it even happened. He saw it play out the instant Devlin flicked his snake-tongue across his thick wet lips.

As Kevin played out the memory, relived every horrific detail as if he was still, in that moment, trapped in the Devlin's dank, windowless basement.

His suffering was *exquisite.*

Raymond gobbled it up, every bite. The energy surged through him, filling him as quickly and completely as it drained from Kevin.

When it was over — when he was full — Raymond slipped his hand away. He left Kevin, sobbing and spent on the bathroom floor.

He wandered downstairs, out the side door, to the playground. He wanted to see the sky.

Raymond lay back on a slide, the metal cool

against his skin. Above him, so many stars, glistening, overlapping, vibrating with thousands of years of memories upon memories.

Bliss. That was the only word for it.

Raymond floated.

Chapter Thirty-Nine

ADA.

Raymond sat up. He had no idea how long he'd been there, but the slide was slick with dew. Raymond squinted into the glare of the yellow bug light in the alcove of the side door. Sure enough, the glint of her glasses caught his eye. They always did.

Ada stood in the alcove, her head tilted upward, smiling as if listening to the music of angels. She *looked* like an angel.

She looks like you feel.

Yes, she did. The weight of Kevin's sadness would come later. But right now, Raymond was warm, blissfully free of pain ... *whole.* And Ada had siphoned some for herself. Taken her share.

But how? *Why?*

Raymond stood slowly, his head still buzzing. Still blissful, still high. And so was she. Would there ever be a better time to ask her?

"Ada?" he whispered.

Her chin dipped and turned toward his voice. Her smile widened.

Raymond went to her, feeling as if he were floating above the grass.

"See? Like falling off a log," she murmured. "Were you scared?"

"Yeah. Then it just … *happened*."

"'A step towards what you fear is a mile towards mastering it.' Matshona Dhliwayo. If you're wondering."

"Okay," Raymond mumbled. "I just want to understand."

"Don't we all." She sighed. "Let's take a walk."

"Now?" Raymond looked around him. It was a moonless night, and the grounds of Haven were steeped in darkness. Though that made no difference to Ada. "Where to?"

"I suppose you'll be wanting the chapel."

"It'll be locked now."

Ada pulled a ring of keys from her pocket and jangled them.

Raymond's mouth dropped open. "Those are Father Galen's."

Ada shrugged with one shoulder and smirked. "He felt I should have them."

She stretched her hand, letting it hover, mid-air, like a featherless bird.

Raymond took it gently, then tucked it into the crook of his arm. She started forward, and he moved with her.

They walked through the damp, shrouded stillness

of Haven's back yard, along the stone path, passed the dark windows of Father Galen's cottage. Finally, they stood outside the thick wooden double doors of Jophiel's Chapel.

Narrow columns of dim, yellow light spilled from the windows. Security lights always burned in the chapel, though Raymond wondered why. Anything of value in a chapel should be there for the taking by those in need, right?

Ada handed Raymond the keys. After he unlocked the door, they stepped inside the vestibule.

"Window seat?" Raymond asked, remembering their last visit here. But Ada kept walking.

"Going all in," she chirped, and headed through the door to the main chapel. Again, as he often did with Ada, Raymond got the sense that she had walked that path a thousand times. He followed behind her.

The first ticks of rain began to patter on the roof and windows. The damp, chill air was sweet with a hundred years of lemon oil and incense.

"It's always raining when I'm here," Raymond said.

"Tears of Jophiel," she murmured.

Jophiel floated above them, life-like. Radiant, as always. She smiled down at him like an old friend. But for the first time, Raymond saw the sadness in her eyes. How could he not have noticed that before?

Ada moved down the narrow center aisle, pausing to trail her fingers along the backs of the worn, wooden pews, as if each held a fragment of a long-forgotten memory. Finally, to Raymond's surprise, she bobbed into a half-curtsey, genuflected, and slipped into an aisle several rows back from the alter.

Raymond followed, sliding into a pew across the aisle. "You believe in all that?"

"All that and more."

"What's the more?"

"The more that I already know but don't remember yet. Anamnesis."

"You're a Tetra, aren't you?"

Ada sighed, heavily. "I used to be."

Raymond's chest fluttered, as hope twitched its wings like a weary bird. "Once? You mean, it can change? *I* can change?"

"Hmm." Ada tilted her head to one side. "Yes and no."

"Just … GIVE ME STRAIGHT ANSWERS!" Raymond's anger and frustration boomed through the chapel.

"You're not asking straight questions!" Ada snapped.

"Okay! Who am I? What am I? Is this it? Is this my life?"

"You want it all to be simple, digestible, tied up with a little bow. Well, it's NOT! Get used to it."

"I don't understand it! How am supposed to get used to it?"

"That's easy. You do as I ask, and I'll give it all to you. When you're *ready*."

"You're gray smoke, Ada. How do I know I can trust you?"

"You don't. But I'll make you a deal."

"NO. I don't want a *deal*."

"Suit yourself, but I'm all you've got, sunshine." Ada stood and pointed up at the saint suspended above them. "And *that* is NOT Jophiel!" She started up the aisle. "Lock the door on your way out."

"What?" Raymond jumped up. "That's bullshit!"

She continued walking as if he were no longer there.

"Ada, WAIT!"

She paused and tilted her head upward. Annoyed, but listening. Smug, like she'd already won.

Raymond shook his head and sighed. "Tell me the deal."

She turned around and held up her index finger. "I'll give you one thing. ONE thing. The rest you have to earn."

"*One* thing? But I have so many questions."

"Then you better get busy earning the answers. For now, I'll answer one. For Kevin. I owe you, I guess."

Images and questions swirled in Raymond's mind like dead leaves in a windstorm. But one image burned brightest. The *only* thing he'd managed to take from Ada. The shiny shoes, swaying beneath khaki pants. The terrible creaking. His name, in bold black ink, on the gray patch.

"What's my name, Ada?"

The question floated through the incensed air like a paper plane and landed at Ada's feet.

Ada did something he'd never seen her do. She *hesitated*. For just a moment, she chewed her lip. Then

371

nodded, in her curt Ada way. "You are Novice Ray. You were named for your father."

And just like that, another door swung open. Raymond gasped and staggered. He gripped the pew to keep from falling over as the full memory revealed itself, crashing down hard.

The sawdust smell of the sun-filled barn. The man, a soldier in full uniform, blue-faced and swollen. The hairy rope wrapped around the thick, wooden beam above him. Rows of shiny metals glistening in the sunlight. Above them, a name tag — not a *patch*. A name tag, for whomever found him.

And that would be his mother, the one who screamed, as she held *him*, just a tiny baby, in her trembling arms.

"*We* found him? My mother and me?"

Ada's lip trembled. She turned her back on him. "I said one thing." She choked and started back up the aisle.

"Ada, wait! Please! Just tell me why. Why did my father kill himself? ADA!"

She paused in the doorway to the chapel just long enough to shrug. "Maybe he was hungry."

Chapter Forty

THE SUN WAS warm on Raymond's back as he swung gently, barely moving. He watched his shadow stretch and extend, beyond his feet, then shrink and contract until it nearly disappeared. Keisha sat on the swing beside him, creaking slowly, back, and forth, in time with his motion. She hadn't said much since the night Kevin came back. She wanted to listen. And he'd promised to tell her everything.

He'd been talking for a while, uninterrupted, about Lisa and Matt. It hurt — the sore spot in his belly throbbed and burned, as he relived that terrible night. But he told Keisha everything … almost.

"So, I know I was mean to Kevin."

"*Really* mean."

"That wasn't me, Keisha. Not the real me. Honest."

She shrugged.

"I was just upset. You know how that is, right?"

Keisha sighed. "I guess so."

"Like, when you first got here."

She nodded, staring off into a memory that shadowed her face with sadness.

"You know, Keisha, you never told me what happened."

"I never told anyone. She was … " Her voice cracked. "She was my *mom*."

"You can trust me. Do you?"

She studied his face, deciding. "Yeah. I trust you, Ray."

"Good. Can I ask you a favor?"

"I guess."

"Will you call me Novice?"

"*Novice*? Why?"

"Because that's my name. Same as my dad. Novice Ray."

She smiled. "I like it."

Novice smiled back. "Me, too."

He reached over and gently took her hand. She slipped her fingers through his, soft and warm.

"Now, about your mom," he whispered. "Tell me everything."

What to read next...

Forgetting is hard, remembering is hell.

Exploring the idea that humans are the scariest monsters of all, this chilling story of a young woman struggling to hold onto her sanity in an insane world is both haunting and unforgettable.

Start reading Victim today

A Quick Favor...

If you enjoyed this book, please take a moment to write a short review on your favorite online bookstore so other readers can enjoy it, too.

Thanks so much!

About the Author

E.G. Rose colors outside the lines. Her stories dive deep into the dark pools we like to pretend aren't there and sometimes drag the unthinkable to the surface. She picks through the busted remains of what once seemed unbreakable and finds the story dying to be shared. In her world, family ties, forever friends, promises, dreams, sanity, and sometimes reality itself, crack and spill their secrets. Rose weaves them into tales that are haunting, gripping, shocking, and thought-provoking, but always entertaining. If you like books by Stephen King, Shirley Jackson, Patricia Highsmith, Daphne Du Maurier and movies like The Other, The Sixth Sense, Get Out, Let The Right One In, Whatever Happened to Baby Jane, anything Hitchcock and all things Twilight Zone, you've met a friend in E G Rose.

www.ingramcontent.com/pod-product-compliance
Lightning Source LLC
Chambersburg PA
CBHW010523100726
47903CB00011B/2872

* 9 7 8 1 6 2 9 5 5 2 1 9 4 *